Not Here to Be Liked

Not Here to Be Liked

MICHELLE QUACH

KATHERINE TEGEN BOOKS
An Imprint of HarperCollins Publishers

Katherine Tegen Books is an imprint of HarperCollins Publishers.

ISBN 978-0-06-303836-3

Typography by Molly Fehr
21 22 23 24 25   PC/LSCH   10 9 8 7 6 5 4 3 2 1
❖
First Edition

To the real J.

1

I SHARE A BEDROOM WITH MY OLDER SISTER KIM, which wouldn't be a problem except she has this habit of making a face whenever I walk in.

"That's what you're wearing?" She points her mascara wand at me, the disbelief thick enough to flake off.

"It's fine." I push up my sleeves and they fall right back down again. "Don't worry about it."

To be fair, what I'm wearing is a big polyester sweater the exact gray of parking-lot asphalt, and it isn't anybody's idea of a good look. But I don't care. In fact, this is basically how I dress every day. I read once that a lot of important people have a "uniform" to save their mental energy for things that actually matter, so I've started doing it, too. Kim thinks this is a horrible way to live.

"Isn't today supposed to be a big deal for you?"

I flop onto my bed with a book, an Eileen Chang novel I found by chance at the library. I like it because the main character is a Chinese girl who's smart but a bit prickly, which is a combination the world could really use more of. Just a personal opinion, of course.

"Well?" Kim asks, after I've turned a page.

I bite into the chewy flour of my Cantonese-style sachima, which is sweet and sticky, like a Rice Krispies treat without the marshmallows. Then, because I can sense Kim's impatience practically forming condensation on my silence, I take a long sip of tea and turn another page.

"Sure," I agree. "It's a big deal."

Today is the day that the staff of the *Willoughby Bugle*, my high school paper, will select its new editor in chief for next year. It's a hallowed ritual, occurring around the same time every spring—and this year, being a junior, I finally get to be in the running.

"So, shouldn't you try to look better?" Kim has switched over to penciling her eyebrows into the thick, horizontal style of K-drama heroines. "Don't you want people to vote for you?"

Now, I don't believe in self-aggrandizing, never have. You're only as good as your facts, I like to say, in journalism and in life. Here are mine:

For almost three years, I've been the most prolific, hardest-working, most no-nonsense staff member the *Bugle* has ever seen. I can write a quality 750-word article in thirty minutes flat, I pitch half the stories that make it onto the front page every month, and I'm already the current managing editor—a position they normally give to a senior. So, no, I don't need people on the *Bugle* to vote for me just because I clean up nice.

They're going to pick me because I'm the most sensible option. Because literally no one else will do a better job.

And also, as it happens, because there is no one else. I'm running unopposed.

"Since I'm the only candidate, I just need enough votes to be confirmed," I explain, finishing off the last bite of sachima. "It's really more like, you know, a Supreme Court appointment than an election."

Kim is unconvinced. "Do you want me to at least curl your hair or something?"

Sometimes, I swear, my sister's perseverance rivals only her denseness. "The *Bugle* isn't like that, Kim. It's a meritocracy." I crumple the crackly sachima wrapper into a ball. "If I wanted to participate in a farce, I'd be running for student council."

"Well, you did, once."

It's an unexpected prick, sharp and inconsequential like a paper cut. "That was a long time ago."

Kim is only two years older than me, so she used to go to Willoughby, too. Last year, when she was a senior, I thought I'd finally be free of her when she graduated, but then of course she ended up at UC Irvine. "So close!" Dad said. "You don't need to stay in the dorms. Waste of money." So here we are. Like old times.

"It wouldn't kill you to look prettier, Eliza. I mean, in general."

I scrunch up my face—one eye squinted, nose wrinkled, tongue lolled out sideways. "You don't think I'm pretty?" I joke, trying to talk and hold the expression at the same time.

Kim answers like I've asked a serious question. "No."

There goes my amusement, dripping down the side of my neck in a cold trickle. I watch for a moment as she dabs on a coral lip stain, and then, half-heartedly, I lob one more shot: "Don't buy into the male gaze, Kim."

But she totally has. See, Kim is one of those girls with the misfortune of thinking she should be pretty. It's not really her fault: she *is* pretty. She has nice eyes, big Fan Bingbing affairs with the kind of double eyelids you might, if not kill for, certainly consider acquiring under a knife. When we were younger, people would exclaim (usually in Cantonese) about how lovely she was: "*Gam leng néuih ā!* She could be in the Miss Hong Kong pageant!"

"Why the hell would you want that?" I'd asked once, and Mom had to shush me: "No one's telling *you* to!"

Mom's at the door now, waiting to see if I'm ready to go. "*Đi được chưa?*" she asks in Vietnamese. That's the other language, besides Cantonese, typically heard in our household. Mandarin, in contrast, only makes an occasional appearance, usually in the form of a wise saying. My family is what Cantonese people call *wàh kìuh*, or "overseas Chinese," which essentially means that despite spending three generations in Vietnam, we never quite gave up on being Chinese. Kim and I understand everything, but we, being lazy Americans, often respond in English.

"Yeah, sure," I say to Mom, as I climb off the bed and start gathering up my books for school.

She takes this opportunity to inspect my outfit. "Are you—"

"Let's go." I leap up to barrel past her, books clutched to my chest, backpack still half unzipped. "Bye, Kim!"

Outside, the air is still cool, as if the sun is up but not quite itself yet. The sprinklers have just kicked off, leaving patches of darkened pavement alongside the lawn. As Mom and I trek past the familiar rows of apartments, I breathe in the evaporating mist. It smells like damp concrete and warm mulch—morning in a stucco wasteland.

We're following the long driveway to our carport when my phone buzzes. The text is from James Jin, the current editor in chief of the *Bugle*:

You might like to know that Len DiMartile emailed me last night.

This is random. Len is this half-Japanese, half-white kid on the *Bugle* staff who's been assigned to the News section this month. James and I have never talked about him before.

Me: Why, is he quitting or something?

James: Actually, he's decided to run for editor in chief.

"Eliza, I told you not to wrinkle your forehead so much," says Mom. Our car is a couple of yards ahead of us, and she unlocks it with a disapproving beep. "You want your face to stay that way? Just like pickled cabbage!"

I fall a few steps behind Mom so my eyebrows can rise in peace.

Me: Is he an egotist or a masochist?

James: Aw, come on, Quan. Be a good sport!

"You definitely get it from your dad." Mom is still pontificating on my facial calisthenics. "It's such a bad habit."

I ignore her and get into the passenger seat, drawing the door shut with one hand so I can keep texting with the other.

Me: I'm a perfectly fine sport.

James: Oh yeah? So you're okay with our boy Leonard giving you a run for your money?

Now my forehead really goes to town. Seriously? "Our boy" Leonard just joined the *Bugle* last year. I don't know what he's thinking, pulling this move, but it doesn't change the very obvious fact that he's greener than an apple Jolly Rancher.

Me: I don't care what he does. A boy can dream. 👧

James: Okay, good. Glad to see you're not afraid of a little competition. 😆

"Eliza, are you even listening?" Mom frowns at me as she starts the car.

"Yeah, definitely."

But my shoulders are tensed up with possibility, the way they get when I'm about to clinch a triple-letter score in Scrabble, and I'm busy typing out my response to James:

Bring it on.

2

THE *BUGLE* WAS FOUNDED THREE YEARS AFTER Willoughby High School opened its doors as Jacaranda Unified's first public college-preparatory academy. The original staff was a small, dedicated group led by Harold "Harry" Sloane, class of '87, a young man with a preternatural view toward posterity. We can trace just about every *Bugle* tradition to this remarkably fertile mind.

Take, for instance, the *Bugle* name itself. Harry picked that to go with the vaguely military associations implied by our school mascot, the Sentinels. At some point that first year, he showed up with an actual brass bugle, which he purportedly stole from St. Agatha's Academy down the street (then known as St. Agatha's Military School for Boys). In reality Harry bought it from an antique shop in Fullerton, which I know because I emailed him about it once, out of curiosity, and he told me. They got it engraved with the *Bugle* motto, *Veritas omnia vincit*, and now it sits on Mr. Powell's desk, a bona fide historic relic. Truth conquers all.

Or take another example: the aforementioned Bugler election. The *Bugle*'s editor in chief is always chosen the way Harry was that very first year—by popular vote among the staff. Harry, as the story goes, maneuvered it so that he, and not Lisa Van Wees, also class of '87, would get to be editor in chief, because everyone knew she was their adviser's favorite. Harry has denied this; Lisa could not be reached for comment.

Then there's the Wall of Editors, which is probably Harry's coolest idea. On the back wall of the newsroom, flanked on one side by a cabinet full of Shakespeare, and on the other, Mr. Powell's poster of Johnny Cash, hangs the face of every editor in chief since Harry, who picked up the tradition from a student paper he'd encountered on a northeast college tour. Eton Kuo, class of '88, the inaugural artist and erstwhile *Bugle* cartoonist, hand drew every portrait with real India ink and continues to do so for each new editor in chief elected (even though he is now an endodontist in Irvine).

The Wall of Editors is the first thing I see every morning when I walk into Mr. Powell's classroom for zero period. And every time, even if just for a second, I pause to admire it, reminding myself of what I'm working toward. Because here's the truth—at Willoughby, when you make it into that lineup, it means you mattered. Like being school president, the other top position on campus, being editor in chief of the *Bugle* means becoming part of an institution. Even if you end up doing a totally worthless job, your spot in history will be preserved forever. You'll always be able to say, "Well, at least I made it on the wall."

This morning, as I linger there, wondering how long it would take my own portrait to start yellowing like the older ones, Cassie Jacinto skips over to join me. A reasonably competent *Bugle* staff photographer, she's a sophomore with a big, bushy ponytail and a toothy smile secured with braces.

"Hey, Eliza!" she exclaims. "Are you excited about today?"

I sidle away from the Wall of Editors and set my backpack down on my usual desk. "Sure—"

"Me too! I mean, I'm totally excited for you."

"Thanks, I—"

"You heard about Len, though, right?" Now her voice drops to a whisper, and before I can even open my mouth again, she rushes to add, "You're not worried about him, are you? Because you really shouldn't be. Like, you're way more qualified, and you have way more—"

"*Cassie.*" I interrupt her this time. "I'm not worried. Really."

"Awesome!" Cassie smiles at me like she knew all along that I'd come through. Then she offers me a fist bump before bouncing away, leaving me to wonder why exactly everyone is assuming that this Len kid's eleventh-hour, third-rate, basically write-in candidacy is something I'd be even remotely threatened by.

A few minutes later, I'm over by the *Bugle* computers, digging through a drawer for a red pen, when a sheet of paper flutters over my shoulder. Startled, I cradle my arms to catch the page awkwardly before it falls to the floor. It's the first draft of an article about Ms. Velazquez, the cafeteria lady who's retiring next month. When I see whose name is in the byline, I turn around, but he's already walking away.

"Thanks," I call out, and Len waves without looking back.

I glance down and pretend to be interested in his draft, but instead I watch him make his way to the back of the room, right near Johnny Cash. He usually spends the entire period in that corner, saying so little to anyone that you can forget he's even there. In a blink-and-you'll-miss-it display of agility, he hops up to sit on a cluster of desks, cross-legged, and settles in with his computer in his lap. It is surprisingly catlike.

"So." James has appeared next to me, and I realize the drawer I was rummaging through is still hanging open. In a hurry, I push it closed.

"Hey," I say loudly, because I can tell he's caught me spying, and the last thing I need right now is some James Jin commentary. I try to think of something to distract him. "You know that new boba tea shop?"

"Yeah?" He pauses, looking interested. James is fond of bubble tea.

"They've set an opening date for the week after next. I found out from Alan Rodriguez." Alan, the kind of senior citizen who runs marathons and wears pastel polos with khaki shorts, is the president of the Jacaranda Chamber of Commerce. I've had an in with him ever since the *Jacaranda Community News* filed for bankruptcy two years ago.

James is pretty excited. "Finally!"

Recently, someone started renovating the abandoned strip mall across the street from school, next to the Presbyterian church that puts up funny sayings on its marquee (*Jesus wants to give you an extreme makeover*). But it's been sitting empty for a few months now, and Boba Bros is the first business to move in. For years, the only other hangout spot within walking distance of campus has been a dingy Dairy Queen two blocks over, so this is definitely news—at least in a month as slow as this one.

"I think we should do a story on it," I say.

"Agreed. Add it to the front page." James gives me a high five. "Way to get the scoop, Quan."

Buoyed by the praise, I sashay back to my desk—but as soon as I sit down with Len's article on Ms. Velazquez, my effervescence takes on a new, competitive charge. Reading it over, I'm reminded that even when his writing is messy and unpolished, it's . . . well, kind of good. I'm weirdly pulled in by his sparse opening line:

> When Maria Elena Velazquez was 12 years
> old, she wanted to be a dancer.

I mean, the woman spent the past twenty-five years of her life assembling school lunches, and that's how he starts the story?

"Hey, Eliza." Aarav Patel, a sophomore, strolls up wearing an absurd leather jacket. "How's it going?"

"It's fine." I flip through my binder to find his draft, which I edited last night. His story is about the annual student-council bake sale, which would be a real snoozer even in more capable hands.

"Just fine? Why just fine?" Aarav asks, like he can't under-stand why I think that's a sane response to his question.

I humor him with an impassive look. "How are *you* doing?"

"I'm great!" He beams. "I'm going to a concert tonight. Super stoked."

"That's good. Here you go." I hand him his draft, which is covered, as usual, with red marks.

"Aw, seriously?" Aarav pouts as he takes the paper from me. "It's not that bad, is it?"

I shrug. When it comes to forming written sentences, Aarav has the proficiency of a third grader.

"Red is such an aggressive pen color, Eliza. Maybe you should try, like, purple. You know, so it's less in your face."

He flashes a contrite smile, trying to smooth things over in that half-needling, half-whining pretty-boy way of his. He hasn't learned that it doesn't work on a girl as charmless as me.

"Maybe you should just write a better draft," I suggest.

Next up is Olivia Nguyen, a freshman, who accepts her story back with trembling hands. Today her fingernails are painted in different shades of pink. She's writing the only real big article this month, about recent cuts to club activity budgets that will disproportionately hit smaller groups—like those dedicated to marginalized student interests.

"Okay," I say, as patiently as possible. "I see you've talked to more people besides your friend Sarah since last time. And actually . . ." I take the draft back from her and skim through it. "We cut Sarah out, right? Remember what we said about 'conflict of interest'?"

"Yes?" Olivia's voice is stuck in her throat.

"Yeah, so this is a huge improvement." I tap the sheet of paper with my pen. "But do you see how every other paragraph is a quote? We need a bit more structure. You're the writer, so you need to actually tell us a story."

Olivia nods solemnly. She always seems so terrified of me, but I don't worry about it—James says she can't keep it together around him either.

The last draft I have belongs to Natalie Weinberg, another sophomore. I scan the room to see if she's here yet, and I spot her approaching Len's corner. Which is a little odd.

He's focused on his laptop and doesn't notice her. But then she says something that makes him look up, and for a second he even smiles, like he's a perfectly normal person rather than the *Bugle*'s resident recluse. She keeps talking, saying things I can't hear, and then he actually laughs, like he thinks she's really funny. Since when has Natalie been funny?

I look away. Now is not the time to ponder enigmas of the universe.

James has climbed on top of a chair at the front of the room and is waving his hands in a way that's both ridiculous and dignified at the same time, like a world leader getting off a plane. "Friends, Buglers, countrymen," he says in his booming voice, "lend me your ears."

Everyone falls silent. Mr. Powell, at the back of the room,

clears his throat and tilts his head. James steps down from the chair but continues, unfazed:

"Today is the annual Bugler election, in which you will have the opportunity to select your next editor in chief. This is, as you know, a unique tradition among student newspapers, one that our forebears instituted out of a deep respect for the power of democracy. Cherish this privilege to choose who leads you, and vote wisely. As your current fearless leader, I know I leave colossal shoes to fill—"

Here, Tim O'Callahan, editor of the Sports section, catcalls from his desk, setting off a wave of tittering and then urgent shushing. James motions for the room to settle down.

"But I also know whoever you choose will no doubt rise to the occasion with courage, conviction, and charisma." James starts pacing back and forth. "They will work hard to deserve their place on the Wall of Editors. They will spend tireless nights living up to the honor bestowed by this inviolable token, this symbol of clarity and responsibility." He picks up the bugle from Mr. Powell's desk like he wants to play a sound for emphasis, but then decides he'd better not.

"Remember, deliberations will take place at lunch, at the end of which we'll take a vote, so come prepared for a lively debate. And don't be late!" He aims the bugle at me, and then Len. "You guys, of course, are mandatorily exempt." Now he brings his hands together. "On that note, let the speeches begin!"

Len and I have to play rock, paper, scissors to determine

who goes first. The first three rounds, we tie: rock first, then scissors, then rock again. "All right, you two," says James, standing between us like a referee. "We don't have all day."

I look up at Len and notice for the first time that he is very tall. I only come up to his shirt collar, which is partially scrunched under his hoodie. Okay, Len, I think, let's get this over with. Whatever you do, *just don't do what I do.* Nervously, I close my hand into a fist, and we start again. Rock, paper . . .

On the third count, as if he heard my silent plea, he puts two fingers out. A sideways peace sign: scissors. My hand's still in a fist. I'm first.

Len and James leave me at the front of the room, and suddenly, everyone is staring at me. I smooth the front of my sweater and try not to feel self-conscious.

"So," I say, clearing my throat. It's always so awkward to start a speech like this, when you more or less know everyone. Are you supposed to say hi, like it's just a conversation? Or are you supposed to just launch in like it's a TED talk? Which one makes you seem less phony? I brush off my jitters and summon up the words I've rehearsed. "I'm up here because I would like to be editor in chief of the *Bugle*." Surveying the room, I catch sight of James leaning against the back wall. His arms remain crossed, but he gives me a thumbs-up. "And, to borrow one of James's favorite phrases, I think I'd be a damn good one."

That gets some chuckles. Everyone knows that if James scribbles DAMN GOOD WORK all over your draft instead of marking it with edits, you've finally really written something.

Emboldened, I charge forward. "I've been a Bugler since I was a freshman. I've written over thirty articles, including sixteen front-page stories. I've placed four times at the Southern California Student Journalism Conference, and two of those times, I won first. Now, of course, I'm the managing editor, in charge of running our biggest team, News, and overseeing the content for all sections. All in all, I've probably spent over three hundred fifty hours of my life working on the *Bugle*, so when it comes to experience, I've definitely got it covered."

I go on to describe my proposed ideas for next year. We should partner with the AP Computer Science kids to build interactive infographics like the ones in the *New York Times*. We should make embedded-journalist videos like the ones on *Vice*. We should scour the district's publicly available data for stories. We should push the envelope on articles about diversity and gun violence.

"I'm excited for us to work on all these projects together," I conclude. "I hope you'll agree I'm the best candidate to lead us next year."

Everyone claps politely when I sit down.

"Len?" James says next, pointing at him.

Len swings his arms back and forth as he ambles to the front of the room, touching his fists together when they meet in front of him. He then rolls his shoulders back a few times before shaking them out. I get the feeling that I'm watching an athlete loosening himself up, preparing for a competition. Which, in a sense, I am.

"Eliza's a tough act to follow," he says, grinning. He's got a wide smile, the kind that crinkles up his eyes so much that you can't doubt he's smiling at you. "But I guess I'll try." He pockets his hands in his hoodie.

"The truth is, I did just join the *Bugle* about a year ago. Maybe a little more. Some of you know I used to play baseball. Everyone has a thing, right? That was my thing. I was the pitcher, and I was pretty good. You could say I was the Eliza Quan of the Willoughby baseball team."

This seems to amuse everyone but me.

"But I had to quit," he continues, "because I tore a ligament in my elbow. And, not gonna lie, that was hard."

I think back to sophomore year, vaguely recalling he had his arm in a brace at one point.

"I couldn't pitch anymore. Not the way I used to. I couldn't play baseball at all. After the surgery, the doctor said I should stay off the field for a while. It seemed like forever." He pauses. "I felt really lost."

Somehow, the room is hanging on his every word. I wonder if this is because everyone else has also realized that, in the entire time he's been on the staff, this is the longest succession of sentences Len has ever uttered.

"But eventually, I knew I had to try something else. I thought, if I couldn't play baseball, what did I want to do?" He shrugs. "There I was, wandering around the spring activities fair, and then I saw the *Bugle* table. I think a few of you were probably there."

I was there. I had volunteered to staff the *Bugle* table all week, because, well, I thought it was the thing to do if you were going to be editor in chief someday. I remember Len better now. He looked more like an athlete then: less pale, more lean than thin, his frame not yet gone soft in its descent back into skinny boy. His hair, still wavy under a Willoughby baseball cap, was longer, poufed out behind his ears, and also lighter, the kind of honey brown that dark hair becomes after spending a lot of time in the sun.

"I joined the *Bugle* because I needed something to do. But I found it was somewhere to belong."

I roll my eyes exaggeratedly at James, but he seems intrigued.

"I learned that I like to write," Len goes on, "and that I'm not too bad at it either. I haven't won as many awards as Eliza, but I did place at last year's conference. First, in fact. For best feature article." He eyes me for a second, coolly combative, and the frisson that passes between us is electric. "It was my first competition."

I cover up my newly racing heartbeat with an unimpressed sneer.

"All this is to say that I'm not totally inept. But for me, that's not what this is really about. No, this is about giving back to the *Bugle*. This is about giving you a choice in who leads you next year. This is about democracy, and making the *Bugle* the best it can be." He runs a couple fingers lightly through the right side of his hair, which I immediately recognize as a subtle mark of anxiety, but everyone else apparently reads as a Mr. Cool gesture.

"I trust you'll all make the right choice," he says, inclining his head, like he's taking the slightest of bows.

Applause fills the room as he heads back to his seat, and I'm smart enough to know that I'm in trouble.

3

"IT WAS COMPLETE BULLSHIT," I GRUMBLE, TEAR-
ing open a shiny green bag of Korean onion-flavored rings.
They're light, crispy, and perfectly salted—a very dangerous
combination. Winona and I are going through a phase right
now where we're addicted to them.

"Well, you don't *know* it's bullshit," Winona says, taking a
ring from the bag.

Neither of us has a seventh period, so we're hanging out
under the one shady tree in the quad, an old oak in a sea of
scraggy palms. Winona is sitting at one of the lunch tables,
ostensibly doing AP Chem homework, and I'm pacing around
with the onion-flavored chips.

"He was saying some nonsense about 'belonging.'" I crush
the bag in my fist. "That's some serious fake news right there.
I swear he's even more antisocial than me."

Winona pushes her glasses up the bridge of her nose. They're
vintage-looking, with a rose-gold brow line, and the lenses do

nothing to obscure the appraisal she levels at me now. "That's possible?"

Winona Wilson, one of the three Black kids in our grade, is my best friend and also the smartest person I know. I met her back in freshman year, when we got assigned to the same group for a Spanish project. At our first meeting, Divya Chadha and Jacob Lang, the other team members, were slightly more astonished than I was by Winona's announcement that we would *not* simply be recording ourselves demonstrating the usage of the verb *gustar*. No, she said, we would be making a *film*.

"But none of these are even in Spanish," protested Divya, when Winona showed us her proposed inspiration—a series of clips from black-and-white movies that required subtitles to understand.

"Can we just make a normal video and get it over with?" said Jacob, before asking whether we thought he should text Zach Reynolds about the upcoming dance.

"Um, yes," said Divya.

Winona looked at me then, eyes narrowing, and it was clear she was expecting me to be a disappointment, too. But in reality, I was much more interested in her idea than anyone's love life.

"No," I said. "Let's make a film."

In practice, what that meant was that Winona and I ended up doing the majority of the work for the project ourselves. (We earned an A-minus, with points marked off for some incorrect conjugations.) But from that day on, we recognized each other as kindred spirits, and I think Winona's had a pretty good idea of who I am ever since.

Even when I wish she didn't.

"All I'm saying is, I spend so much of my life at the *Bugle*. How is it that I never noticed Len 'belonging' there?"

"Maybe it's because you have a jock blind spot."

"What's that?"

"It's like your brain shuts down when asked to process anything related to sports. Sometimes I feel like you physically can't see jocks, or people you think are jocks—like Len."

"Well, he's an ex-jock."

"Yeah, now you know that, so now you see him."

In the distance, I spot James heading our way, most likely en route to the parking lot. When he notices me, he stops in his tracks—which is odd, because he's normally the type of guy who would shout your name across a crowded room and insist on elbowing past a hundred strangers just to clap you on the back.

Before I have time to process what this could mean, I've already got my hand halfway up for a wave, and it's too late for both of us.

"Hey, Quan," he says, approaching the table. He tries to sound jovial but can't quite hit the right note. "Hey, Winona." Seeing the onion-flavored rings, he helps himself to one. "Oh, nice, I love these."

"So . . ." I hand him the whole bag. "How'd the voting go?"

"Oh." James chomps on a chip. "It was fine."

The little waver in his voice instantly curdles the onion-flavored mush at the bottom of my stomach. "James, tell me what happened."

"You'll find out soon." His skin, already ghostlike under ordinary circumstances, has acquired an unhealthy sheen. "I'm supposed to send the results out tonight."

Winona, who by this point has dropped all pretense of working on her chem homework, stretches her arms across the tabletop. "Just tell her!"

James rubs the asphalt with the tips of his high-tops, first the left side, and then the right. "All right," he says eventually, scratching the back of his head. "Fuck, I'm sorry, Eliza, but they picked Len."

I knew it. I knew this was going to happen. I knew it, but somehow that doesn't make it any easier to believe.

"*They* picked Len?"

James's eyebrows leap together defensively. "Yeah, *they*. I voted for you."

I glance over at Winona, who seems as shocked as I am.

"They picked *Len*?" I say again, louder.

James swivels around to see if anyone has heard. "Yeah, but keep it to yourself for now, will you?"

I gape at the ground, where the grass has been flattened by the metal legs of the picnic table. I've wanted to be editor in chief of the paper for so long, the dream was basically a life function: eat, sleep, plan to run the *Bugle*. Now, though, it's over. Totally crushed. And all because of some *jock*?

"He's not even qualified," I croak. "At all."

I thought this type of nonsense didn't happen on the *Bugle*. That was the whole reason I joined in the first place. That's why I've been so goddamn dyed-in-the-wool about it. The *Bugle* was supposed to be the kind of organization where paying your dues mattered. Where being good at your job mattered. Where having some fucking integrity mattered.

"I don't know." James's shoulders have sagged so much they can't even muster a shrug. "He gave a good speech, I guess."

"*That's* what it came down to?" I flail my arms out and almost wallop Winona in the face.

"Sort of. I mean, I don't know."

"What do you mean you don't know? You were there!"

"I know. I know."

"So, what happened?"

James looks pained.

"Just spit it out, dude," Winona says. She retrieves the onion-flavored rings from him and starts munching on them nonstop, like she's watching a movie and the good part is just about to begin.

"Well," says James. Every syllable is an effort, which is also unusual for him. "I guess some people voted for Len because they thought he seemed . . . well, they thought he seemed more like a leader."

"What?" Winona and I both react at the same time.

"What does that even mean?" I say.

James fiddles with the strap of his backpack. "I don't know if you want to—"

"I want to know."

He surrenders then, and I can see it in his spine, the stiffness melting away with any last attempts at sugarcoating. "People said you're kind of intense, Eliza. And harsh with edits. Overly critical, I guess, was the general gist."

I feel my face go warm. It's one thing to imagine that people are saying negative things about you; it's another to know for certain that they are.

"I just have high standards." My throat is strangely dry. "Like you."

"I know," he says. "And that's what makes you a damn good reporter—"

"*You're* intense," I argue. "*You're* critical. And nobody had a problem voting for *you* last year."

"I know, but . . . come on, Eliza, you know you can sometimes be kind of, well, cold. You just don't even try."

I can't believe I'm hearing this.

"Up until that ridiculous revisionist speech, *Len* is the one who didn't try." I kick the leg of the picnic table, but it doesn't budge. I thwack it again anyway. "When has he ever said two words to you that weren't absolutely necessary?"

"I don't know, people seemed to think he was more . . . approachable. Like he wasn't trying too hard."

"So first it's because I don't try, and now it's because I try too hard? Which is it?"

The exhale from James is weary. "You know what I mean, Eliza."

"No," I say. "No, I do *not* know what you mean."

"Look, if it were up to me, you'd be the new editor in chief. Hands down." He deflates further. "But there wasn't anything I could do. I tried to convince the rest of them, but they weren't having it. They said you were too 'establishment.'"

"Too *establishment*?" I repeat, dumbly.

"Yeah, right? Just because we're friends. But since when have I been 'establishment'?" He seems genuinely nettled by this.

"I—" But I can't decide what to say. I have too many thoughts, all of them caustic.

James shifts his backpack to his other shoulder. "Anyway, I gotta go, Eliza, but I am really sorry." Even though he sounds as if he means it, I feel myself sinking into a sulk. "Hey, are you okay?" He puts a tentative hand on my shoulder.

Stone-faced, I manage two words. "I'll live."

"Okay, well, text me if you want." He holds up his phone as he shuffles backward, away from me, and finally waves before he turns around.

After he's gone, I dig my heel into the grass, each twist more forceful than the last, not caring how deep the divot gets. "Winona," I say, after several seething minutes. "I think the *Bugle* might be as full of misogynistic bullshit as the rest of the world."

Nodding, she bites into another onion-flavored ring and crunches sympathetically. "I think you're right."

When it's time for Winona to go pick up her brother from St. Agatha's, I head to the newsroom to talk to Mr. Powell. I'm not exactly sure yet what I'm going to say, but it'll probably be something along the lines of "this is misogynistic bullshit." Except, you know, in a way that makes me come off as reasonable.

Mr. Powell, however, isn't in the room when I get there, and neither is anyone else. Sighing, I dump my backpack on my desk and approach the Wall of Editors. I stare up at those portraits for a long time. There's good old Harry at the start of the lineup, same as always, with those big eighties glasses that are back in style, and a hair part that hasn't quite come back yet. And there's James at the end, giving side-eye but also grinning, so you can see some of his front teeth. I think it looks just like him, but James complained that his eyes aren't actually that small when he smiles. (They are, though.)

Now Len's portrait is the next one going up there. The guy decided less than twenty-four hours before the election to throw his hat in the ring, and no one asks whether he's committed enough. He decided, today, that he would be charming and friendly, and no one asks whether he actually gives a damn.

I, on the other hand, am a try-hard.

What really gets me is this idea that Len is "more like a leader" than me. I have just as many flaws as anybody else, probably more. But one thing I do have going for me, which seems pretty relevant right now to this question of whether or not I'm leadership material, is that I'm already leading a fucking team. In what way could Len possibly be more qualified than the managing editor herself?

And yet. There is maybe something. I know it, because it kind of worked on me, too, even though I tried to throw it off angrily. It was something in the way he spoke, the baritone equivalent of putting an arm around you, of looking into your eyes as if to say, "I got this," even though you know he's got no such thing. It reassured me even as it caused me to doubt myself. What if he *is* actually better? Why is he so *effortlessly* better?

It's the reason why the majority of the *Bugle* staff voted him to be editor in chief, despite everything. It's also the reason why James can be bombastic and particular, but why I can't be . . . whatever I am.

Because everyone loves a girlboss until she tries to tell you what to do.

Mr. Powell still hasn't shown up, so I go back to my desk and open my laptop. Unfortunately, it's dead, and of course on a day like this, I've forgotten my charger at home. I poke around the room to see if anyone's left one lying around, but after a few minutes, I resort to hunkering down at a *Bugle* computer. Maybe, I reason, I should do some homework while I wait. No need to let this sorry affair waste more time than it already has. Right?

I fish out an AP US History essay prompt from my binder. *Using historical evidence,* it begins, *argue the extent to which scientific or technological change affected the US economy between 1950 and 2000.* Okay, yes, I can do that. With an air of renewed purpose, I open a blank Google Doc and begin typing:

The US economy was significantly impacted by technological change during the second half of the 20th century. Many scientific developments

Ugh, who am I kidding? I jab the backspace key until my intellectually milquetoast drivel disappears. The truth is, I have nothing original to say about the US economy right now. Not one thing. All I can think of is how pissed off I am about this whole Len situation.

So I switch topics, and, just like that, the words flow out in a torrent:

Today, I was passed over for the position of editor in chief of the Bugle. *My fellow classmates have chosen another to be their leader next year. This would be fine, except that it's a blatant gesture of misogyny and I am appalled that in spite of our enlightened age and the supposed progressiveness of our generation, it is an outcome that we are forced to confront. Yes, friends, democracy is not immune to sexism.*

I admit that I am not a likable person. This is not my goal in life. One might say, and many have, that I'm a real bitch. Others have said that I'm "intense" and "overly critical" and "cold." But I am also the most qualified candidate for editor in chief this year, and that is an unequivocal fact.

Facts, however, are not of primary concern to my dear Buglers. No, they are not interested in how much experience a candidate has, or how many hours she has put in. They are not interested in the number of articles she has written, or what concrete plans she has. No, they will be won over by nothing less than the patriarchy, cloaked in cheap sentimentality.

This is where we come to the subject of the chosen one: Len DiMartile, the washed-up baseball star turned boy reporter whose only real talent lies in the occasional clever turn of phrase. But it doesn't matter, because he's tall, because he's got dark wavy hair, and because he sports a sprinkling of acne across his cheekbones the way a supermodel pulls off thick glasses.

But most importantly, he's a guy.

You all know what I mean. This is how it is with all elections, at Willoughby and beyond. A girl who seeks a leadership position must be smart, competent, hardworking, attractive, and, above all, nice. She must be all of those things in order to stand a chance against a male opponent, who frequently only has to be some of those things, and sometimes isn't any of them. A guy who seeks a leadership position just has to try not to mess up too much. Girls get judged for their past; guys get judged for their potential.

This is how I, the current managing editor of the Bugle, *lost out to DiMartile, whose stories I have edited all year. Because I'm "not very nice." Because I "try too hard." Because DiMartile told a good story in his speech, and that was enough to convince everyone that he, despite his typical reserve, is more of a leader than I am. Because DiMartile presented himself as approachable, and that was taken as a revelation, not a fluke.*

I thought my esteemed colleagues at the Bugle *were better than this. They are not. They*

The newsroom door swings open abruptly, and I spin around, reaching behind me to shut off the computer. I somehow failed to notice that classes had ended for the day, and *Bugle* staffers are filling up the room. Although I'm pretty sure no one saw my screen, I'm still seized with a compulsion to get the hell out of there. I decide my talk with Mr. Powell can wait.

"Oh, hey, Eliza!" Cassie, with infallible timing, jumps into my escape path. Maybe I'm imagining it, but I swear she's turned up the force of her cheeriness just for my benefit. "You need a photo of Ms. Velazquez, right? Like an action shot in the cafeteria or something?"

"Uh, yeah," I say, "that would be good."

"Okay, what about the botany-club thing?"

I struggle to remember the botany-club thing. "Oh, uh, Gene Lim said something about how they got local drought-resistant grass that he wants the school to plant in place of the non-local drought-resistant grass they already have."

"Ooooh, right. You thought it would be cool to have a slideshow, right? Of the different kinds of plants?"

"Yeah, something like that. Hey, I actually have to run, so I'll see you later." I start to edge toward my desk.

"Oh, okay. By the way"—Cassie darts her gaze around, then resumes the whisper from this morning—"I'm not supposed to tell you who won the election, so I won't, but I just wanted to let you know that I voted for you."

I blink at her for a second before pulling it together enough to say, "Thanks."

Cassie smiles at me kindly, and then, with the giant camera around her neck, bounds off in her usual way, like a kangaroo.

I don't say a word to anyone else as I gather up my things. I feel awkward, even though it's not like they're huddled together whispering about me. But they know, and, worse, they think I don't. I'm not sure if the distance between us is filled with satisfaction or pity.

Outside, I'm barely through the door when I almost collide with Len.

"Whoa," he says. "Breaking news?"

"No," I snap, and then I suck in a breath. "I mean, sorry," I say again, more calmly. "I wasn't paying attention."

"That's unusual."

I'm holding the door open, and when I look back into the classroom, I see that everyone is watching. They all avert their eyes when they realize I've noticed.

What else is there to do? I gesture at the doorway, as if I'm a goddamn usher, and after a second of hesitation, he steps inside. "Thanks," he says.

"No problem," I reply, and slam the door shut behind him.

4

JAMES DOESN'T SEND OUT THE ANNOUNCEMENT about Len's victory until late Saturday morning.

Sorry, Quan, he texts me afterward. **I had to do it eventually.**
☹

As if I *asked* him to put it off, dragging out my dread like gum clinging to the bottom of a shoe.

I get the email while I'm standing under the fluorescent light of the seafood section in Viet Hoa, a Vietnamese supermarket in Little Saigon. In the background, the tinny crooning of *cải lương* mixes with the sounds of the fish counter: water sloshed from tanks, fins detached in quick cuts, scales scraped off and hosed away in heavy sprays. The cacophony, briny and cold, is indifferent to my dismay.

YOUR NEW LEADER reads the email subject line in James's customary fashion, milking the drama even when it's a tragedy.

I delete his message without opening it.

Kim, bent over the shopping cart with her own phone, is not yet aware of this turn of events. Neither is Mom, who is ripping off a pink ticket from the Please Take a Number dispenser. And I get the feeling that I want to keep it that way.

The three of us are regular visitors to Viet Hoa because it's where Mom likes to do her weekly grocery shopping. She'd really prefer a Chinese market, but the Vietnamese ones are closer, plus they have better prices—and Viet Hoa's can't be beat. Some of Mom's mainland-Chinese friends drive all the way to San Gabriel Valley to do their shopping, but she thinks that's a waste of gas. Her *wàh kìuh* roots run deep, but not that deep.

Still, even though we come here so often, I sometimes don't quite feel as though we belong. Little Saigon, sprawled across multiple cities in Orange County's heartland, is a midcentury suburban hangover made over in the image of the Vietnamese American dream. It's named after the capital of the former South Vietnam, which is where most of the residents are from originally (and the side that the US supported during the war). The South Vietnamese flag, yellow with three red stripes, still flies proudly over Little Saigon's strip malls and office buildings, symbolizing everything the south fought for. But my family, like a lot of ethnic Chinese caught in the crosshairs of that conflict, actually lived in North Vietnam before being forced to flee. Let's just say we didn't fight for much.

"Did you believe in communism?" I asked Mom once.

"We had to learn about it in school, but I found it boring."

"So you wanted the Americans to win?"

"No, they were dropping bombs on us in Hanoi, so I went around insulting Nixon just like everyone else."

Mom's general philosophy is that all wars are futile. "Look at us—after all that, here we are in America. It always happens that way. All that killing and dying, and then the leaders shake hands and it's over. Life goes back to normal. That's why the only thing you should ever care about is making sure you have a bowl of rice to eat."

If our family had a motto, it would probably be that: Make sure you have enough rice to eat. I wish we stood for more, but it seems I'm the only one who cares.

"Please give me a small fish," Mom is saying now, gesturing with her hands. She's speaking in English because the man behind the counter today is neither Vietnamese nor Chinese, but Mexican. Such is the beauty of life in Southern California.

The man grabs his net and dips it into the tank full of swimming tilapia, catching the unsuspecting individual that will go home with us. He lifts our fish into the air, and it flops around frenetically. "This one okay?" he asks Mom.

"Yes," she says, nodding.

"Fry?"

"No, just clean."

There's a sign hanging overhead, with diagrams, that helpfully explains all the options offered by the Viet Hoa fish counter. Option one is to simply have the fish cleaned of its scales, which is Mom's go-to pick. Option two is to have it cleaned and its head chopped off. Option three is all of the above, but also to have its tail chopped off. Option four is to have the thing deep-fried (presumably you can specify which parts you want chopped off in that case, too). The last option is what fills the air with the aroma of freshly fried fish, which smells pretty good until you catch a whiff of it from your clothes later, long after you've left the supermarket.

While Mom waits for our fish to be prepared, I decide to make a quick pit stop in the snack aisle. Maybe it's because I'd prefer not to be interrogated about my bad mood, or maybe it's because I need a break from the mounds of seafood close enough to look in the eye. Hard to say.

But when I reappear at the cart a couple of minutes later, my arms full of enough onion-flavored rings to feed Winona and me for a week, Kim only has one question.

"You guys are still obsessed with those?" She plucks a bag from my hoard and suspends it in the air with the kind of distaste ordinarily reserved for, say, a dying cephalopod.

Mom comes up behind me with our fish wrapped in white paper. "Leave your sister alone. It's good she likes to snack," she says. "You're both too skinny and need to eat more."

Dumping the bags in the cart, I smile sweetly at Kim. She turns back to her phone, but a second later, with the bored finesse of a poker player who's been sitting on a winning hand for a while, she tosses out a question—in Cantonese, just to make sure Mom doesn't miss it. "Hey, I never asked you, how did the *Bugle* election go?"

Mom, who has been marking off her shopping list, recenters her attention on me. Goddamn Kim.

"Oh, you know," I hedge. "It happened."

"It's official, then? You're the new editor in chief?" says Kim.

"Not exactly." I study a nearby pile of little blue crabs pinching slowly at the air. "There was . . . a complication."

"You lost when no one was running against you?" My own sister is gleeful about this possibility.

"No, that was the complication." One of the crabs has climbed on top of another, and I watch as it claws at the rim of the container, so close to escaping and yet not really. "Someone did run against me."

"And now they're going to be editor in chief?"

"Brilliant deductive reasoning, Kim. Can we go now?"

Kim, satisfied with my takedown, pushes the cart forward. But now Mom is involved.

"Who was the winner?" she inquires in Cantonese.

"You don't know him," I say.

"What's his name?" she asks anyway.

I mumble the syllables. "Len DiMartile."

"Huh," she observes. "White-people names are always so hard to say."

We've made it to the front of the store, where the checkout lines are. It's crowded, so Kim tries to maneuver the cart into what seems like the shortest line. I make a show of examining the Marukawa bubble-gum rack while also hoping Mom is done questioning me about Len.

Apparently, she isn't. "Is he very talented?" Mom asks. "More than you?"

It's the second part that makes it such a typically unanswerable Mom question. "I don't know," I manage.

"He must have been talented if people voted for him," says Mom.

I don't respond, instead giving Kim a nasty look as I hand her a package of baby bok choy from the bottom of the cart. She places it carefully onto the conveyor belt, feigning ignorance.

"Well," says Mom, "don't feel too sad. All you can do is your best. There are always mountains beyond mountains." She intones this last piece of wisdom in Mandarin: *Yī shān hái yǒu yī shān gāo.*

It's a weirdly reasonable thing for Mom to say in the face of my defeat, and I'm so surprised that I almost drop a carton of eggs. This is a woman who, like many Chinese mothers, views being second best at anything to be a moral failure. I was sure I would be in for a lecture, but it seems like maybe I won't be getting one after all.

"Yeah," I say. "I guess so."

The subject gets cast aside as Mom focuses her concentration on the cash-register monitor, which displays a running tally of our items as they get rung up. The cashier, a girl with a round face framed in wispy baby hairs, wears a name tag that says *Hello my name is PHUONG*. Over the chorus of chimes emitted by the scanner, she and the bag boy discuss why another girl, named Tuyet, hasn't shown up for work today.

They either do not realize that we understand Vietnamese, or, possibly, do not care.

"Maybe she found a boyfriend," says the bag boy, tossing hunks of lotus root into a tote bag with an abandon that displeases Mom.

"Hopefully one with American citizenship!" Laughing, Phuong shakes her head as she types in a code, from memory, for a package of leafy ong choy. "I think maybe she just quit. She said she wanted to get into doing nails."

The bag boy seems grossed out by this prospect. "I'd rather work here than do other people's nails. Especially their feet." He shudders as he scoops up the ong choy. "Wouldn't you?"

Phuong barely looks at a bag containing beefsteak tomatoes before keying in the code and sliding them down. "*Anh ơi*, why do you think I'm still here?" To Mom, she reads out the total in accented English.

After we're done checking out, Mom makes us wait behind the bag boy as she goes through every item on the receipt.

"We're blocking the way," says Kim, still at the helm of the shopping cart.

"No, we're fine, let's just stand off to the side." Mom drags us over so that we're almost flush against a display of *Paris by Night* DVDs. An episode of that Vietnamese musical variety show is playing on a fuzzy little flat-screen in the corner, and the DVD vendor, an old man in a fleece vest, has been watching it intently. He seems perplexed by our invasion of his sales floor.

"That cashier was too busy chitchatting," says Mom. She apparently did not appreciate the intrigue surrounding Tuyet. "I need to make sure she didn't ring anything up wrong."

Kim and I collectively shrink into ourselves. Hating this ritual is one of the few things in life that we agree on, but there's no fighting against it. Ever since that one time some unfortunate cashier accidentally rang up a bag of Gala apples as Fuji apples, resulting in an unfair overcharge, Mom has been certain something like that is bound to happen again.

Today, though, this rite of frugality seems almost acceptable. Why *not* take time to be a vigilant consumer? Why *not* be so engrossed in such a preoccupation that you don't have a chance to lecture your aggrieved daughter?

But later, when we're all sitting in the car, with our seat belts fastened and all the groceries loaded in the trunk, Mom says, "Eliza, I know you're not going to like hearing this, but I have to tell you because I'm your mother."

Nothing in the history of the universe has ever followed such a preamble without being extremely bad news. Even Kim, a bystander in this conversation, goes still in the front seat, her thumbs held motionless over her phone.

"Okay." I keep my voice monotone as Mom backs out of the parking spot.

"I just think that maybe next time you have to give a speech or do something important, you should dress a little more nicely."

You know how there's often that one thing someone, usually

a parent, becomes convinced is the solution to all your problems? And even though the thing is so specific and trivial that
no otherwise rational person could possibly believe it's the
driving factor behind anything, they still manage, with pro-
digious creativity, to find ways to make everything about it?

This is Mom's thing.

What I should have done was nod and say, "Yes, Mom,
you're right. The reason I did not get elected editor in chief is
absolutely that I dress like a slob."

Unfortunately, what I actually say is "Are you *serious*?"

"Yes, I'm *serious*," says Mom, as she turns out of the parking lot. Even though she's still speaking mostly Cantonese, she
enunciates that one word, *serious*, in English. "I tried to mention it yesterday morning, but you're so stubborn, and to tell
you the truth, sometimes I just don't have the energy to argue
with you."

"I really don't think this was about how I was dressed," I say
peevishly, less because I think she's wrong and more because
I'm afraid she's right.

"Isn't it, though? People always judge you based on your
appearance. Like when you wear that sweater, it looks like
you're wearing someone else's clothes." She means in a bad
way, of course. "You know, you're lucky you're not A Pòh's
daughter. When I was a kid, if we left the house looking like a
mess, she would hit us. It didn't matter that we were poor. We
had to look respectable."

Kim turns around, and her face is a combination of *I'm
sorry* and *I told you so.*

"A Pòh is the one who gave me this sweater," I point out.

"*Aiyah*, only because she was being nice to you. She probably didn't know you were actually going to wear it outside the house. It's a man's sweater. Even A Gūng didn't want it because it was too big for him."

I pull down the sleeves of the sweater in question, completely hiding my hands. Mom hates this move, probably because it emphasizes the fact that I'm wearing an article of clothing that my grandpa rejected.

"At least it's machine washable," I say.

"Too bad it didn't shrink," says Kim.

Mom ignores us both. "I'm not saying you have to be stylish, because that's a waste of money. But at the very least you need to dress neatly and comb your hair properly. I don't want people insulting you, saying that you didn't have a mother to raise you."

Leaning against the window, I watch through half-closed eyes as we drive by a big shopping plaza with another Vietnamese market, a pretty good pho place, and a sandwich shop where you can get three banh mi for the price of two.

"I also don't understand why you like to wear those dark colors," Mom continues. "It makes you seem sickly. You don't have the look of a leader at all."

I finally lose it. "It's not like the other guy was dressed like the president or something, okay?" I say. "He was just wearing a hoodie and a wrinkled shirt."

"So?" Mom pauses, like she seems surprised to have to explain this. "He's a boy. It's different."

I crumble in my seat and cover my face with my arms, hiding beneath the generous folds of my objectionable sweater. "Can we not talk about this anymore?"

Mom clicks her tongue. "That's what you always say, can we not talk about this, can we not talk about that," she chides. "What I'm saying is reality. It's my responsibility to tell you, even if you don't want to hear it." Then, as an aside to Kim: "She gets mad so easily."

"I do not," I say, muffled.

I hear Mom sigh. "*Bǎo bèi*, I know you're a smart girl," she says. I let my arms drop to my side, and Mom regards me through the rearview mirror. "You'd be smarter, though, if you listened to me."

I bury my face back under my sleeves.

5

ON MONDAY MORNING, I'M IN A CONTEMPLATIVE mood as I cut across the quad to the newsroom, threading absently between the lunch tables. At this hour, the air still has that nice chill to it, and I wrap my cardigan more tightly around me. I don't bother to button it, though, because the cold would just blow into the gap between me and the polyester. But I don't mind, because it's comforting to hug it close.

I considered boycotting the *Bugle*—you know, showing up only so that I could then storm off dramatically, maybe brandishing a big sign that said *I'M TOO GOOD FOR SEXISM* or something. *That* would show them.

Only it wouldn't. I came to the conclusion that my continued presence would probably be worse for everyone than my sudden absence, and I decided that I would much prefer to make it worse.

When I get to the newsroom, I'm expecting it to be empty, since it's still pretty early. But Len is already there, sitting cross-legged in his usual spot, and there's also a fresh cup of coffee on Mr. Powell's desk. His favorite Oscar Wilde quote is printed on the mug, each word a different color of the rainbow: *The truth is rarely pure and never simple.*

Len doesn't acknowledge me when I come in, which is fine. I don't acknowledge him either. His computer, balanced in his lap, appears to have a complete monopoly on his attention. When I walk by him, though, he clears his throat.

"'This is where we come to the subject of the chosen one,'" he begins. "'Len DiMartile, the washed-up baseball star turned boy reporter whose only real talent lies in the occasional clever turn of phrase.'"

I freeze at the familiar words.

"What are you reading?" I say, feeling desperation creep up hot on my cheeks.

"'But,'" Len continues, ignoring me, "'it doesn't matter, because he's tall, because he's got dark wavy hair, and because he sports a sprinkling of acne across his cheekbones the way a supermodel pulls off thick glasses.'"

Len looks up at this point. "So," he says. "You've noticed my acne?"

"What are you reading," I repeat, my horror growing.

"The *Bugle*," he says, pivoting the laptop to show me his screen.

I drop my backpack and dive toward the computers lined up against the wall. Frantically, I open a window and wait for it to load. Then, as a cruel reward, the article appears, as it would on every browser with the *Bugle* set as its default home page (which is to say, every browser on every computer on the Willoughby network, thanks to my own enterprising efforts to make that happen sophomore year):

THE PATRIARCHY LIVES!
By Eliza Quan

"Who wrote this headline?" I say, aghast.

"What's wrong with it?" Len asks, as if he doesn't know.

"It's absurd and completely . . . melodramatic," I say weakly.

"Well . . ." Len turns back to his laptop with an implicating eyebrow raise.

"I swear I didn't post this," I insist. "I didn't mean for anyone to read it."

"That much does seem clear."

I slump in the chair, sliding lower and lower until I notice something that makes me bolt upright. Someone—probably whoever posted it—has added a conclusion, picking up where I stopped midsentence:

I thought my esteemed colleagues at the Bugle *were better than this. They are not. They never have been. In the three decades that this paper has been in existence, only seven of the editors in chief have been female. That's 19 percent. That's lower than the percentage of women*

currently in Congress. We're talking about Con-
gress, people.

Today, the Bugle *could have done a small part*
to bend the arc of the moral universe. Instead, it
has elected yet another male to do a job that, on
just about every criterion, should have gone to
a far more deserving female. I'm disappointed,
I'm indignant, and I'm insulted—but maybe I'm
not surprised.

"I didn't even write . . . part of this," I say, seeming increasingly like I did.

Len shrugs. "I don't know, it kind of sounds like you," he says. "Lots of facts."

He's wearing the same gray hoodie as last week, and right now he's got the end of one drawstring in his mouth; the other also seems regularly subjected to this unfortunate habit. He's looking down at his computer screen, and I notice that his eyelashes are longer, more like a girl's, than mine.

I waffle over how to respond. "Listen, I didn't mean it. What I wrote. I mean, the part I actually wrote."

"You did," Len says, almost before I can get the words out. He's typing something now, fingers flying over the keyboard. "I wouldn't say it was your best work, but you weren't wrong."

Mr. Powell pops in at that moment, holding a stack of copies.

"Quan and DiMartile," he says, radiating pride at us. "The new twin pillars of the *Bugle*."

Mr. Powell is a nice guy. He's not that old, but I overheard Ms. Norman, who is ancient, say that he "dresses like he campaigned for Bobby Kennedy in 1968." She means this as a compliment, I think.

I attempt a smile, but it turns into a grimace. Mr. Powell looks from Len to me. "Is everything okay?"

"Eliza's written a manifesto," Len says matter-of-factly, and suddenly, I decide he's kind of the worst.

"There's something I need to take down from the *Bugle* website," I say.

Mr. Powell's concern grows as he reads the manifesto, scrolling through it silently. Watching him, I feel like I'm stuck in a nightmare, one of those awful ones that keeps on going even after your dream self gets suspicious enough to ask, "Am I dreaming?" I've convinced myself on numerous occasions that I was definitely not asleep, only to wake eventually in a cold sweat, fists clenched, relieved that I hadn't actually taken the SAT without studying after all.

"Well," Mr. Powell says when he is finished reading, "it seems like we have a lot to talk about."

"We can start with the fact that I didn't post it," I propose.

Mr. Powell considers me for a moment. "Okay," he says. "Let's see who did."

We uncover that the manifesto was published on Friday . . . by me. There it is, in the log. Posted by equan at 3:17 p.m. Pacific time.

"What!" I exclaim. "Someone must have used my account."

Mr. Powell, to his credit, is doing a pretty good impression of believing I am not completely unhinged. "Okay," he says again, scratching his head. "Did you actually write this?"

Inwardly, I curse my words, which parade flamboyantly across the screen with no shame whatsoever. But I can't disown them. "Yeah . . ."

"Though apparently not all of it," Len offers helpfully.

"Not the last two paragraphs," I clarify.

"Okay." Mr. Powell seems to realize this is not a terribly useful detail. "You wrote some of this. How did someone else get access to it?"

"I don't know." I try to remember that afternoon. "I mean, I was writing it here." This new information deepens the lines in Mr. Powell's face. "That probably didn't help," I admit. "Maybe my Google Drive account was still signed in somehow. I thought I turned off the computer before I left, but I guess I was in a hurry." I'm struck by a frightening thought. What *else* could this person have accessed?

"I'm surprised I haven't gotten any calls about this," muses Mr. Powell, as I desperately change my password. "It's been up for a couple of days."

"No one reads the *Bugle* over the weekend," I say hopefully.

"What the fuck, Eliza?" James's voice comes from the door. "You are one ballsy son of a bitch."

Ugh, James. Of course *he's* seen it. Though probably only recently, because otherwise I would have heard about it via a flurry of animated texts.

James barges into the room and dumps his books, full of

loose papers, in front of me. "Jesus!" He sees that we have the manifesto pulled up on the screen. "Did you approve this?" he asks Mr. Powell, who says, delicately, that he did not.

James looks dumbfounded as I explain what happened. "What the—"

"Yes," I interject, "so can we please get on with taking it down?"

"Wait." James holds up a hand. "Are we sure we should?"

Len, who has been silent for most of the conversation, immediately says, "Yes, we should definitely take it down," at the same time that I say, "Are you kidding me?"

"Well," James reflects, "it's technically not good journalistic form to remove something we've already published."

"I don't know how the administration and other faculty will feel about our leaving this up," says Mr. Powell.

"Anyway," Len chips in, "if we're talking about good form, this should have been published as an op-ed, not as front-page news."

"Yeah, but maybe this is what the *Bugle* needs. Some chutzpah. Something in your face. We're apparently at risk of becoming 'establishment,' and we can't have that. I don't agree with everything Eliza said, but this . . . *this* is a point of view."

I slam my hands onto the desk, startling all three of them. "I wrote it," I say. "I wrote it for myself. Someone violated my privacy by posting it, and that is not okay. I was hacked, and that is not the same thing as 'being published,' which indicates intent. And *consent*." I take a calming breath before continuing. "All of your arguments are valid, but the point is, none of them matter."

Mr. Powell, Len, and James look at me blankly for a second. Then James recovers. "Like I said," he says, "a point of view."

They let me have the honor of unchecking the "publish" box, and, just like that, upon refresh, the front page of the *Bugle* is back to its regularly scheduled programming.

If only life were that simple. I've barely gathered my thoughts when other members of the *Bugle* staff begin filtering in.

"Hey," Natalie says, keying in on me but addressing the others. She wields her phone with a threatening waggle. "Did you guys see the front page?"

"Natalie, could you please put your phone away?" Mr. Powell marshals everyone away from the door. "How about we all take a seat?"

A few minutes later, once most of the staff has arrived, Mr. Powell stands at the front of the classroom with his hands on his hips. "Okay, folks," he says. "Some of you may have seen that a piece was published on the *Bugle* website without approval. We've taken it down, but I want to emphasize that this is unacceptable on a number of levels. First, as you should know, I expect you all to treat the *Bugle* as a newspaper of record, which means you should behave with professionalism and journalistic integrity at all times. The editorial process exists for a reason, and all content that we publish under the *Bugle* banner needs to go through it." Mr. Powell pauses. "Yes, Aarav."

Aarav lowers his hand. "Does this mean Eliza is in trouble?"

The room erupts in murmured speculation. I glance at James, who shakes his head, like he can't believe this is happening to me. Len is watching me, too, but his eyes shift away when I notice.

"That brings me to my second point," Mr. Powell goes on. "Eliza says she didn't post the piece, and she is entitled to our trust, as befits our belief in the presumption of innocence until proven guilty. Which means that someone else published her writing without her permission, and that is also against *Bugle* policies. Uh, yes, Cassie?"

"Did Eliza actually write that stuff?" Cassie's voice trembles, and I feel like the kind of person who drowns baby marsupials for fun.

"Ah . . ." Mr. Powell adjusts his sleeve cuffs before answering. "I know that Eliza may have expressed some controversial opinions, but they were also shared prematurely—if they were meant to be shared at all. Those who are interested in exploring the concerns she raised should feel free to come talk to me, and perhaps we can organize a broader discussion. But in the meantime, I'd recommend that everyone respect Eliza's privacy in this situation."

Sometimes, I seriously think Mr. Powell deserves a standing ovation.

"Now, how about we get back to business?" he says.

The News team is supposed to have a weekly status meeting every Monday, so I lug myself over to the cluster of desks where they've assembled, spread before me like the world's most hostile Socratic circle. There's Aarav, typing something on his phone. Olivia, drumming her manicured fingernails on the desk. Natalie, observing me like an insect she has pinned by the wing. And Len, back on his computer, pretending that nothing unusual is happening.

"So," I say, peering down at the spreadsheet that I have open on my laptop. "Any story updates?"

"I actually have a question." Natalie raises her hand, deciding halfway through to catch a lock of hair, which she winds around her finger.

We all look at her.

"Do you really think the *Bugle* is misogynistic?"

Len and I exchange a glance. It happens before I realize what's happening: I look around, my face contorting into *Ugh, kill me now*, and Len's is the only one that responds with *Sorry, dude*.

"I never said that, exactly." My cheeks feel like they probably match the shade of nail polish on Olivia's left ring finger.

"You implied that was why Len got picked for editor in chief instead of you. Didn't you?"

Natalie is asking hard questions, like a good news reporter. I would appreciate this more if I were not the one being cross-examined. I decide to deploy a classic deflection technique.

"You were there, weren't you?" I say serenely. "Why don't you tell us why you voted for Len?"

"Actually, how about not?" Len's interruption is nonchalant, like a throwaway joke, but I learn that he, too, can turn bright pink.

"Hey, Eliza." Mr. Powell has stopped by. "A word, when you have a minute?"

I wave a resigned hand at the News team. "If no one has any updates, I guess we're done," I say, and they scatter like a group of hostages suddenly released.

I follow Mr. Powell outside, and he eases the door closed behind us. "How are you doing?" He sounds worried.

"Oh, you know, no one in there liked me, so I called them a bunch of misogynists, and now they like me even less."

Mr. Powell's laugh is more of a sigh. "I was wondering if you wanted to talk about what you wrote," he says. "It was quite the manifesto."

I trace a crevice in the concrete with my toe. "I don't know." For a second, the anger rises up inside me again. "Don't get me wrong. I definitely think this did have something to do with sexism." All of a sudden I picture Len, and I can't decide whether I'm more humiliated by the fact that I called him the patriarchy cloaked in cheap sentimentality, or that I basically said he makes acne look good.

"Ughhh." Hiding my hands in my sweater sleeves, I press my palms into my face and pull down on my cheeks. "I really just want it all to go away."

Mr. Powell nods supportively. "I'm sorry it's not easier for us to figure out who posted it," he says. "But look on the bright side—even though you didn't intend it, I think you've provoked some serious discussion among the staff, which is always good. And at least the piece has been taken down, right? The worst is over."

I let myself relax a little. Maybe that's true. Maybe I just need to maintain some perspective on the situation, and everything will turn out fine. Totally, absolutely fine.

6

WINONA HOLDS HER PHONE IN FRONT OF MY FACE. "What . . . is . . . this?"

On the screen, there's a Boomerang video of me with my arms crossed, rolling my eyes. To the right, and then back. Over and over. To be honest, I kind of want to download it to use as a personal meme for when Kim sends me annoying texts.

Unfortunately, the Instagram post also consists of screenshots that I don't like as much—along with the following helpful commentary:

@nattieweinberg: In case you missed it: @elizquan wrote this very interesting "manifesto" that was published on the Bugle front page, though it has since been taken down (see screenshots). In it, she accused the Bugle staff of being sexist because we picked @lendimartile to be the editor in chief next year. Dramatic much? Eliza claims she didn't post it. I kind of doubt it. But hey, I'll support free speech.

Eliza can say whatever she wants, and so can we. Is she just being a sore loser or is there something to this whole misogyny thing? Does sexism actually exist at Willoughby? Discuss.

"That's what you call serious service journalism," I gripe to Winona.

"What a load of shit!" she declares.

We're walking to Winona's house with her little brother, Doug, who is still dressed in his St. Agatha's cadet uniform.

"Winona, language," says Doug, who's eleven. He has not yet succumbed to the pull of foulmouthed adolescence, which one day comes for all of us.

"What a load of sheeeeeeeeeee-it," Winona replies.

The Wilsons live in a planned community called Palermo, which is within walking distance of both Willoughby and St. Agatha's. Like the Sicilian city that provided its name, this Palermo is enclosed by brick walls around its perimeter. Unlike the original, this one boasts curving streets wide enough to park four BMWs side by side, as well as pristine sidewalks and lawns lusher than any grass in a desert climate has the right to be.

Right now we're making our way down Palermo Avenue, the neighborhood's central thoroughfare. All the houses on the street are facing the other way, so there's nothing to see except the tops of backyard trees and an occasional basketball hoop. Sometimes it's so quiet that you can hear the gurgling of a faux Italianate fountain.

Today, though, Winona and I are causing a ruckus.

"I could *kill* her." I yank on the ends of my hair. "I don't even know when she took that video."

"Seriously, that's so messed up," agrees Winona. "What are you going to do?"

"I have no idea," I say. "I told her to take it down, but something tells me that's not gonna happen."

The larger problem is that there are already a ton of comments, chiefly from members of the *Bugle* staff, who unsurprisingly think I've gone off the deep end of political correctness.

@livvynguyen: OMG right? I was so shocked.

@heyitsaarav: Dude, sorry @elizquan, but you're totally cray. We're not sexist.

@ocallahant: Uh news flash: @lendimartile was just a better candidate. Not everything has to be about sexism.

@auteurwinona: Can we stop calling every girl who speaks her mind "crazy"? That's sexism right there, in case you didn't notice. Also, since when has it been cool to post someone else's content without their permission?

"Good old Winona," I say. "You tell 'em."

"Girl, you know I got you."

As we turn onto Terrazzo Way, the Wilsons' street, Doug greets a neighbor who is walking a golden retriever. "Hi, Mrs. Singh! Is Sai home yet?"

"Soon, Doug," she replies, waving. "When he gets back, I'll send him right over."

"Dad says he likes those new poppies you put in," Winona reports, nodding at the explosion of shrubbery that has recently replaced the Singhs' lawn. As if on cue, the golden retriever trots over to the tallest plant and raises a leg.

"They are quite hardy, aren't they?" Mrs. Singh pauses to admire her own yard. "Can you believe I ordered them from the internet?"

"No way." Winona's incredulity is flat-out chipper.

"I'll email your parents the name of the company. Your mom was asking."

"Awesome, thanks, Mrs. Singh. I'm sure Mom will really appreciate it." And with that, Winona deftly wraps up the conversation, all the while herding Doug and me up the stone path to her front door.

The Wilsons are the only Black family for blocks, so Winona's parents have always made it a point to get to know all their neighbors. Winona says her dad believes it will ensure that the Wilsons are seen as part of the community, which is otherwise mostly white and Asian. Mr. Wilson, a colossus of a man with broad shoulders and an even bigger smile, is a former college football player and current vice president at an apparel company—the kind of success who believes he owes everything he's achieved to God, country, and decorum. "Never get noticed for the wrong reason," he likes to say. "Don't give them a chance to take you down."

Winona plays by her dad's rules, but only for now. "I obviously get where he's coming from," she often explains. "But becoming the unofficial mayor of McMansion Land isn't gonna fix everything."

For Winona, the real dream involves one thing: making movies. Since that first Spanish class project, she's become a lot more well-known at Willoughby for her videos, nearly all of which have garnered rave reviews (the sole exception, a satirical piece on climate truthers, is a work that Winona feels has been misunderstood to this day). Her current project, a short film starring Doug and Sai, is called *Driveways*, which Winona describes as "a meditation on two boys, their friendship, and the different ways of being dark-skinned in suburbia." She's planning to enter it into the National Young Filmmakers Festival—which is basically, as she puts it, "Sundance for high schoolers, so, yeah, kind of a big deal."

Last year, her entry to the festival was rejected, and I know that really bummed her out. That film had been a bit of an experiment—instead of leaning into the social justice topics that she typically explores, she decided to tell a semiautobiographical story about a doll that her grandma had given her years ago. The feedback, however, was that the piece was "charming, but could have tackled larger themes." I wasn't sure that was entirely fair, but the comments seemed to really stick with Winona, who insisted she wasn't going to be the kind of artist who cried over criticism. Since then, she has spent a lot of time trying to figure out an idea that feels weighty enough to be a contender for this year's competition, and it wasn't until last month that she came up with *Driveways*. She's convinced, though, that this is going to be a winner—her most important work yet.

That's why, in the roughly three weeks we have left, we're going to work extra hard to make *Driveways* the absolute best it can be. I'm the producer on the project—which, because it's a Winona Wilson production, means I also spend a lot of time being a story editor, production assistant, gofer, boom operator, and everything else in between. We're a lean team, but it works.

"Hi, Smokey!" Doug bends over to hug their family dog, a gray-blue Bouvier des Flandres and schnauzer mix who has come over to welcome us, wagging her tail. Smokey is both the first Bouvier des Flandres and the first schnauzer that I've ever met, and also one of the cleverest dogs I know. She has an extremely magnetic personality and more fans than I could acquire in a lifetime.

"By the way, did I tell you that Serena Hwangbo talked to me today?" Winona asks, as I find myself sinking into the low-pile carpet to pet Smokey.

"Really?" Serena, the junior-class president, is one of those popular girls whose social standing has been built primarily on her being the girlfriend of a series of Willoughby heart-throbs (currently Jason Lee, a senior on the baseball team) and secondarily on her being Korean, which is the largest Asian demographic on campus and therefore the coolest. She's also known for being "nice," which Winona has always considered a mild form of acquiescence to the patriarchy: "She smiles too much to ever be told that she needs to smile more!"

Apparently, however, Serena has now had the gall to request a favor from Winona. "She asked if I wanted to make the prom promo video," says Winona, sounding as if the request involves squashing a nest of cockroaches.

"Are you gonna do it?"

"I don't know," she says. We stampede up the spiral staircase that leads to Winona's room. "I'm over here struggling to make art, and she wants me to film a glorified commercial?" Her lips compress into a thin line. "Also, the theme is *Pretty in Pink*, and I feel like I might be philosophically opposed to it."

"The theme, or prom itself?"

Winona tosses her backpack on the floor and thinks for a second. "Both. But I meant the theme."

"Because you're against John Hughes?"

"Am I against prom being an homage to a man who, despite his gift for chronicling adolescence with ingenious sensitivity, was also probably sexist, racist, and homophobic? Yes." Winona transfers a pile of clothes from her chair to her bed. "But I'm probably giving Serena Hwangbo too much credit. Maybe she doesn't even know who John Hughes is. Maybe she just likes pink."

"No way. She has to know."

Winona sniffs. "Have you met her?"

Now she starts sifting through the mess on her desk. A book of movie reviews by Pauline Kael gets placed carefully on a shelf, but just about everything else finds itself on the floor. A plastic bag that used to contain baby carrots is thrown in the trash, but not before the last dried-up piece gets fed to an enthusiastic Smokey, who has followed us upstairs.

"Here it is." Triumphant, Winona holds up the tattered pages of a script. "I made some notes since our last shoot."

Twenty minutes later, we're outside on the sidewalk in front of the Wilsons' house. Sai, a round-faced kid with thick hair that sticks up in the back, stands in front of Doug. The two of them play a hand-slap game while Winona crouches next to them with her camera and I hold the boom mic overhead.

Sai and Doug stare at their hands intensely, just as Winona directed them to. Sai's palms are facing up, while Doug's are on top, facing down. When Sai's hands quiver, Doug snatches his away. Then, just as quickly, he stretches them out again, and it's back on.

The sun is directly overhead, and a shiny layer has developed on Doug's forehead. Sai leans forward, his face imperturbable. His hands remain still. Then, *slap*! His attack makes contact.

"Damn it, Sai!" Winona drops the camera from her face, which I take as a sign to mean that it's okay to lower the boom mic. Carrying that thing is tiring!

"Language, Winona," says Doug.

Winona ignores him. "You're not supposed to actually get him, Sai. We went over this."

Sai is grinning like he's just stuffed a ton of candy in his mouth. "I know, but I can't help it."

Winona turns to Doug. "Also, why are you so bad at this? Did I teach you nothing?"

I block their impending squabble with the boom mic. "How about we just try it again?"

We set up the scene once more and start from the top. Again, Sai and Doug stare at their hands. Again, Winona trains the camera on them. Then, just as Sai is about to make his move, my phone buzzes. Everyone's attention fixes on me.

"Damn it, Eliza!" says Winona.

"Language—" Doug begins.

"Damn it, Doug!"

"Sorry, my bad." I pull my phone out of my pocket under the guise of silencing it, but instead find myself checking the notification.

"Give me that!" Winona swipes the phone out from under my fingertips and stomps toward the front door. "I'm enforcing a new rule: no devices on set." She pops inside and reappears a few seconds later, empty-handed. "Let's focus now, okay?"

Nodding, I lift the boom mic into the air, and we all return to our places—just as a faint buzz wafts through the window. And then another. And another.

I fidget, fighting the urge to run up the steps, but Winona wags a finger at me. "Nuh-uh, Eliza," she warns. "Don't even *think* about it."

7

BUT HERE'S THE FUNNY THING ABOUT COM-
ments on social media: just because you don't think about
them doesn't mean people stop posting them.

By the next morning, Natalie's post has, to my consterna-
tion, gone positively viral by Willoughby standards. I'm pretty
sure more people have read the manifesto in the past twenty-
four hours than everything I've ever written for the *Bugle*
from the past three years combined. I don't even know all the
commenters, but they definitely seem to think they've got me
figured out. And most aren't fans:

@joeschmoez01: Poor guy. This bitch is going OFF on
him for no good reason.

@gracenluv: What is she even talking about? What sexism do we experience here? The junior class president is a
girl! 🙋🏻

@walkerboynt: When's the last time we had a Black or
Latinx school president though? #realquestion

Occasionally, a few throw me a bone by saying I made some good points but am ultimately misguided:

@hannale02: I get what she's saying, but NO ONE cares who's in charge of the Bugle. Can't she make a fuss about something actually important?

@lacampanaaa: Okay but it's not enough to just have women take over. The WHOLE SYSTEM has to be reimagined.

There are also a lot of comments about my appearance, which, apparently, is relevant after all:

@getitriteyo: She needs a haircut.

@notyourlilsis: Honey, you need to take better care of yourself. That sweater ain't doing you any favors.

@andmanymore502: She's sorta cute for an Asian girl. Not much ass though.

Most humiliating, though, is this preposterous backstory involving a failed romance between Len and me:

@benimator: Did he start screwing another chick or something? She sounds real pissed off 🌀

@socalsurf18: He must have dumped her. She just needs to get laid.

@78coffeeabs: Dude I don't blame him. She's def not hot enough to be that extra.

When the bell rings for lunch, I wrap my sweater around me and walk to my locker with my head down, eyes glued to my phone. All around me, people are pouring out of the classrooms and crisscrossing the quad, but I ignore them all. Even though I know I shouldn't, I scroll obsessively through the latest comments, each one a platitude sharp as a knife. I'm so focused on following my social evisceration online that I don't realize that I'm about to stumble onto a related discussion happening in real life.

"I always knew Eliza was intense, but that manifesto was just so over the top, don't you think?" From around the corner, I hear Natalie before I see her, and I freeze. My locker is just a few feet away, but it's also *toward* the direction that Natalie's voice seems to be coming from, and despite all evidence to the contrary so far, I do possess some semblance of self-preservation. I'm about to bail when I recognize the other voice.

"Yeah, she can be a little . . . tightly wound," says Len.

The sting burns up everything on its way to my face.

Suddenly, I no longer feel like running off. Instead I march toward my locker, even as Natalie, getting closer, says, "Honestly, I'm glad you're going to be the editor in chief next year. It's about time for a change. The way Mr. Powell just let her off the hook . . . what's up with that?"

I tell myself that I'm just going to open my locker, get my lunch bag, close my locker, and act like I can't hear a word either of them is saying. Just open my locker, get my lunch bag—

"What the hell?" I sputter, in spite of myself.

I stare at my locker, which has been newly emblazoned with a single word, written jaggedly with permanent marker: *FEMINAZI.*

Because speaking out against sexism is exactly like

supporting a political regime that committed one of the worst atrocities in human history. Ludicrous.

I look around for the culprit, but the only thing I register is Natalie and Len rounding the corner, both surprised to see me. Natalie regains her composure first. "Let's talk later," she says to Len. And then, for my benefit, she adds, "Hi, Eliza," before flouncing away.

I reach for my combination lock, thinking that if I busy myself with it long enough, Len will just walk right past me and the situation will be over. But as soon as I touch the lock, it pops open—even before I've entered the combination. I'm instantly suspicious, because this is not, under normal circumstances, how you want your combination lock to work. Slowly, I unhook it and crack open the door.

I yelp as an avalanche of tampons tumbles out, spilling onto the concrete.

"What the *hell*?" I stagger backward. Unfortunately, Len is right behind me and reacts a moment too late. He gets shoved in the side by the double-compartment behemoth that is my backpack, that eternal armor against coolness, fortified as usual by the weight of too many textbooks.

"Geez, what do you have in there?" says Len. He rubs his arm reflexively, and I am mortified.

"Books," I say, my cheeks achieving a level of heat that I did not realize was possible in so few seconds. "I didn't . . ." I find myself gesticulating feebly at the tampons on the ground, as if they will offer a rational explanation for what just happened, but I stop because I realize that what I'm doing is calling a boy's attention to the fact that there are a bunch of tampons on the ground. Presumably mine.

Len, in a reasonable if somewhat mindless response, bends over to help collect the tampons that have rolled over to his feet. But then something dawns on him.

"Wait, are these . . . ?"

"Yes," I say, numb to all feelings at this point. "They're tampons." I clamber onto my hands and knees to gather up as many as I can.

"Are you sure you have enough?"

I shoot him a silent killer of a glare, then resume my furious raking.

Len eyes the *FEMINAZI* on my locker door. "Do you, uh, need help?"

"No thanks." I stand up to stuff fistfuls of tampons back into my locker. "I'm beyond your help. Too 'tightly wound' is what I've heard."

This makes Len go pink, but he seems otherwise unbothered. "Well, why do you care what a washed-up baseball star has to say?" he replies, handing me the tampons he's picked up. I open my mouth to respond but nothing comes out. He smiles at me, wryly, and walks away.

I feel this strange urge to run after him, to grab his arm and say, "Hey, I didn't mean it like that. There's nothing wrong with being a washed-up baseball star. I don't even like baseball stars."

But the explanation is falling apart even in my fantasy, so I don't say anything. Instead, I just stand there, watching his loping gait reveal slivers of white sock at his ankles.

Sighing, I stoop down to corral more of the tampons. I have no idea what to do with them all, because I don't even *use* tampons. It seems like a waste to throw them away, but I can't exactly leave them in my locker forever. I start loading them into my backpack instead—maybe I can disperse them among the girls' bathrooms?

I slam my locker door shut, and the *FEMINAZI* scrawl stares back at me. I try to rub at it with my cardigan sleeve, but it doesn't come off. Not even a little bit. I take out my phone and start to google *how to remove Sharpie from a metal locker* when the absurdity of this whole situation hits me. But ignoring it hasn't worked, and lashing out is only going to make me seem even more like a hysterical female.

And that, with my backpack full of tampons, is when I figure out exactly what I need to do.

8

WINONA IS SKEPTICAL. "I DON'T KNOW ABOUT this."

"It's taking back the narrative," I say. "I'm telling you, it's a brilliant move, because no one expects it. No one thinks you're going to agree with them when they shit on you. It'll totally throw them off."

We're in the multipurpose room, which is where the morning announcements are broadcast live every day at eight a.m. sharp. I've snuck out of the *Bugle* ten minutes early to join Winona, who has a shift working the camera this morning, and who has begrudgingly agreed to help me.

"While it's great that you're the kind of person who refers to her own plans as 'brilliant,' I don't think this is going to get people to stop calling you a feminazi," she says, adjusting the tripod. "If anything, it's probably going to get worse."

"Yeah, but it won't matter, because I'll have owned it," I explain. "The only thing worse than being insulted is being insulted for something you haven't owned."

"Interesting philosophy on insult," says Winona.

The announcers today are Serena Hwangbo and Philip Mendoza, who is the school treasurer. It's not a requirement to be involved with student council in order to read the morning announcements, but there's a high overlap between our leaders and the population of Willoughby students who think they look good on camera.

"Hi, Eliza," Serena says, in a tone that manages to question my presence and convey a warm welcome at the same time. She flashes a smile that can only be described as megawatt. Man, that girl had a good orthodontist.

"Hi," I say, but that's it. I'm not about to explain myself to Serena Hwangbo, which is okay, because she loses interest in half a second.

"Okay, places everyone," Winona calls out, getting behind the camera. She loves saying things that make her sound like a director. "Five, four, three . . ." She finishes the countdown silently, with just her fingers, and then they're live.

"Hello, Sentinels!" says Serena. "It's Serena Hwangbo here . . ."

"And Philip Mendoza."

"Please stand for the Pledge of Allegiance."

I zone out during the recitation of today's cafeteria menu, reminders about upcoming standardized testing dates, and a bunch of other boring stuff that is normally the soundtrack to my last-minute studying. I wonder if Mr. Pham, whose AP

Chem class is my first period of the day, will mark me tardy.

Winona pokes me. *Get ready,* she mouths. I step in front of the maroon backdrop that has been set up next to where Serena and Philip are sitting.

"And now for today's special guest," Philip is saying.

Normally, this segment of the morning announcements is reserved for people like the basketball-team captain urging everyone to attend a home game, or the Key Club president asking people to please donate canned food. It's not hard to get this airtime, but you do have to submit a request for approval by Ms. Greenberg, the faculty adviser who oversees the announcements.

Today, though, the special guest is me, and I haven't submitted any request. Winona, in an act of true friendship, has just slotted me in.

She swivels the camera over to me, and it's now or never.

"Thanks, Philip," I say, like this is totally supposed to be happening. "I'm Eliza Quan, managing editor of the *Bugle*. Most of you probably know me because I wrote that manifesto. You know, the one about sexism and the *Bugle*. The one that's been getting *lots* of attention."

Ms. Greenberg has gotten up from her desk, where she was on her computer, and is looking very confused. I figure I have about sixty seconds before her disorientation turns into disapproval and she tries to get me yanked off the air.

"First," I say, "for the record, the manifesto wasn't meant to be published. Someone did it without asking me. So I apologize for any comments that may be misconstrued as a personal attack against a specific individual. However, I stand by my observation that Willoughby is not, as so many are trying to claim, beyond sexism."

Ms. Greenberg is now gesturing at Winona, who is making a valiant effort to appear as though she does not understand what the problem is. She puts a finger to her lips and points to me, like she's saying, *Can't talk, we're recording!*

"We all know that the two oldest—and, some might say, most venerable—student groups on campus are the Willoughby Student Council and the *Willoughby Bugle*. Most Willoughby students who go on to the Ivy League and other elite colleges invariably pass through one or the other. But did you know that girls rarely get elected to the top leadership position of either organization?"

I spent yesterday afternoon in the Willoughby library, trawling through old yearbooks with a spreadsheet, and as a result, unearthed some very interesting numbers.

"The student council has an even worse track record than the *Bugle*—in almost forty years, during which female students have consistently comprised at least half of the Willoughby population, there have only been five girls elected school president. Sure, we get female class officers and female treasurers and vice presidents, just like we at the *Bugle* get female section editors and even female managing editors." I cross my arms. "But what does it say that the *top* positions remain so unequivocally, stubbornly male?"

I glance over at Ms. Greenberg, who has now stopped trying to interfere and is actually just standing there, listening. Time to throw down the gauntlet.

"So, today, I'm here to take my manifesto one step further," I say. "I challenge us to make this the first time in Willoughby history that we get both a female school president and a female editor in chief in the same year. That means I'm calling for every qualified girl to run for school president in next month's student-council election." Then I make sure to look directly into the camera. "That also means I'm calling for Len DiMartile to step down from his position as next year's editor in chief."

I pick up my backpack, unzip the main compartment, and pull out a giant pin that says *I AM A FEMINIST*. I made a couple dozen last night, using those clear plastic buttons that you insert paper into, and I've left a bowl of them in the girls' locker room. *Take one if you believe in gender equality*, I wrote on a sign.

I attach the button to my shirt now. "Some of you may think this makes me a 'feminazi.' But really, the only thing it makes me is a feminist."

Now I flash a smile to rival Serena's. "And the next time you want to fill my locker with menstrual products"—I grasp the sides of my backpack with both hands—"do me a favor and make them pads." I dump all the tampons onto the floor. "I've never been a tampon girl myself."

Then I walk off-screen.

Winona rotates the camera back to Serena and Philip, who both still have their heads turned, staring at me. Winona waves at them, and Serena recovers first.

"And that's all we've got," she says, laughing like she's not sure just what happened, but she manages to remember the sign-off. "Good morning, and good luck!"

9

DR. GUINN, PEAR-SHAPED AND BALDING, LEANS
back in his chair and smiles at me. I've always thought he was
an okay guy, but as his eyes crease up now, I wonder if what
Winona has been saying for years is actually true: that's not
a twinkle behind those round Santa glasses. It's something a
little more sinister. Like a glint.

"How are you doing, Eliza?" he asks.

I'm sitting on the edge of a district-issued armchair with my
backpack still on, like I'm convinced Ms. Wilder, the admin,
will come in any minute and tell me this is all a mistake. That
it wasn't me Dr. Guinn wanted to see at all, it was the *other*
Eliza Quan. The one who does shit outrageous enough to war-
rant being called to the principal's office.

"I'm fine," I reply. "How are you?"

Dr. Guinn sits up and rests his arms on the desk, hands
clasped. "To be honest, my dear, I'm feeling a little surprised.
Normally, you're the one setting up our meetings."

I've interviewed Dr. Guinn loads of times for the *Bugle* over the years, and I have to say, this seat has never been as uncomfortable as it is right now.

"Well, I guess you'll be asking the questions today," I say cheerfully.

"Very true." Dr. Guinn chortles. "Very true." He leans back again, smoothing his tie, which is printed with mallard ducks. "How about we dive right in? Do you know why I've asked you to come in today?"

I look down at the little tray of butterscotch candies that Dr. Guinn keeps near the edge of his desk. I think about taking one, but decide against it. "Because of my unscheduled morning announcement?"

Dr. Guinn smiles again. "This conversation isn't meant to be punitive, Eliza. I'd just like to have a discussion." He taps his fingers on the armrests of his chair. "You've brought up some interesting points about gender and leadership at Willoughby, both in your essay—or manifesto, as I think you call it—and, yes, your announcement this morning. It's true that we still have work to do when it comes to those numbers you cited."

I brace myself, because that can't be all that he wants to say.

"And, of course, as an educator, I always encourage students to think critically and express their opinions, as you have done. However."

He crosses his arms, revealing thinning leather patches on his elbows, worn down by many years' worth of arm crossing. "It's also my job to make it clear that there is a time and place to express rational dissent. And, unfortunately, Eliza, the morning announcements, hijacked in the manner that they were, is neither the time nor the place."

At this point, he pulls open his desk drawer and produces an *I AM A FEMINIST* button identical to the one I'm wearing. He must have gotten someone to take it from the girls' locker room for him.

"I see you believe in gender equality," I say.

Dr. Guinn chuckles. "I do," he says, setting the button in front of me. "Very much so. I just wanted to posit, however, that perhaps your cause would be better served by a less antagonistic approach?"

I inspect the button, which lies there like an arraigned criminal. "Is it antagonistic to be a feminist?"

Dr. Guinn folds his hands on top of his desk. "We live in extremely pugilistic times, Eliza. Proponents on both sides of every issue are increasingly entrenched, often with little to no space for reconciliation. I worry sometimes what impact such a culture has on young people." He does, in fact, look aggrieved by this. "It is my hope, you see, that your generation will emerge as a new vanguard of civility and compromise. In fact, I consider it my responsibility to make sure you do."

"I see." I'm not sure how else to respond.

"So, no, my dear, it is not antagonistic to be a feminist, per se. But perhaps think about all the ways you have presented your arguments so far, and evaluate whether you have done so from a place of exclusion or inclusion. For example, encouraging girls to run for school president is one thing. But demanding Len's resignation is quite another."

I mull this over. "That's fair," I say. "But I guess I'm just wondering . . . what would have been a conciliatory response to, for example, the fact that someone Sharpied my locker and filled it with tampons?"

"To start, perhaps not dumping them like that during a live broadcast?"

I mean, I'm not saying the man doesn't have a point.

"Certainly, the original stunt involving your locker was itself unacceptable, and rest assured there will be consequences for the culprit, should he or she be discovered," he goes on. "But frankly, I was disappointed with your own lack of judgment in perpetuating the offense. To discuss such, ah, personal matters on the air, especially in an educational setting, is really quite in poor taste."

"It wasn't that personal," I say. "Everyone who's been on social media knows what happened with the *Bugle* stuff. Also, you know, my locker still says *FEMINAZI*."

Dr. Guinn clears his throat. "I meant your discussion about . . . feminine hygiene."

It takes me a minute to understand. "Are you trying to say that tampons aren't allowed on the morning announcements?"

Dr. Guinn studies me for a moment. "Perhaps Ms. Wilder can help explain." He shrugs, like it's not up to him. "I'm just trying to ensure that this is an environment where everyone feels comfortable."

Look, I get it. Tampons are embarrassing. Periods are embarrassing. PMS, for some reason, is not, but that's because it has somehow become a synonym for being in a bad mood while female. The whole specific business with the *bleeding*, though, is still not cool, except in certain woke corners of the internet. And yes, I admit that before my own recent scorched-earth tampon dumping, I was as complicit as the next girl. I even had a whole maneuver worked out to retrieve a pad in class without anyone knowing (reach into backpack under innocuous pretenses, tuck pad into the extremely roomy arm of my sweater, raise hand to go to the bathroom without anyone knowing what I've got up my sleeve).

But it's weird to have Dr. Guinn tell me how embarrassing periods are. The man has never had one in his life—why does he get to have an opinion about it?

"Could it be," I say, in as conciliatory a tone as I can manage, "that maybe it's *not* an environment where everyone feels comfortable . . . if we're not allowed to talk publicly about something that is a normal, healthy part of life for every menstruating student and teacher at Willoughby?"

The old-school intercom on Dr. Guinn's desk buzzes, and it's Ms. Wilder, making an ominous announcement. "Mr. DiMartile is here to see you," she says, and then the static clicks off.

Dr. Guinn holds down the button and replies, "Thank you, Claire, we'll be ready for him shortly." He doesn't say anything to me for a while, long enough for me to start wondering what he meant by "*we'll* be ready."

Finally, he smiles. "Very good, Eliza. It seems we all need, from time to time, to reexamine our worldviews. I take your point." He gestures again at the *I AM A FEMINIST* button. "But I hope you'll also take mine."

He removes his glasses and opens another drawer, producing a microfiber cloth. "You'll find, as you move through the world, that you may feel a lot of anger about the way things are," he says, polishing his lenses. "Part of becoming an adult is learning how to respond in productive ways."

He takes his time with the glasses, every second increasingly harrowing because I have a feeling I'm not going to like what's coming next.

"Let's talk, for instance, about your relationship with Len."

"I—"

"Hear me out, Eliza. You're colleagues. You're peers. Right now, it seems like you're feeling a lot of resentment toward Len, and that's understandable. You feel that something is being taken away from you. And perhaps, in some ways, the situation has been unfair. But life, my dear, is often unfair. The solution, however, is never to dig in deeper where you are. The solution is to reach a hand over the trenches and, as our dear friend Forster would say, connect. Only connect."

He stands up and steps over to the closed door. "To that end, I've asked Len to join our conversation. I hope you don't mind?"

"Ah . . . ," I say, as he opens the door.

Len looks up from where he's sitting, on one of those plastic chairs directly across from Dr. Guinn's office. He's stooped over, elbows resting on his legs like he's been benched. Fanned open in his hands is a thick paperback.

"Hello, Len," says Dr. Guinn, like we're all about to sit down for a nice lunch. "Come on in."

Shutting the book with a soft thud, Len stands and scoops up his backpack in one swooping motion. He drops into the chair next to me and immediately leans back so that the front two legs lift off the floor. His knees almost reach the top of Dr. Guinn's desk.

I feel, suddenly, that the office is too small for the three of us. My backpack is starting to get uncomfortable, but to take it off now feels somehow like a declaration of surrender.

"As I was just telling Eliza," Dr. Guinn begins, "given everything that has transpired, it would be a good idea for you both to put aside hostilities and establish, if not a friendship, then at least a collegial working relationship. Especially since Mr. Powell tells me that Eliza will likely be the managing editor again next year." Dr. Guinn motions at Len. "Unless, Len, you have decided to acquiesce to Eliza's . . . ah, call to action?"

Len unwraps a butterscotch candy. "Not yet," he says, and I have to physically stop myself from rolling my eyes.

"Wonderful." Dr. Guinn looks pleased, as if Len has spoken for both of us. "I've proposed to Mr. Powell that the two of you write all your *Bugle* stories together through the end of the year."

Both Len and I start talking at once.

"I'm the managing editor, that means I *edit*—"

"We don't need to—"

"I'm not supposed to write that many stories anymore—"

"We get along fine—"

Dr. Guinn raises a hand, and we fall silent. "One at a time, please," he says. "Eliza?"

"I spend most of my time editing these days," I explain. "I don't know if I'll have time to cowrite that many stories."

"You're actually working on a story now, aren't you? Mr. Powell mentioned as much, I believe. About the new boba shop across the street? That seems fun. You guys can start with that one."

Mr. Powell, the unwitting traitor. I sag against my backpack a little.

"But you do make a good point, Eliza. Len, since Eliza will be helping with your writing and reporting duties, you can help with her editing duties. Sharing responsibilities will help you learn to work together better."

I start to object to what is clearly a de facto (not to mention premature) demotion, but Len beats me to it.

"Dr. Guinn, I agree with everything you're saying, a hundred percent." He rolls the butterscotch up against the inside of his cheek. "But I guess I'm confused about why all this is necessary, because Eliza and I are already friends."

Both Dr. Guinn and I gawk at him.

"Right, Eliza?" Len says, grinning at me like we hang out all the time. I search his face for some kind of explanation, but I learn nothing except that green flannel makes his eyes look more hazel than brown.

A reasonable response right now, I think, would be to explain to Dr. Guinn that I have no idea what the hell Len is talking about because he is undeniably lying his ass off, so maybe whatever punishment he gets should be twice as bad as mine, and on top of that should not involve me.

But Len is watching me, as if waiting to see if I'll say exactly that, his curiosity draping over me like a poised net. So I don't.

"We're . . . friendly," I say.

"Really," says Dr. Guinn.

"She lent me this, actually," Len says, holding up the book he was reading. It's called *Life: A User's Manual*. I have never seen this book in my life.

"How intriguing." Dr. Guinn examines the cover along with me. It is impossible to tell whether he has read the book or not. "What made you suggest it, Eliza?"

Len starts to say something, but Dr. Guinn shakes his head. "Eliza?" he repeats.

Straightening in my seat, I steal another glance at the book. There really isn't much to go on, besides the fact that it was written by some guy named Georges Perec and apparently was translated from French.

I go with that. "Len is a fan of French literature."

"That's right," Len agrees quickly.

"In translation, though."

"Definitely only in translation."

"And mostly male authors, now that I think of it."

"Maybe you should recommend a female writer next time."

"You know what? Maybe I will."

Dr. Guinn looks from me to Len. The pause feels interminable. "Well," he says at last, oddly amused. "It does seem like you two will make a good team."

Exhaling, I catch myself relief-grinning at Len, who runs two fingers through his hair again, that flick that isn't as casual as it seems—sort of like the boy equivalent, now that I think about it more, of tucking your hair behind your ears. But when he notices my contemplation, he gives me a little smile back, and for a hot second I'm almost sorry that his ploy to foil Dr. Guinn's plan actually worked.

Then Dr. Guinn continues. "Which is why you shouldn't have any problems following through on our plan." He leans so far back that his shiny head almost touches the back wall, and his chair creaks with foreboding. "I look forward to seeing your co-bylines."

10

"WHAT THE HELL WAS THAT?"

Len is traversing across the asphalt in long strides, and I am scurrying to keep up. We're both headed to fifth-period English, pink late slips in hand.

"That was me trying to get us out of this Woodward and Bernstein situation," he says.

"Yeah, I got that," I say, "but what made you think it was a good idea to make up that stuff about me and your book?"

"I needed a detail that would sell the story." He shrugs and pops a second butterscotch candy into his mouth. "It was the first thing I could think of."

"Well, maybe you should've thought about it more. That book is like some random French novel. There's no way I would've known anything about it."

"Now I'm aware."

I trip a little over my irritation.

"So, what's the real story?"

"Hmm?"

"How did you really come across the book?"

"Oh. I found it on one of my dad's bookshelves."

"What's it about?"

He pauses so that I can catch up. "It's about this fictional apartment building in Paris and everyone who lives in it."

I expect there to be more to the synopsis, but I am wrong. I get nothing. We walk a few steps in silence, and I'm about to pronounce this conversation's time of death when he decides to continue after all.

"One of the residents, this rich guy named Bartlebooth, is on a lifelong quest."

I'm mildly curious now. "What kind of quest?"

"A very demanding, very specific one." Len glances over at me, as if to see whether I really want to know. "Involving paintings and jigsaw puzzles and a lot of misery."

"That sounds . . . random."

Len laughs. "It's just an elaborate way to consume his entire life without having anything to show for it. And the sad thing is, he doesn't even succeed. He ends up failing at his own commitment to a pointless existence."

We climb the stairs that lead up to the one indoor hallway on campus, which has been immortalized in a number of Winona Wilson films. Len takes the steps two at a time, like it's easier for him that way.

I give up trying to match his pace. "Did you just spoil the book for me?"

He waits for me at the top of the staircase as I jog up behind him. "Were you going to read it?"

"If I supposedly recommended it to you," I huff, slightly out of breath, "shouldn't I?"

His face splits into a grin, like he's remembering one of his own good jokes. "That was a pretty terrible performance you gave in there."

"I had zero notice! I had no idea what to say."

"You were in a tight spot, I agree."

We make our way toward Ms. Boskovic's classroom, which is at the other end of the hall. Len runs his hand along the top row of lockers, disrupting each combination lock as he brushes past.

"Honestly, I don't see why you had to lie at all."

"It was in the service of a greater truth. See, Guinn's angle is that he just wants us to get along. But we don't *need* to cowrite every story in order to learn to work together. I mean, look at us now, we're already kind of friends."

The claim seems, at best, a gross overstatement. "Still, I wish you'd left me out of it."

Len opens the door for me. "Only because it didn't work."

Our entrance is, regrettably, an interruption. "Hello, love-lies," says Ms. Boskovic from the front, waving her hand out expectantly. As usual, she has on several chunky gemstone rings. ("The only real one is the turquoise," she's admitted.)

The entire class watches as we make the walk of shame to give her the late slips and then duck into our seats on opposite sides of the room.

"As I was saying." Ms. Boskovic barely skims the pink sheets before flicking them into the recycling bin. "Today we're beginning a play that explores gargantuan themes. Ambition. Morality. Violence. One of Shakespeare's greatest works." From her desk, she picks up a book that explodes with Post-its of various neon colors. She holds it with both hands, like a prize, against the black cashmere that enshrouds her generous middle. "That masterpiece, of course, is *Macbeth*."

Ms. Boskovic goes on to explain that we'll not only be reading the play, but also performing it. "Never forget that Shakespeare wrote for the stage," she enthuses. "He wanted his words to be spoken—to be *lived*."

Most of the class stays inert, but Serena Hwangbo, sitting one desk cluster away from me, nods.

"Ideally, we would stage the play in its glorious entirety," says Ms. Boskovic, "but, sadly, we don't have time for such a luxury. We'll just have to make do with some key parts." She trades her book for a can of wide Popsicle sticks, each labeled with a student's name. "I'll divide you into groups and assign each one a scene or two, which you will then perform over the next few weeks."

Winona raises her hand. "No, Winona, as much as I enjoy your auteurship, you may not do a video for this project."

Winona drops back into her chair, like she doesn't see how it makes a difference.

"I want you to experience the thrill of live theater!" Ms. Boskovic shakes the can like it's a maraca. "This is your chance to truly feel the highs and lows of Shakespearean drama."

When no one responds with enough zeal to match hers, she sighs. "If you dress up in costumes, you'll get extra credit." At her last two words, a significant portion of the room becomes visibly more interested.

Ms. Boskovic picks the groups by randomly drawing Popsicle sticks. I end up with a truly unfortunate mix that includes Ryan Kim, Korean bro and all-around goofball; Serena; and, because Dr. Guinn has apparently paid off the gods of chance, Len.

"Okay, everyone, do a quick huddle with your group," Ms. Boskovic calls out. "Try to get a feel for who you'd like to cast in each part. You have fifteen minutes."

"Dude." Ryan saunters over with his No Fear Shakespeare edition of *Macbeth* already rolled up into a U shape. He looks at me and Len. "Is this gonna be awkward?"

"Why?" Serena is already sitting, her back straight and long ponytail swishing. I can't tell if she's being dense intentionally or not.

"Eliza hates Len." Ryan points at us with his thumb. "Everyone knows that."

"I don't *hate* Len," I say.

"Yeah, I don't think she hates me," says Len, and I decide that actually, I do hate him a little bit.

"Okay, if I say that Len should play Macbeth," Ryan counters, "is Eliza gonna say I'm being sexist?"

I'm not sure if I'm more annoyed or confused. "How is that sexist?" I scrunch my forehead.

"Well, it's the lead role."

"And?"

"You're a feminist, right?" He points to the button that is still pinned to my shirt.

"And . . . ?"

"Maybe you think it should go to *you*."

I roll my eyes so far back, it almost hurts. "I said I was a feminist, Ryan, not a narcissist."

"I think I'll just be Fleance," says Len from behind his copy of *Macbeth*.

"Come on, Ryan." Serena surprises all of us. "Leave her alone."

Ryan backs down, and in the silence, something clicks in my mind. "Hey," I say, "what if Serena plays Macbeth?"

"Ooh!" Ms. Boskovic pops into the discussion as she walks past. "Gender-bending casting. What an inspired choice!" She loops her beaded necklace around her finger. "There's a tradition of that in Shakespearean theater, you know. Women weren't allowed to perform onstage, so all female roles were played by men. I love that you're inverting that. Very *au courant*."

As she leaves us, I say, "See? Ms. Boskovic is a fan."

Serena leafs through her crisp paperback, one of those fancy new Shakespeare reissues with a minimalist illustration on the cover. "I guess I could do it?"

"Sure you can," I assure her. "I think you're gonna be great. Plus, Ryan's right."

It's Ryan's turn to be confused. "I am?"

"Yeah, why not make this a feminist performance? Why not cast a girl in the lead?" I'm already warming up to the prospect myself.

"True," says Serena, and you can tell she likes the idea, too.

Len raises a hand. "Who's gonna play Lady Macbeth?"

"I'll do it," I decide. "Unless Ryan wants to . . ."

"Uh, no," says Ryan. "No, it's fine. I'll be, uh . . ." He flips a page. "Banquo. That's a dude, right?"

"Yeah, man, you'd be my dad," says Len.

"Oh, for real?" Ryan seems tickled by this. He puts on a deep voice. "Len, *I am your father.*"

Len busts up laughing, which makes me think he has a bad sense of humor.

"Okay, then." I close my own copy of *Macbeth*, a hand-me-down from Kim that's still in pretty good condition because she's fussy about books (not sure why, considering how little she reads). "Any objections to our casting plan?"

Serena shakes her head while Ryan shrugs. Len leans back, clasping his hands behind his neck.

"Hard to argue with Lady Macbeth."

11

"OH, ELIZA," MOM SAYS WITHOUT LOOKING UP. "I got a voice mail today, but I don't understand it. Can you help me to check?"

She and Kim sit at the dining table, and in front of them, Kim's laptop is surrounded by a spread of paperwork. The fluorescence of the ceiling lamp, and their gravely intense focus, is reminiscent of an operating room. It's almost ten o'clock, and they are still deeply engaged in the annual ritual known as TurboTax.

"Employer's federal ID number," Kim prompts from the screen, and Mom, armed with her W-2, reads it aloud.

The kitchen, which is at the back of the apartment, is separated from the living room only by a counter that functions as a room divider. On one side, there's the stove, overhung by cabinets and the built-in range hood, and on the other, a line of plastic bar stools. Even though I am sprawled out on the couch, trying to read *Macbeth*, I can see Mom and Kim bent over the computer.

"Right now?" I say, dog-earing a page.

"In the front pocket." Mom indicates her lunch bag, which sits on the counter.

Sighing, I drag myself over to dig out her phone. I assume it's just going to be a particularly committed telemarketer, because Mom is always getting worked up about things like that: salesy voice messages, official-looking letters, class-action settlement notification postcards.

But then I see the transcription:

> *Hello, this message is for the parents of Eliza*
> *Wand. This is Dr. Quinn . . .*

Dr. Guinn! Could the man be any more diabolical? Does he not realize how much a phone call like this can set an Asian kid back?

Reluctantly, I bring the phone up to my ear. A distorted version of Dr. Guinn's voice blares so loudly, it sounds like I've got him on speaker:

"Hello, this message is for the parents of Eliza Quan. This is Dr. Guinn, the principal at Willoughby. It's Wednesday, about ten thirty a.m., and I'd just like to chat with you about how Eliza is doing, and some concerns I have about her recent behavior. Please give me a call back at . . ."

Maybe I can delete the voice mail and tell her it wasn't anything important. A reminder about an upcoming fundraiser, maybe. Or a survey for parents. Mom hates both fundraisers and surveys.

"Um, it's just my school." I zip the phone snugly back into the lunch bag.

Mom cranes her neck so that she can examine me over her reading glasses. "Your school?"

"Yeah . . . my *haauh jéung* wants you to call him back," I say, hoping that the Cantonese will make the whole thing go down easier.

"*Há?*" Mom glances at Kim, who shrugs. "Why?"

Through the front door, I hear the sound of fumbling keys, which means that Dad is home. I run over to unlock the door for him, but he's already opening it, appearing now in the doorway with a large cardboard box.

"Look what I found," he says, slipping off his workman's shoes by the door.

Dad is a cook at a Chinese restaurant called Seafood Island, where he spends most of his work hours in the oil-soaked glow of a kitchen range. As a side effect of the job, his clothes get coated with a persistent layer of grease that comes out only when Mom uses dish detergent in the wash. His footwear, though, becomes unsalvageable every six months, so that's why he only ever buys the cheap stuff from Walmart. Dad hates to throw away anything as sturdy as a pair of shoes, but once they've become misshapen with grime, what choice do you have?

"*Aiyah,* why are you always bringing trash into the house?" Mom complains, as Dad parades his box into the living room. Considering that he almost definitely retrieved whatever he's carrying from the side of the road, this is technically a fair question.

"What trash?" Dad sets the box down on the coffee table.

"This is something valuable."

"What is it?" I steal over to get a closer look.

"Wait a second," Mom says. "We're not done talking." To Dad, she reports, "Eliza's *haauh jéung* called me. I don't know what she did."

"Is that right?" Dad says, but he opens the flaps of the box so I can peer inside. I'm surprised to see that it contains what appears to be a record player, the kind that also has a built-in cassette player and AM/FM radio.

"Cool!" I say. "When do you think this is from?"

Dad considers the knobs. "1980s."

"Does it work?"

"No, but I can fix it." Dad fiddles with the turntable arm. "So easy."

"Eliza, come back here," Mom commands.

I follow Dad into the kitchen, but we both get stopped. "Shoes," Mom reminds us, pointing at the house slippers that we use exclusively in the kitchen. Dad puts on a pair and proceeds to heat up the fried rice he's brought home from the restaurant. Because there aren't any slippers left, I hover by the counter, toeing the border where low-pile carpet meets floral-printed laminate.

"Box one," says Kim, as if she's the only one in the room. She reaches for the W-2 form.

"So?" Mom waits.

I let out a deep sigh, and then I explain what happened. The accidentally posted rant. The backlash. The morning announcement. The conversation with Dr. Guinn.

Dad sits down at the table with his bowl of rice, making no comment, while Kim seems almost sorry for me. Mom, thoroughly scandalized, has many questions. The first one: "Why didn't you bring home the *waih sāng gān*? If they were still wrapped, we could have used them."

Not knowing the Cantonese word for "tampon," I had referred to them as *waih sāng gān*, which means "pads."

"No, they're the other kind. The skinny ones. The kind—"

"Oh, those are no good. Don't use them unless you want to die." Having gotten that Asian-mother propaganda out of the way, she moves on to the heart of the matter. "Will this impact your report card?"

"What? No, it doesn't have anything to do with grades."

"Will he write a bad letter when you apply to college?"

"It's fine, I just won't ask him to write me one."

Mom shakes her head. "Really, Eliza. What a loss of face. Now I have to call your school? If this had happened to me when I was your age—"

"A Pòh would have hit you," I interrupt.

"Exactly," Mom says.

"But Dr. Guinn isn't Chinese, so maybe there's been no face lost. No need to hit anyone."

"*Néih góng māt gwái ā?*" Mom waves away my nonsense. Turning to Dad, she says, "This daughter is always getting told off by teachers."

"What? When has that ever happened?" I've never gotten a

detention in my life. I haven't even gotten one for this!"

"Like how in elementary school, you never got an award for 'outstanding citizenship' like all the other kids. You just got it for 'great spelling.'"

I look at Kim, who coughs into the W-2 form.

"It's not my fault I was actually good at something that required skill!"

Mom ignores me. "This whole business with the *Bugle* election. I thought we talked about this." A sudden insight strikes her. "You know what the real problem is? *Néih dōu meih yihng cho.* You still think you're right. If you lost, then you need to accept it and learn to do better next time. Girl or boy, both have to do that. Don't blame outside people for your own mistakes."

I lean over one of the bar stools and rest my elbows on the counter. "But don't you think it's harder to be a woman sometimes?"

"Of course it's harder," Mom says. "I wish I were a man all the time."

It's true. She is always wishing that. She's probably been wishing it since before she was born. Mom, as the story goes, was the fourth daughter in a family with no sons, so A Gūng wanted to trade her for a male child. He even found a local Hanoi Chinese family that was open to the exchange—because they had too many boys already. But A Pòh changed her mind at the last minute, and so they were stuck with Mom.

"Yeah, but what if it didn't have to be like that?" I argue. "What if things could be better?"

"They already are for you," Mom replies. "Even though *your* dad has only two daughters, he is not sad." She turns to Dad. "Are you sad because you have no sons?"

Dad, who has just finished wolfing down his fried rice, stands up to rinse his bowl and chopsticks. His reply is succinct. "No."

"See?" Mom says, like that settles it.

"But I want to make things better *overall*. Starting with what happens at school."

"How have you made anything better? You just got yourself in trouble." Mom sighs. "You already know that the thing that scares your mom most is having to talk to these *gwái lóu*. Yet you insist on making trouble so that your *haauh jéung* calls me?"

Dad places his clean bowl in the plastic dish rack, on top of the dishes that Mom washed earlier. He tries to escape from the kitchen unnoticed, but she catches him.

"Don't you have anything to say to your daughter?"

Dad rubs his nose. "*Aiyah*, this is small stuff," he says, stepping toward the living room. "Just talk to the *haauh jéung* and it'll be fine."

"*Haih lā!* Everything is small stuff. Everything is easy. But I don't see you doing it." Mom adjusts her glasses and refocuses on the computer screen. "Your dad," she says to Kim, "*jihng haih dāk bá háu*. All talk."

As Dad heads to the bathroom to shower, he laughs, imitating Mom. "All talk."

"Exactly!" Mom shouts after him. To us, she adds, "He's

too scared to death to do anything."

"Employer federal ID number," reads Kim. She picks up another W-2 form and places it in front of Mom. "For Dad this time."

12

"HAPPY THURSDAY, SENTINELS!"

I'm hunched over my calculus homework in first-period chemistry, trying to solve for the vertex of a parabola, when Serena Hwangbo's voice bursts forth from the TV.

"Hey." James, bleary-eyed and looking particularly like a nocturnal animal this morning, is taking AP Chem as a senior-year elective to appease his mother, who still thinks he could become a doctor someday. His seat is next to mine, and while he normally crashes from his *Bugle* high around now, today he is trying to get my attention with an uncharacteristic sense of urgency.

I ignore him because I don't want to lose my place in the problem, but he nudges my arm again, causing my pencil to veer off. "You might want to pay attention to the morning announcements," he says in a low voice.

I'm about to tell him to quit trolling when I catch a glimpse of Serena wearing one of my giant *I AM A FEMINIST* buttons. On air.

What the . . . ? Did I just get Oprah-ed by Serena Hwangbo?

The other kids in my class have noticed as well, and they start eyeing the button that I'm still wearing on my cardigan. As we stand for the Pledge of Allegiance, we're all thinking the same thing about Serena's sartorial choice: What could it possibly mean?

We find out near the end of the announcements, when Philip, like the *Good Morning America* anchor he was born to be, tees up the subject. "Serena, I have to ask," he begins. "What's that on your shirt?"

Serena looks into the camera. "Now, Philip, I don't know if you're aware, but I'm a feminist, too. And I'm wearing this to show support for my friend Eliza Quan."

James seems truly befuddled, like he'd sooner get into med school than believe that Serena Hwangbo just called me her friend.

"Sexism does exist at Willoughby, even though we don't like to admit it. And I admire Eliza for taking a stand. It's tough being a leader when you're a girl. People are judging you all the time." Serena steadies herself, her doe eyes nearly welling over with emotion. "People might be judging me now, for agreeing with Eliza. But she's right. I think she should be editor in chief of the *Bugle* next year. And we should all give this inequality thing another look."

This declaration shocks me as much as the rest of the room, and we're all watching the screen to see what else will happen.

"Well, Eliza also wants a girl to be school president next

year," says Philip, who is rumored to be a contender himself. "Does this mean you're planning to run?"

Serena flashes a demure smile. "Never say never."

As they sign off, James jokes, "What the hell, Quan? You're supposed to write the news, not be in it."

"Hey, Eliza." Mariposa Abarca, who up to this point has known me mostly as the girl who routinely disappoints our PE class volleyball team, calls out from across the room. "Got any of those buttons left?"

At the lunch bell, Winona and I head to our usual spot by the library, where there's a nice concrete slab just outside the door, a quiet place shaded by the eaves. As we make the trek out to that far-flung corner of campus, I see Serena and her friends in the center of the quad, under that one shady oak. Though Winona and I like to sit there *after* school, it's too much trouble to fight for it during the prime time that is lunch.

"Honestly," says Winona, "I'm surprised Serena had a coherent thought about any of this." When I give her a look, she shrugs. "What? Don't act like you weren't thinking the same thing."

Still, it's hard to deny that Serena is a force to be reckoned with. Thirty seconds of her goodwill and the comments about me online have, like magic, already started to turn:

@iluvtoast: I'm so glad @princessserenabo stood up for @elizquan. People were being nastyyyy and it's about time they got called out. 🖤

@lavender1890: Loving the sisterhood right now! Gurls run the world. @princessserenabo @elizquan

@dottieingo: I've been saying this all along. @elizquan is speaking the truth.

"The thing is, what did Serena even add to the conversation?" Winona is flummoxed. "She just HuffPo-ed what you said."

Right that second, Serena spots us and waves from atop the table, where she's sitting with her feet up, like she's modeling her white tennis shoes for an ad. She leans playfully against Jason, who is shaking half a carton of orange curly fries into his mouth.

There is no way for Winona and me to pretend that we haven't seen her, so I give a little wave back.

"Come sit with us," she calls out.

"What have you done?" says Winona through gritted teeth.

As we approach the table, I'm conscious of the fact that my lunch bag is bulkier than the canvas tote that Serena uses as her book bag, which lies flat next to her and appears to be filled with nothing. Some girls manage life without a backpack, effortlessly free from the burdens of nerdhood. Serena is one of those girls.

"You know everyone, right?" Serena flits her hand around. "Jason, this is—"

"Oh, yeah, I've heard of you." Jason has turned to face us. "Eliza the feminist."

I'm not sure which is more unnerving, the fact that Jason

Lee knows who I am, or that he knows me as "Eliza the feminist."

"And Winona the filmmaker," I say, pointing at her. Winona waves like she'd rather be anywhere but here.

Jason stares at me, and I wonder if it's out of stupidity or judgment, but then he says, "Right on."

Serena's eyes light up. "Winona, you're doing the prom promo video, right?"

Winona assesses Serena for a minute. Then she says, "Sure," and I can tell she's decided to do it simply so that she never has to have this conversation again.

Oblivious, Serena beams and scoots over, a clear sign that she expects us to sit. A resigned Winona plops down at the table and boldly unzips her lunch bag like she's right at home. As for me, I have to swing my legs awkwardly over the seat, because between Serena and Winona, there's no other way for me to get in.

"Hey, um, thanks for the shout-out today," I say, unwrapping the sandwich Mom packed me. It contains a full inch's worth of turkey cold cuts because she's convinced anything less would be "not enough food." This is an incorrect assumption, but I'm also afraid of throwing away any part of my lunch. She would know.

"Dude, of course," Serena gushes. "We girls gotta stick together, right?"

Winona crunches on a celery stick. "So, Serena," she says. "I didn't know you were interested in feminism."

Serena's eyes widen. "Me neither!"

"She's been going off about it ever since Eliza made her big speech," says Jason, scrolling through his phone. "What are you gonna do next, babe? Burn bras?" Now he looks interested. "Wait, would that mean you'd go braless?"

"Can you not?" she whines, jostling him, and he complies by getting up from the table, chuckling.

"It sounds like you're planning to run for school president?" I ask Serena.

"Yes," she replies, her voice turning resolute. "I haven't announced it yet, but I think so."

"That's really cool," I tell her. "If any girl could win, it'd be you."

Serena gives me a curious once-over. "What about you and the *Bugle*? Is Len going to resign?"

I think back to him sitting in Dr. Guinn's office, popping butterscotch candies into his mouth, and a gloom settles over me. "Not that I've heard."

"Why not?" Serena is indignant.

"Who's going to make him?" I take a disgruntled bite of sandwich. "Not Dr. Guinn. He thinks I'm just being antagonistic."

Mom did call Dr. Guinn back during a break earlier today, but luckily for me, she found the conversation mostly incomprehensible. She managed, however, to confirm that I was not "in big trouble" and that this would not go on my report card, which was all she really wanted to know.

Serena frowns. "So what are you going to do now?"

The question, and her tone, catches me off guard. It's like she's saying, *I'm trying to become only the sixth female school president in Willoughby history—what are* you *doing for the cause?* I look over at Winona, and she apparently wasn't anticipating this either. When did Serena Hwangbo, Willoughby's sweetheart, become a taskmaster for feminism?

I struggle to form a response. What *can* I do? I've published a de facto open letter. I've dumped tampons live on air. How much further can a girl really go to protest something?

"A walkout," I say, suddenly. "I'm going to plan a walkout."

"A walkout?" Both Serena and Winona echo it back to me, Serena sounding intrigued, Winona sounding, as usual, skeptical.

"Yeah," I say. "A walkout to protest Len's election to *Bugle* editor in chief. If we can get him to resign, it'll be a major symbolic win against sexism at Willoughby."

"That sounds kind of 'antagonistic,'" Winona observes, arching an eyebrow. "Just quoting Dr. Guinn, of course."

"Well, both guys and girls can participate," I reason. "Anyone who thinks gender equality is important can be part of it."

Serena bobs her head earnestly, like I am espousing something very profound. "I love that," she says. "I'm in."

Winona, however, has a more probing take. "I'm obviously all for fighting inequality, but I don't know if we should be wasting time on performative gestures." Here, she covertly indicates Serena with her eyes. And it's true, maybe Serena, with her track record of conventional girliness, *is* only getting involved because she thinks it'll somehow be good for her brand. But maybe not? Either way, I'm riled up enough now to take the chance.

"I just think we shouldn't waste all this momentum," I say. "Because if we let it go, Len isn't going to resign, and everything we've said so far will have been just noise. And yet another year will go by in which an important position at Willoughby is held by a boy when it really should have been a girl." I picture the Wall of Editors, with its rows and rows of boys, and it makes my throat catch in a funny way. "You heard what James told me, how everyone said I'm not as good a leader as Len. You *know* that's bullshit."

The criticism in Winona's face fades into something more uncertain, and she pokes a half-bitten celery stalk into a ziplock bag. "Have we weighed all the consequences, though? Like, my dad would . . ." She stops, looking troubled. I know she's thinking about what he'd say, and she hates it when he gets in her head.

"Oh, my parents tell me to keep my head down, too," Serena pipes up. "They especially don't like the idea of girls making a scene. It's totally annoying, but they're all about that 'good Asian' thing."

I cock my head at her. "You mean . . . the model-minority myth?"

"Yeah, exactly!" Serena snaps her fingers in recognition. "But we want to break out of stereotypes, right? Wouldn't this be a great way to do that?"

Winona takes stock of the crowd in our immediate vicinity, which is entirely Korean besides me, and entirely Asian except for her. "It's a little different when the stereotype you're dealing with is 'angry Black woman,'" she says dryly.

Immediately, I realize I should've thought of this earlier—that part of the reason for Winona's hesitation might have to do with something bigger than her or her dad. Fortunately, Serena, with surprising nimbleness, seems to understand as well.

"You're so right, Winona," she says. "And you definitely shouldn't do anything that makes you uncomfortable."

"Yeah," I jump in, "maybe it's a rash idea anyway."

Winona smooths out each edge of her celery bag, considering every side. "Well, I haven't said I won't do it." She shakes the remaining stalks around, thinking aloud. "You know I'm not afraid to speak up when it's important." Her voice gets defiant. "No matter what my dad says. No matter what *anyone* says."

I nod, reflecting on *Driveways* and Winona's past filmography. "Right, like in your movies."

"Yeah. But I guess I've always just preferred to be behind the scenes. That way, at least you get more control over how the story gets told."

At that, an idea pops into my head. "What if you directed the walkout?" I say. "Then you could decide exactly what role you want to take."

Winona perks up at this suggestion, and I can see her filmmaker's mind clicking into action.

"Ooh, I love it!" Serena exclaims. "You'd be so amazing, Winona."

I'm a little worried that this bit of overexuberance might backfire, but Winona, already energized by the potential creative challenge, doesn't reject it.

"All right," she says finally. "I'll see what I come up with."

Esther Chung glides up to us then, and I notice she, too, is wearing an *I AM A FEMINIST* button on her shirt. In fact, every single one of Serena's female friends is wearing one. All the buttons that I put in the girls' locker room have disappeared, and now I know where they went.

"So, Eliza," says Esther, like she's about to dish something juicy. Her hair, dyed an impressively silky shade of platinum, falls over her eyes. "What—"

"Hey, Esther. Wanna hear a joke?" Dylan Park, who is wearing a jersey with his name on the back, hurries over in an exaggerated scamper. Jason, languidly, follows behind him.

"What?" Esther is annoyed by the interruption but also into it.

"If you want to make a blonde laugh on Wednesday," he says slowly, "tell her a joke . . . on Monday."

Jason loses it completely, while Winona and I exchange a glance. Esther appears to ponder this for a full ten seconds before erupting in fury. "Oh my *Godddd*!" she shrieks. "Are you saying I'm dumb?" She shoves Dylan, who cackles in delight. "You're the idiot! This isn't even my natural color!"

Serena crosses her arms. "Dylan, that is so not okay."

Dylan seems unconcerned. "You've become so humorless since becoming a feminist," he remarks, before both he and Jason, satisfied with their obnoxious performance, mosey away.

"Anyway," says Esther, her dignity only slightly ruffled, "you guys are talking about Len, right? What's the deal with you two?" She purses her lips together. "You were, like, together, right?"

Winona guffaws, so loudly that she doubles over. "Eliza would burn the *Bugle* newsroom down before she'd date a jock," she proclaims, which strikes me as a tad hyperbolic. Not that I'd ever admit it to anyone, but I don't know if I'd go *that* far.

Serena, for her part, is mortified. "God, Esther, Eliza was talking about a *walkout* to protest Len being editor in chief." She flips her ponytail over her shoulder. "Clearly there is nothing going on between them. There never was. That was just some bullshit people made up online."

"Yeah, but yesterday Heppy saw them walking up the stairs together," Esther challenges. "Right, Heppy?"

"Yah, totally." Hepsibah Yi nods from where she's perched on the oak-tree planter.

All eyes fall on me, waiting for a defense. "We got let out of Dr. Guinn's office at the same time," I explain, a little flushed.

"They're just in the same fifth period," says Serena, remembering. "We all have English together." She tuts at her friends. "You heard Winona—Eliza would never be into Len. He stands for everything we're fighting against. What did you call him, Eliza, the 'face of the patriarchy'?"

"Basically," says Winona.

"This is about something important." Serena taps Esther's *I AM A FEMINIST* button. "If you girls want to be part of the movement, then you'd better shape up."

"He's cute, though," sighs Heppy, and we all turn to follow her gaze across the quad. Len, thumbs hooked under his backpack straps, is striding past with his baseball friends. He's laughing, like he's having a grand old time chumming it up with privilege. He seems different from how he looks indoors. Handsomer, and also, somehow, worse.

"The patriarchy often is," I say, watching him walk away.

13

"SO WHERE CAN I GET ONE OF THOSE?" LEN POINTS at the *I AM A FEMINIST* button that I'm still wearing pinned to my chest every day.

"You're out of luck," I say. "There aren't any left."

We're standing at the corner, waiting for the crosswalk signal, because we're about to head over to Boba Bros. It's fantastic weather for the grand opening of an establishment planning to sell iced drinks. Which is to say, it's really effing hot.

I fan myself with my notebook. We haven't been outside for that long, but the top of my head has already absorbed an alarming amount of afternoon sun, which continues to beat down around us, luxurious and brutal at the same time. I've tied my hair up, but now I feel a burn building on the back of my neck. I should take off my cardigan, but it's too late to run back to my locker, and I hate to carry it. So I roll up the sleeves instead.

Len wipes his forehead with his arm and looks out toward the Boba Bros strip mall. "This feminism thing has gotten to be a big deal, huh?"

The light changes, and we step off the curb at the same time.

"Yeah," I say. "I guess so." I don't mention the walkout, obviously, but the Hwangbo halo effect has continued in full force: suddenly, feminism is *very* cool at Willoughby. A select group of girls, including Serena and her friends, continue to wear my *I AM A FEMINIST* buttons conspicuously displayed on their shirts, and I feel a little bit like I've joined an elite cohort that owns the same limited-edition handbag.

But there's no denying that the atmospheric shift is real. Overnight, the girls' field hockey team pulled together a petition to replace their decade-old uniforms, preferably with the money that the football program squanders on new tackling dummies every year. The entire drama club—guys included—voted unanimously to substitute next fall's production of Arthur Miller's *Death of a Salesman* with Genny Lim's *Paper Angels*. And the newly formed Willoughby Intersectional Feminist Book Club, led by a trio of freshmen I'd never met, invited me to pick their inaugural title (I decided we could start with bell hooks's *Feminism Is for Everybody*). People are talking about sexism even beyond what I've brought up, sometimes even challenging their preconceptions of feminism, and I have to say . . . overall, it's pretty neat.

Things for Len, however, haven't been as great: this morning, before he had a chance to take it down, I saw that someone had covered his locker with pink gift wrap, like it was his birthday, but instead of *Happy Birthday* the person had written *THE PATRIARCHY*. Serena swears she doesn't know who did it.

Boba Bros is at the very end of the strip, a lone sign of life in an otherwise deserted row of storefronts. A riot of gold and white balloons surrounds the entrance, framing a sign that reads: *Grand Opening Special: Buy One, Get One Free!* Oldies music floats over the din of the crowd, and it's livelier than I expected.

"Here's the plan," I say, flipping open my notebook. "I've talked to one of the owners, Kevin Cheng, on the phone, but we've never met in person. Let's start by finding either him or his brother."

Len, who has brought one of the *Bugle* cameras, photographs someone walking by with four boba teas. "Sure thing, boss."

Inside, everything gleams white, as severe and comforting as a Nordic bathroom. One wall features the name *BOBA BROS* arched over a drawing, done in the style of a *New Yorker* cartoon, of an unidentified hamster-like mammal sipping boba. ("I think it's a wombat," Len suggests, though I didn't ask.) Over by the window there's a wooden ledge, where you can sip your drink while enjoying a lovely vista of the parking lot.

"There are a lot of options," Len says, as we both check out the menu, a black panel that also includes step-by-step instructions: choose a tea, choose a topping, choose a milk, choose a sweetness level.

The prep area behind the counter is thronged with employees, and one of them, in the process of pouring creamy liquid over ice, catches sight of us. He's wearing rectangular-rimmed glasses and a black apron that says *I'm one of the bros.* If you ask me, though, he seems more like a nerd than a bro. "Welcome to Boba Bros!" he bellows, beckoning us forward. "What can I get you guys?"

I start to explain that we're not here to order any drinks, but Len replies, "I'll have a regular milk tea with boba. With the normal amount of sweetener."

I give him an irritated look, but he just shrugs. "It's hot outside."

Turning back to the nerd-bro, I say, "We're actually from Willoughby, across the street? We write for the school paper, the *Bugle*, and we're doing a story about the grand opening. We're here to talk to Ian and Kevin Cheng."

"Oh! I'm Ian." He sticks out a hand. "Nice to meet you. Eliza, right?"

"Yup." I give him my best firm handshake. "And this is Len."

"Got it, a classic milk tea for Len. How about you, Eliza? Both your drinks are on the house!"

"Oh no," I insist. "Thank you, but it's against the *Bugle*'s journalistic code of ethics for us to accept gifts of any kind."

"What she means," says Len, pulling out his wallet, "is that I'll pay for the drinks."

"Oh no," I repeat, waving my arms. "He's not paying for anything for me."

"Okay, well, I'll pay for mine, and she can have the free one that comes with it." When I protest again, he says, "You can pay me back for half of the one that isn't free."

Ian nods at my button and smiles in a friendly way. "Is it because you're a feminist?" he asks knowingly.

"No, it's because—" I stop myself. "You know what, I'll just have a lavender tea, but with soy milk. Oh, and with almond jelly instead of boba. And only half the sweetener, please." Then I point at Len. "He's paying."

"Coming right up." Ian hits some buttons on his tablet.

Len and I head over to one of the booths, which have benches made from wooden slats. Exposed Edison bulbs hang low from the ceiling, and Len bats at one playfully before sitting down.

"That was a very specific drink order for someone who wasn't planning to get anything." He takes up the entire bench on his side.

"It's easy." I slide in across from him. "In my head, I know exactly what my perfect milk-tea drink is, so I always just try to get the closest thing to that."

"You always want the same thing, every time?"

"Yeah, of course."

"Just like how you wear the same thing every day."

It suddenly feels kind of warm in this booth, especially around my neck. I take off my sweater, which, in this light, seems heavy and maybe a little too oversized after all. I just never thought it was something for anyone to notice.

I dig into my backpack for my own wallet and throw two dollars at him.

"I thought you said I was paying."

"I changed my mind."

"You do that?"

He is trying not to let his smirk ruin his joke. I straighten up. "Not often," I say. "You've witnessed possibly a once-in-a-lifetime event."

Before I realize it, he has snapped a photo of me.

"What the hell?"

"Pics or it didn't happen."

When Ian calls our names, I tell Len that I'll go get the drinks. What I don't tell him is that it's because I'm already kind of sick of him.

"Here." I set the teas down on the table, inspecting them both. Each of the cups has a label with the order details printed on it. "This one is yours." I rotate it around to face him. "The *basic* one."

"I believe the term Ian used was 'classic.'"

In response, I pop my straw out of its wrapper and stab it into my drink, a one-fisted maneuver as natural as taking a breath. Len, however, struggles with his, so I reach over and do it for him.

"What kind of Asian are you?" I shake my head as I push his drink back to him.

"Half," he says, leaning forward to take a sip.

"Eliza, Len, this is my brother Kevin," says Ian, and I whirl around. Kevin, whose hair swoops up to an impressive height, is wearing the same apron as Ian. He's slightly shorter, older, and maybe just a bit more of a bro. His handshake, unlike Ian's jaunty squeeze, is a real solid grip.

"Nice to finally meet you, Eliza," says Kevin. He settles into the side of the booth opposite Len, and Ian follows. Which leaves only one spot for me.

Len scoots toward the wall, either to make more room for me or to distance himself—it's not exactly clear which. Resting his elbow on the table, he touches his hair with that quick, light tousle that is becoming strangely familiar to me. I want to tell him that his thicket of hair, even with its usual touch of frizz, looks fine. It always looks annoyingly fine. If anyone should be concerned about their hair, it's me. Strands from my bun have plastered themselves to my neck and are only just now unsticking themselves, feeling cool and gross in the throes of evaporating sweat.

"You're covering the grand opening for the Willoughby paper, right?" says Kevin. "You know, I used to be on the newspaper staff when I was in high school. On the biz side, though. I sold ads. Do you guys still do that?"

"Sure," I tell him. "But it's not a major source of revenue."

Kevin laughs. "Yeah, it wasn't back when I was doing it, either. Of course, that could have been because I was doing it."

"Where did you go to high school?" asks Len. Out of nowhere, he has produced his own notebook and turned to an empty page.

"Hargis High," says Ian. "We both went there."

"Our rival school." Len grins at me like this is supposed to mean something.

"Suck it, Sentinels!" Kevin coughs into his hand.

Remarkably, Len knows the appropriate response. "Bears blow!"

"Just to make sure we get all these quotes right," I break in, "do you mind if we record the interview?"

"No problem," says Kevin. "Make sure the thing about the Sentinels gets in, though."

I smile agreeably. "Well, I really appreciate your taking the time to chat with us, and congrats on opening the shop—"

"Thanks," Kevin interrupts, leaning back so that his arm stretches across the top of the booth. "We're really excited." He gestures at our drinks. "What do you think?"

Len stops chewing on the end of his straw and looks at his cup, which is empty except for ice and left-behind tapioca balls. "Pretty good," he says.

"You know what sets us apart?" Kevin reaches for my cup and lifts it like a gemstone. "High-quality ingredients."

"We only use tea brewed from real tea leaves," explains Ian. "Not tea powders like our competitors."

"Did either of you try our limited-edition oolong?" Kevin asks. When he finds out we haven't, he's flabbergasted. "Aw, man, you gotta. Ian, can you grab the tin?"

Ian retrieves a shiny metal canister from the kitchen and cracks it open for us. Both Len and I lean in to sniff it, and I'm momentarily distracted by how close I am to the face of the patriarchy.

As Kevin moves onto the merits of Boba Bros' proprietary syrup, I inch away from Len, reminding myself to keep an eye on the story.

"Question for you, Kevin," I say. "When we last talked on the phone, you mentioned that the grand opening was slated for last October. What happened?"

This topic seems to upset Kevin as much as our failure to try the oolong tea.

"I'll tell you *exactly* what happened, Eliza." He pounds a fist on the table. "Red tape. Bureaucracy. The number of hoops we've had to jump through to get here has been truly farcical."

"What kind of hoops?" I inquire.

"We had to do a ton of work to get the space up to code," Kevin groans. "And don't get me started on the *landscaping* regulations."

He goes on for a while about how unnecessary all those rules are, and I'm taking notes as fast as I can. Len, though, barely writes anything down at all.

"But what would you say to someone who argues that regulations exist for a reason—like public safety, for example?" I ask. "How would you determine what to roll back?"

Kevin considers this for less than a second. "Look, I'm a business owner," he says. "But I'm also a member of this community. I'm not going to make irresponsible choices just because there's no law telling me what to do."

I notice Len watching me then, so I give him an opening. He takes the cue and bends forward. "What did you do before this?"

That has got to be the lamest question ever, but I stay quiet because the first rule of co-reporting is no undermining your partner.

"I worked in tech," Kevin replies. "At a few startups in SF, most recently as an account manager."

"Kevin has an MBA from Stanford," says Ian. "Our mom would want you to include that, so people know he has marketable skills even though he's now running a boba shop."

"Nah, Ian's the one with skills," Kevin demurs. "He was a software engineer."

Len nods at them. "So, why boba?"

The three of us pause, and I wonder if Ian and Kevin are also puzzling over why Len didn't just read their About page.

Kevin, in fact, starts to recite the story from the Boba Bros website. The brothers are Taiwanese, and they got their love of boba from their dad, a tea connoisseur and tapioca lover. He always wanted to run his own business, but he spent all of his working life as a corporate accountant. Boba Bros is an homage to his American dream. The perfect tech-bro-turned-entrepreneur story, with just enough child-of-immigrant pathos thrown in.

"Your dad must be really proud," says Len.

"Yeah, he's been really supportive," Ian agrees. "The Boba Bros tapioca balls are based on a recipe he created."

"What about your mom?" asks Len. I picture their About page, and I realize I don't know the answer because she is, peculiarly, not mentioned.

There's some hesitation before Kevin speaks up. "She wasn't thrilled when we told her we were both quitting high-paying jobs to do this. She was an accountant, too, and always believed in working hard, getting a good education, doing something lucrative and prestigious. Running a small business like this, selling boba." He laughs. "It's not exactly what she wanted for us. It's risky. Unstable."

"Her face when we told her how much of our savings we had poured in." Ian presses his fingertips into his temples.

"She didn't understand your motivation?" Len, who has his pen cap between his teeth, removes it long enough to ask the question.

"Not really." Ian rolls one of the empty straw wrappers into a tight cylinder. "For our parents' generation, opening a restaurant—that was something you did if you were unedu-cated, if you didn't have another choice. For them, work was about survival. But for us, it's about something else."

"It's like that saying," adds Kevin. "Your parents want what's good for you, but they don't always know what's best for you." He motions around at the shop. "For us, this is what's best for us. A kind of coming home."

My eyes fall upon Len, who is now very intently filling up a notebook page with his scribblings. As he finishes the last few words, he glances up at me. "Any more questions?"

◆◆◆

After we're done interviewing the Cheng brothers and a bunch of their customers, Len and I wander over to the opposite end of the strip mall and find a bit of shade to sit in. Today, the sign in front of the church next door reads: *There are some questions that can't be answered by Google.*

Len unloops the camera from his neck and sets it aside, reclining into the grass, hands behind his head. His T-shirt pulls up slightly, revealing a bit of plaid peeking up from the waistband of his jeans.

I refocus my attention on my notebook. "Let's talk about our angle."

"Sure," he says, without sitting up.

"I think it might be the whole regulation thing," I say. "The opening was delayed for six months. That's not an insignificant amount of time. Maybe I could talk to Alan—"

"Who's Alan?"

"The president of the city chamber of commerce."

"Right, of course. Go on."

"Alan might know if this is a pattern for new businesses in Jacaranda. If everyone faces these same delays due to regulations, maybe Kevin is right. Maybe the city codes are too onerous. Or maybe something is up with the department in charge of that stuff."

"But what's the story *really* about?"

I ruminate on this before responding. "It's about how hard it is to identify the balance between the need for regulation and the desire to encourage business development."

"Is that interesting, though?"

"Yeah," I say, like I can't imagine why he would have to ask. Len shoots a doubtful look at me from the ground. I sigh. "Okay, it's not the sexiest topic, but it's *important*. It's the type of story you would see in a real newspaper. And if you want to be taken seriously, you have to write about serious things."

"Kids at school don't care about that stuff."

I pluck a blade of grass from the lawn and throw it at him. "It's our job to write what's significant, not just pander to the masses."

"But it's also our job to serve our community. So we should consider what would interest them."

I cross my arms over my chest. "All right, what do you think the story is about?"

Len props his head up with one hand. "It's interesting how there's some tension between the Cheng brothers and their mom. The Asian kids at Willoughby would get *that*."

I gaze out at the church parking lot and review the conversation in my head. "I mean, yeah, there was some drama there. The subtext seemed to be that they think she's the reason their dad never realized his life's goal."

"Yeah, I kind of want to talk to her and find out what she has to say." He grins. "You're the feminist—shouldn't you be interested in this conflict?"

"Sure," I say. "But not all conflict is necessarily newsworthy. Like, my mom also didn't want my dad to open a restaurant. I didn't see anyone writing a story about that."

"Maybe they should have."

I've got a scowl all queued up for him until I realize he's not entirely joking.

"What'd your dad end up doing?" he wants to know.

"He did open a restaurant, briefly. And then it hemorrhaged a decade's worth of savings quicker than you could say 'Great Wall Restaurant' three times fast."

"That bad, huh?"

"Yeah. But it's not something special that happened to us. Restaurants fail. Immigrants lose money. There isn't always a redemptive arc. Now my dad still works in a restaurant—just someone else's."

Len is quiet for a minute. "You don't think that's a story worth telling?"

"I'm just saying it's not news." I try to slip away from Len's unexpected pensiveness, which has unfurled like a too-warm blanket across my lap. "Take the thing with the Cheng brothers' mom—what would be the point of that story?"

Len lies back down in the grass, contemplating the question. For a moment, the only sound is a Motown song drifting over faintly from the Boba Bros shop, and the occasional car passing by. "Maybe it's about the different ways that immigrants approach the American dream," he says, finally. "Maybe it's about gender, and how that affects your willingness to take entrepreneurial risks."

I lean over to get a better view of his face. "You're literally making all this up right now, aren't you?"

He laughs. "Yeah."

A light breeze picks up, blowing a few strands of hair in my face, and I reach up to retie my bun. When I look down, Len turns his head away.

I suddenly can't think of anything to say.

"Okay," he concedes, sitting up. "We can write about regulations." He brushes the grass out of his hair, a bigger, looser move than his usual one.

"Well," I say, picking up the camera, just to have something to do. "We can write about the American dream, too." I start flipping through to see what photos Len has taken. There are pictures of the customers, of Ian and Kevin, of the booth inside the shop. "These are pretty good." I sound more surprised than I mean to.

"Thanks."

"I'm not saying it to be nice."

"I know." He laughs again, lifting a shoulder. "My dad's always been into photography, so he taught me how to use his camera. He lets me mess around with it sometimes."

"I see." I sort of hate that he's also good at this, that yet another talent seems to be his birthright.

Then I get to the photo that he took of me while we were sitting in the booth. My hair is a mess, but I'm kind of smiling, like I'm about to say something clever. It is very strange, but I look . . . pretty.

I flip back a little further and find a few more pictures of me, which I'd assumed at the time would be throwaway shots. But here they are, alive with light and beautifully composed.

There's me furrowing my forehead as I read my notebook, standing against the backdrop of a blurred crowd. There's me turning around to peer at something beyond the lens, wreathed by the gold and white balloons.

I put the camera down, pretending I haven't seen anything.

"I think I have to go," I say, standing up.

14

THE NEXT MORNING, I REALIZE SOMETHING TER-
rible.

"Where's my sweater?" I ask Kim, rifling through a pile of
clothes that I've left on a chair.

"How would I know?" She combs out her hair. "If you
only—"

"Don't say it." I put up a hand to stop her.

I search all over the apartment, but I can't find the sweater
anywhere. Then I remember. Boba Bros. The booth. Did I
leave it there? I pick up my phone to text Len, but that makes
me think of the photos again, and my stomach does a funny
little jump.

I shake it off and type:

Do you remember if I had my sweater when we left Boba Bros?

I don't get an immediate response, so I throw my phone in
my backpack. I put on another cardigan that I don't like nearly
as much—this one is oatmeal-colored, and smaller, with

sleeves that won't cover my hands no matter how much I try to pull them down. Mom is overjoyed.

"See?" she says. "You look so much better!"

Len doesn't text me back until I'm already walking up to the door of the newsroom, and it's just one line:

No?

The brevity simultaneously irritates and embarrasses me. At the same time, I am sort of relieved that his message was so useless, because it means . . . well, I don't know what it means, so why *am* I relieved?

Neither of us says much as James reads through our Boba Bros article on one of the *Bugle* computers. We wrote it last night collaboratively, if not together—Len emailed me an initial draft, and I finished it up. The whole process had been, thankfully, almost businesslike.

Now I'm sitting next to James, while Len stands on the other side with his arms crossed. "This is pretty damn good, guys," James tells us, after he's done editing. "The political stuff is first-rate, as usual." In response, I give Len an imperious look, but then James adds, "I think you've done a decent job sketching out who these guys are, too. Interesting stuff."

I expect Len to return my self-congratulation with his own, but he doesn't.

"Thanks," he says, as James gets up from the computer.

I start to slide over so that I can take care of the edits, but then James pauses. "Wait, Eliza," he says, studying me. "You look kind of different."

"It's her sweater," Len interrupts. He shrugs as we both regard him curiously. "She doesn't usually wear that sweater."

These short cardigan sleeves are more uncomfortable than I thought. "I seem to have left my usual one at Boba Bros," I explain to James, wringing my bare wrists. "I'm going to call them when they open to see if anyone found it."

As I turn back to the computer, I spy Cassie Jacinto walking past. She's wearing what appears to be one of my *I AM A FEMINIST* buttons, but the font is hot pink.

I did not make any buttons with hot-pink font.

"Cassie." I stop her. "What's that?"

"Oh," says Cassie. "Well, I thought a lot about what you wrote, and I agree with your overall point. Even though it was super unfair that you dissed everyone on the staff, considering I voted for you." At this, I wince. "But you are more qualified, and Len's speech didn't have much substance. No offense, Len." He puts up both hands in a gesture of capitulation. "So, I wanted to show support." She beams at me. "Like Serena did."

"But where did you get that?" I'm still confused.

"The button?" Cassie points. "I bought it from Natalie."

"You . . . bought it?" Bristling, I zero in on Natalie chatting with Aarav across the room. "From *Natalie*?"

I leap up from the chair and stumble over to her. Len, uninvited, follows me.

"Are you selling *I AM A FEMINIST* buttons?" I demand.

Aarav and Natalie break off their conversation. "Yeah." Natalie eyes my empty chest. "You want one? They're two dollars each."

"What . . . ?" I struggle to speak coherently. "Why are you doing this?"

"Why not? There's a huge demand for these buttons right now." She turns to Aarav, who nods like a henchman. "I'm just meeting a need."

"But you said I was overreacting when I brought up the stuff about sexism." I thrust my finger toward her. "Now you're profiting off something you don't even believe in?"

Natalie doesn't bat an eye. "I never said I didn't believe in feminism," she says. "I just didn't necessarily agree with *you*." She gathers her curly hair and twists it into the most malicious side bun I've ever seen.

Suddenly, the realization comes to me, so clearly that I can't believe I didn't think of it before. "It was you, wasn't it? You were the one who posted the manifesto on the *Bugle* to begin with. *You're* the one who started all this drama!"

Natalie scoffs, letting her hair cascade back down. "Don't get so worked up about this, Eliza. They're just *buttons*."

"They're not just buttons!" I'm trying not to shout, but it's hard. "And it's not just about the buttons."

Natalie glances over at Len, as if wondering why he's standing there. I wonder, too.

"What do you think, Len?" Natalie asks.

For a moment, he considers the counterfeit button that Natalie is wearing. He doesn't look at me.

"I'll take one," he says.

"Everything's just a big joke to you, isn't it," I say, walking away.

◆◆◆

After school, Winona and I stand over her dining table, where we've spread out in our own walkout war room. Serena couldn't make it because of a student-council meeting, but as Winona notes, what we really need her for—mobilizing the ranks—is out in the field anyway. "Assuming, of course, she's actually planning to follow through with this whole thing."

Serena has mentioned the walkout to me every time I've seen her, so I wonder if Winona's skepticism is, for once, misplaced. "She seems pretty enthusiastic," I say. I mean, I'm not joining the Serena Hwangbo Fan Club any time soon, but sometimes you have to give credit where it's due.

"Yeah, but does she really understand the things she's enthusiastic about?"

This seems like a rhetorical question, so I silently concede the point and hand Winona a marker, which she uses to sketch a map of the Willoughby campus onto a giant sheet of drafting paper. Mrs. Wilson, who is an architect, keeps a large roll in her office and always lets us use as much as we want.

"All right, the walkout is in a little over a week. We need to outline our vision." Winona dumps a jarful of Doug's little green army men onto the map.

"Didn't you say that we still have stuff to film?" Doug himself appears in the kitchen doorway.

"We're taking a break." Winona remains focused on her map. "Go away."

"She's just procrastinating," Doug says to me.

I frown, feeling suddenly bad that we're working on this

walkout instead of filming *Driveways*. "Hey, that festival deadline is getting closer, isn't it?"

"We have two weeks. Ava DuVernay shot her first feature in that much time."

"Yeah, but—"

Winona interrupts me with a labored sigh. "I just feel like the story isn't quite right anymore, but I need some time to figure it out." She taps the marker against her chin. "All this feminism stuff has me reevaluating what I want to do with it. Like, right now, it's kind of just about boys, isn't it?"

She's right—the plot of *Driveways*, as it stands, involves Doug's character being accused of stealing a pack of gum and then getting into an argument with Sai.

"I do still think it's a good story, but I wonder—how much of that is because I believe the festival judges will find it interesting?" Winona notices a wrinkle in the drafting paper and reaches over to straighten it. "I probably should've considered this before, but maybe they didn't appreciate my entry from last year, the one about the doll, because they're a bunch of white dudes. It made me question why I feel like I have to talk about race in a way *they* understand—or like I have to talk about it at all, just to be taken seriously."

"Does this mean you're scrapping your movie?" Doug sounds hopeful.

"No, it means I'm still thinking about it." Winona begins moving the army men around on the map. "In the meantime, I told you, we're *busy*."

Doug inches closer to the table. "With what?"

"Did I not say 'go away'?"

"I'm gonna tell Dad you're planning to make a spectacle of yourself."

"You want to kiss that Xbox goodbye?" Winona delivers this threat with a gaze I've seen from her mother, and Doug retreats—but not before mouthing, *Procrastinating!* to me.

"Should we talk more about *Driveways*?" I suggest. "Maybe we could—"

"It's fine. I'll come up with something." Winona jabs at the drafting paper. "Let's just concentrate on this now."

A nagging voice, like Mom's when she hassles me about blow-drying my hair before going to bed, tells me that Doug might be right. It's not exactly out of character for Winona to deal with a creative block this way—she's no stranger to the 11:59 p.m. essay submission, and in fact often claims that her best ideas spring forth, with Athena-like clarity, only under pressure.

But I let it go, because I can't argue with the fact that she's in the middle of helping me—and the one thing she would not appreciate right now is hearing that I agree with her brother.

"Okay," I say. "What's the plan?"

Winona places a girl Lego minifig in Mr. Schlesinger's class-room. It's got black hair and an angry face. "That's you."

"It looks just like me!"

"Yup. So I think we should do it at some point during sixth period. For a number of reasons." Winona starts counting on her fingers. "First, we want to maximize participation, and too many juniors and seniors don't have a seventh period. Second, it's near enough to the end of the day that they can't be too hard on us for being disruptive. And third, we have sixth period together."

"Why does that matter?"

"Because you're going to do the walkout blindfolded, so you might need some help."

"*Blindfolded?*"

Winona heaves an oversized book from the edge of the table and opens it to a section in the middle, the place marked with an envelope covered in her mom's handwriting. "You'll be dressed as Lady Justice," she declares.

The spread in front of us features full-color images of paintings, carvings, and sculptures, all depicting the same subject: a female figure, usually holding a sword and a set of scales. Sometimes, though not always, her eyes are covered.

I point to one of the photos, which shows a statue of a woman tying a blindfold on herself. "Because 'justice is blind'?"

"Yeah. Except it's not, obviously. At least, not for everybody." Winona rests her elbows on the table and flips to another page full of personified Justices. "My mom's firm is renovating the courthouse on La Salle Avenue, and I heard her on the phone yesterday, debating about whether they should keep this old mural of Lady Justice. That's what got me thinking." She runs her finger down the crease between the pages. "According to my mom, it's misleading to have a blindfolded

Justice when the legal system—and society, really—still discriminates based on gender, race, and class. Which means, of course, the group that usually gets screwed over most is Black women."

I examine the photos in the book again. Most of the Lady Justices also have one other thing in common: they're white. "Yeah, it does sometimes seem like Justice is blind to the wrong things."

"Right, the symbolism is convoluted, and it's been manipulated by all kinds of groups, especially those supporting the patriarchy. But that's why I think we should take it back. Take *her* back."

"By making me Lady Justice."

"Exactly. Especially because American feminism has a history of middle-class white women erasing POC voices. Black voices in particular, but Asian ones, too."

And it's true. Even though Asian American girls haven't had to deal with the same level of bullshit that Black girls do, I've often felt a kind of invisibility when it comes to these discussions—especially in the "real" world, beyond the Asian-majority community of Willoughby. So maybe Winona's right. Maybe it *would* mean something for me to be the face of this movement.

"Okay," I say. "But we're keeping the blindfold?"

"To begin with, yes." Winona draws a line from Mr. Schlesinger's room to the quad area, which she circles twice. "Once we get here, though, you'll do a big speech and then make a grand gesture of taking it off. Because even though I like the idea of Lady Justice being blind, we gotta be real here. In our world, she needs to see things the way they are." Winona recaps her marker and raps the map emphatically. "And that's what we're doing with this walkout—making inequalities seen."

I bow down before Winona. "You're a genius."

Winona grins. "What else is new?"

15

THE NEXT AFTERNOON, OUR *MACBETH* GROUP IS supposed to meet at Len's house, despite my best attempts to derail the plan.

"Don't you live close to school?" I ask Serena.

"Yeah, I'd totally have you guys come over," she says, "but my mom is redoing the kitchen and doesn't want us to get into the mess."

"What about Ryan?"

"He just uses his grandma's address to go to Willoughby, so his actual house is kind of far. What about your place?"

I try to imagine the three of them in my living room: Serena inspecting the faded carpet, Ryan swiveling on the office chair Dad plucked from the sidewalk, Len studying the red-papered bookshelf that Mom has set up as a shrine to Buddha, our family ancestors, and Deih Jyú Gūng, the Chinese Lord of the Landlord.

"I live on the other side of town, so it's probably not ideal."

Serena grabs a tasseled key chain from her bag. "Yeah, so I guess we have to go to Len's?"

I make a last-ditch effort to come up with another possibility. "Why can't we just meet in the quad?"

Serena makes a face. "It's so hot, though."

This is true. It's another blistering day in Jacaranda, maybe even worse than when Len and I went to Boba Bros. Which, Kevin has confirmed, is not where my missing sweater is. "I'll let you know if it turns up," he said when I called.

"Ugh, thank God for AC," says Serena, cranking it up so high that the roar is like a third presence in her car.

We're on our way to Len's house, and Serena has offered to drive me, a gesture I appreciate until I properly belt myself into the front seat and witness the phenomenon that is Serena behind the wheel.

"Where exactly does Len live again?" Serena asks, as we tear down Lemon Avenue at least twenty miles over the speed limit.

I pull up the text with shaky hands. "On Holyoke Lane," I tell her, my voice slightly shrill. I'm mostly used to being in a car with Mom, who drives as if she is chauffeuring senior citizens to their medical appointments, so this is somewhat of . . . an adjustment.

"Oh yeah, I know where that is. That's super close to my house."

In between praying to an uncertain deity that I will make it to Len's alive, I find myself contemplating what his house is like. I wonder, especially, if it is more Japanese or white.

"By the way, did you hear?" Serena chats nonstop, blithely unaware of my terror. "Half the speech-and-debate team threatened to quit when their president tried to argue that you were wrong about sexism at Willoughby."

I clutch the sides of the leather seat as she lurches to a stop at a busy intersection. "Really?" I manage to eke out.

"Yup. And, as of this morning, all of the improv club's new *I'm with Him* T-shirts are missing." Serena looks impish. *"Mysteriously."*

The car revs into motion again, and I am too queasy to respond except by giving a thumbs-up.

"As for our protest," Serena chatters on, "we have fifty-seven people committed, and I think I can get . . ." She counts in her head, diverting more attention from the road to this calculation than seems necessary. ". . . eight more by the end of this week."

Someday, I want Serena to be a real elected politician, maybe even president, because once the girl makes a promise, she moves fast.

"That's great," I say, as Serena accelerates with gusto through a green light.

"I'm so happy this is all happening!" She grins at me. "Especially the walkout. That's gonna be *so* big, Eliza. You're destined to be editor in chief—I can feel it. Len isn't gonna know what hit him."

I do my best not to strain against the car-door handle as

we continue barreling down the street. "Well, let's not get too hostile. We need him to be our Fleance."

"Who's being hostile?" says Serena, blasting a car with her horn for not reacting quickly enough to a light change. As soon as she gets the chance, she zooms ahead, leaving the offending driver behind.

"Don't take this the wrong way," I say after she's returned to her normal level of speeding, "but how come you care about this so much?"

Serena drives quietly for the next few seconds, long enough for me to assume that maybe she's decided not to answer the question, and this is just the Hwangbo way of letting you down easy—pretending you didn't ask.

Finally, she says, "I try really hard to make everything seem easy." She glances in my direction through the amber of her oversized sunglasses, as if to see whether this declaration surprises me. It does. "I didn't realize it until I read what you wrote in the manifesto, but I try really hard, all the time." She taps the steering wheel with her fingers, nails painted with pristine French tips. "I just never thought about sexism being the reason why."

"Hmm," I say, "yeah."

"Your whole 'not here to be liked' thing is so gutsy," she says. "But I could never in a million years be as chill as you about the fact that no one liked me."

I decide not to protest the assertion that *no one* likes me, because I guess it's close enough to the truth. "Life seems to work out better for girls who care about stuff like that, though."

"Mostly," she agrees. "But it's also so exhausting, worrying what everyone thinks all the time." In the rearview mirror, she adjusts a single hair that has slipped out of her otherwise flawless ponytail. "And if I feel that way, what must it be like for everyone else?"

I don't have an answer for this question.

In front of us, there's another car moving slower than the flow of traffic, and naturally Serena has no patience for that. She threads—with fabulous finesse, I have to say—in and out of our lane to circumvent the car.

"Wait, I think that's Ryan," I say, peering into the driver's seat.

"It is?" Serena seems delighted. "He's probably texting, that asshole. Hold on." She lowers my window and slows down so we're next to Ryan. Then she honks the horn, which makes him jump.

"Don't text and drive!" I yell, before we hurtle down the street with a satisfying screech. Serena is in a fit of laughter, and so am I, and it's exhilarating to see Ryan's middle finger receding into the distance.

"Anyway," says Serena, after we've sort of calmed down and she makes a left turn onto Holyoke Lane, "I like Len just fine. But you can tell, he just doesn't really have to try." She eases to a stop in front of his house and shuts off the engine, restoring a calm around us. "Maybe it's time that mattered."

It occurs to me then what a singular moment this is: here I am, inexplicably in solidarity with Serena Hwangbo, the girl whose entire student-council tenure has been based on nothing but marginally considerate behavior and attractive boyfriends. Feminism is a funny thing.

16

LEN'S NEIGHBORHOOD IS A LITTLE FARTHER FROM Willoughby than Winona's, but not by much. It's just as nice as Palermo, though a lot older, with two-story residences straight out of a vintage photo. His house has a pitched, asymmetrical roof, with wooden double doors nestled into a stone-and-glass facade, and the lawn, not subject to the smaller lot constraints of newer subdivisions, is generous—maybe the size of my living room and kitchen put together.

Serena and I walk up the curved path, and Len opens the door before I can knock. "Come on in," he says. Following his example, Serena and I leave our shoes by the door.

Inside, there's a cathedral ceiling over a sunken living room, with hardwood floors and a brick fireplace. The armchairs are refined but worn, their peacock-blue upholstery sagging slightly in the seats. In the corner, there's a grand piano with the lid up and books layered over one another on the music rack. The top one is open to a piece called "Polonaise." Underneath the title, in smaller type, it says *Opus 53*.

"Oh, I know that one." Serena tries out the first few notes with her right hand. "Do you play?"

Len is already walking toward the kitchen. "Yeah."

"Are you good?"

"No."

Serena and I exchange a glance, and I wonder if he's lying.

"Do either of you want anything?" he says.

"Nope." Serena flops onto the angular sofa, which looks stiff and uninviting. But when I sit down next to her, the cushions are softer than I expected.

"Eliza?" Len is still waiting.

"No thanks," I say, and he disappears.

Serena immediately starts scrolling through her phone, but I find my attention drifting over the room. Someone stylish has decorated it, with objects that feel collected from faraway places. An assortment of vintage illustrations, inked over with Japanese characters. A vase glazed with a blue wave pattern. A Turkish rug, floral and faded. And books—lots and lots of books. Large, glossy compendiums of art on the coffee table, whole series of Latin-etched volumes on the built-in shelves, and paperbacks stacked on side tables as if there just isn't enough room for them anywhere else.

There are also some photographs hanging on the wall by the dining room, so I get up for a closer look.

In one, there's a little Asian kid with light brown hair, much lighter than Len's, and it takes me a second before I realize it *is* Len. He's beaming up at the camera, more exuberant than

I've ever seen him, holding a baseball in two hands like it's the most precious thing in the world.

In another, there's a young Japanese woman, dressed in a ribbed turtleneck sweater and a suede skirt that goes to her knees. Next to her, there's a very tall young white man with olive eyes that match his plaid shirt, and behind them are the grays and greens of gothic architecture in springtime. She's looking at something off-camera out of the corner of her eye, smiling wide. He's looking at her.

Len, it seems, has grown into an exceptionally faithful adaptation of his dad, except for his eyes, which crinkle up just the way his mom's do when he smiles. They're mainly what make him look Japanese now.

I hear a loud crunch and turn to see Len draped over one of the dining chairs, biting into an apple as he watches me. "So, are we gonna practice some *Macbeth*?" he asks, and I sidle away from the wall, like I haven't been studying any photographs at all.

The front door opens, and it's Ryan. "You made it," says Len, in between bites of apple.

"Yeah, no thanks to these two." He points at Serena and me. "They tried to get me into an accident."

Serena's well-shaped brows arch behind her phone. "Says the guy who was texting while driving."

"I was checking Len's address," Ryan grouses.

"How about we just get started," I say, pulling *Macbeth* from my backpack.

The scenes that Ms. Boskovic assigned to us are from act 2. Basically, this is what happens: Banquo, who, like Macbeth, received a prophecy from the witches at the beginning of the play, is still feeling pretty unsettled by it. He and his son, Fleance, are walking the halls at Macbeth's castle after midnight when they run into Macbeth, who, unbeknownst to them, has plotted with Lady Macbeth to kill King Duncan. Eventually, Macbeth carries out the deed but forgets to leave the murder weapons in the room to frame the sleeping chamberlains. He is too freaked out to go back and put them there, so Lady Macbeth has to do it, and she has a lot to say about *that*.

About twenty lines into the first scene, a few things become clear to me.

The first is that Len, who holds up a flashlight like a torch, has chosen to be Fleance because it involves only two lines.

The second is that Ryan, who is supposed to play Banquo, should have been given a part with only two lines.

"Ryan," I say, imagining Winona yelling, *"Cut!"* at this dismal performance. "Did you not memorize your lines?"

"I did, but I forgot them." Ryan holds his sword, a.k.a. Len's fireplace poker. "There are so many!"

We try again, this time allowing Ryan to simply read his lines, but he still struggles, delivering the words with all the vivacity of a toaster oven.

"Okay, sorry, Ryan, but you're not playing Banquo," I say. "Len, maybe you should switch parts with him."

Len flips the flashlight in the air and catches it. "Who made you the director?"

In search of a softer target, I turn back to Ryan. "Do you want to switch parts with Len, or are you going to be able to pull it together to do this properly?"

Ryan lowers the fireplace poker. "I'll switch."

Len tries to object with a straight face, but he fails. "Okay, fine."

Our scenes improve significantly after that. Len as Banquo is serviceable, but the real star is Serena as Macbeth.

"'To know my deed, 'twere best not know myself,'" she recites, looking forlorn. Len, leaning against the fireplace, knocks on the mantel, per the stage instructions. "'Wake Duncan with thy knocking! I would thou couldst!'" Serena's last lines are filled with agony, and she pauses. Then she takes a deep bow as we all applaud.

"I think we're pretty good!" Serena says, falling dramatically onto the couch.

"Well, most of us." I eye Ryan, who sulks in response.

"Can we call it a wrap for today?" says Len. He is asking me and making fun of me at the same time, but it's Serena who answers.

"Yeah, sure." She hops back to her feet.

I check the time on my phone. It's only three thirty, which means Mom won't be able to pick me up for another half hour at least. I wonder if there's a way I can extend this meeting so that Serena and Ryan don't leave me alone here with Len. But

Serena is already picking up her tote bag, tapping out replies to text messages that have come in while we were rehearsing, and Ryan is crouching down to tie his shoes.

I feel bad about asking Serena to go out of her way to drop me off, but I am so desperate not to be left here that I briefly entertain the idea of asking Ryan. I decide I must be losing it if I am considering voluntarily spending time with him.

"I don't have a ride until around four," I say to Len. "Do you mind if I wait here?"

Len couldn't care less. "No."

"Okay, bye, guys!" says Serena, waving her keys at us. Ryan also puts up a hand and then follows her out the door, letting it shut behind him.

So now it's just Len and me, standing around in his living room.

"I have some homework to do," I say.

"You can sit in the dining room if you want." He gestures halfheartedly toward it.

"Okay." I walk over and sit down, sliding my math book out of my backpack like I solve differential equations at his dining table every day.

Len picks up his own backpack and approaches with it slung over his shoulder. He rests his hands on the back of a chair, and it's unclear whether he's trying to start a conversation or end one. "I guess I have some more lines to memorize now."

I don't look up from my problem set. "Is that going to be an issue for you?"

Len starts to make some kind of snide comeback, but I don't get to hear it because the sound of a garage door opening just then does something very interesting to his face.

"Is that . . . ?"

"My mom." He actually winces. "I guess she's home early today."

I listen as the back door opens and closes, and the clack of high heels gives way to the soft patter of stockinged feet against tile. "Len?" A petite woman dressed in a silk tee and dark pants appears at the kitchen doorway. "Oh, hello," she says, noticing me. We look at each other curiously.

"Hello," I reply.

"This is Eliza," says Len.

"Hi, I'm Naomi." She smiles, and I recognize the girl from the photo, all grown up.

"We're gonna be working upstairs." Len steps away from the table and pauses, like I'm supposed to follow.

His mom, noting that I have clearly already settled into my spread of math homework, ignores him. "Do you go to Willoughby, Eliza?"

"Yes," I say. "Len and I are in the same English class." His mom nods warmly, and I won't lie—I'm too busy enjoying the fact that Len seems genuinely weirded out to be weirded out myself. Even though it is, I admit, totally weird that I am chatting with his mom. "We also know each other from the *Bugle*."

"Oh, that's nice. Len, you just joined the *Bugle*, didn't you?"

She grins at me and leans in, like we're conspirators. "It's good that he is finally getting involved with something again."

I understand then that Len's mom doesn't know that he's been elected next year's editor in chief, and also, she thinks Len has invited me over because he likes me. Len and I realize this second thing at the same time.

"Eliza's waiting for her mom," he explains quickly. "A group of us were here earlier practicing our scenes from *Macbeth*."

"Your dad would be excited about that. He loves *Macbeth*." Len's mom says this in a way that is hard to read, dipped in a kind of sardonic subtlety that could be either disdain or affection. This seems to be something else Len has picked up from her.

Len reaches over and closes my textbook, taking it under his arm with finality. "We're gonna go do some calculus now."

Len's mom turns toward the kitchen, but not before she says, "Okay, well, once you're done carrying Eliza's books to your room, come help me take in these groceries."

I jog behind him up the stairs, because he can't seem to climb them fast enough—it's three steps at a time today. At the landing, once we're out of earshot and I am thoroughly winded, I say, "Why didn't you tell your mom that you're the new *Bugle* editor in chief?"

He slaps the calculus book into my chest, like he just remembered he was carrying it and definitely doesn't want to anymore. "It never came up."

"You're lying." I clutch the textbook as I follow him into his room.

"I'm not," says Len, dropping his backpack onto a gray wool rug that covers the hardwood floor.

I cross my arms over my book. "Would it kill you to just tell the truth for once?"

This sounds exactly as belligerent as I intended, but the way he falters, almost like I've struck him, makes me second-guess myself.

Not for long, though. "I thought you weren't talking to me anymore," he replies affably, and I'm annoyed all over again.

"When did I say that?"

"That's the thing, you didn't. Because you stopped talking to me."

"Don't try to change the subject!"

He waves at me, completely innocent. "I'll be right back," he says, and heads downstairs.

I realize that I've never been in a boy's room before, and it feels kind of surreal to find myself in Len's. It's cleaner than I expected. His bed is neatly made, covered with a plaid comforter that I feel weird about sitting on. Instead, I take a seat at his desk. His chair is a real classic number, one of those old-fashioned Windsor armchairs finished with black lacquer and a faded Princeton seal. I wonder where he got it.

I place both my elbows on the armrests and try to imagine him sitting here every night, doing super-mundane stuff, like homework, or writing *Bugle* articles. I lean back in the chair so that only the back legs stay on the floor, just like he's always doing. In a lot of ways, this does feel like a room that would belong to Len. It smells like the soap he uses. There are shiny plaques and signed baseballs on the shelf, bats propped up in the corner, and a jacket with a big W on the front, hanging over his closet door. There's even a funny little bobblehead of a Dodgers player on his desk, some Japanese pitcher named Hideo Nomo whose body is twisted, enigmatically, into a rather extreme contortion.

Also on his desk: a plush Totoro (not expected) and *Life: A User's Manual* (more expected).

I check over my shoulder, but there's still no sign of Len. So I pick up the Totoro, its fur fuzzed up and soft from what seems like many washes, and peer into its embroidered eyes. *What can you tell me about Len?* I ask it telepathically. But the Totoro remains silent, as cagey as its owner.

I put it down and open the novel, which has *J. DiMartile* scrawled inside the front cover. When I turn to the first page, I see that the text has been extensively marked up in now-faded pencil.

"What do you have there?"

I jump, dropping the book onto my lap like I've been caught snooping in a diary. Len is back, and he is more inquisitive than accusatory. But also a little bit accusatory.

"It's the book I lent you," I say, setting it back on the desk.

Len laughs. "Oh yeah." He comes over and sits on the edge of the bed, resting his foot on my chair. I feel the weight shift a bit under the seat. "What do you think?"

I eye the massive stack of pages. "Too early to say."

A hint of his smirk appears, slight but self-assured. "You'd like Perec," he tells me. "He's all about rules."

Len's presumption annoys me, but it's true: I am intrigued. I don't remember the last time I talked to a boy who'd read something I hadn't, and it is both disturbing and, perversely, thrilling.

He picks up the book and flips through it. "Have you heard of the Oulipo?" I shake my head. "My dad told me about them. It's this movement that Perec was part of, a group of French writers and mathematicians who believed in creating artistic work with specific constraints."

"Like what?"

"Like in this case, the novel is about an apartment building, right? So Perec envisions it as a ten-by-ten grid of rooms and moves through them, one per chapter." Len shows me the table of contents. "But the catch is, he has to do it following a knight's tour."

The knight's tour problem is a famous logic challenge requiring you to move a knight piece across the chessboard, hitting every square just once. I only know this because there was a brief period in my life, shortly after reading *The Joy Luck Club*, when I became obsessed with chess, hoping (with no success) that it would make me into a prodigy like Waverly Jong.

"How come *you're* into this book?" I ask. "You don't seem to like rules as much as I do, but it sounds as though they're the whole point of Perec."

"They are, and they aren't." Scooping up a mini basketball from under his bed, Len falls back against the pillows. A hoop is attached to the far wall, and after a moment of evaluation, he aims the ball at it. He makes the shot. "The point of Perec is that he was writing about 'life,' which in some ways is bigger than any constraint you can impose on it." He shoots the ball again, and this time he misses, but he doesn't seem to mind. Instead, he grins at me. "And for a rule follower, Perec knew that pretty well."

I make a mental note to check out *Life: A User's Manual* from the library and decide what Perec's deal was for myself.

"I thought your elbow was supposed to be injured." I pick up the basketball from the floor and throw it at the hoop, achieving an impressive airball.

"It is." Len retrieves the ball and tosses it lazily with one hand, sending it in clean through the net. Then he raises his other arm. "But I'm a lefty." He stretches out his fingers, one by one. "Like you."

When the hell did he notice that?

I clear my throat. "Hey, you never answered my question."

Len sits up and spins the basketball on his (right) index finger. "Which question?"

"Why haven't you updated your mom on your *Bugle* involvement?"

"What's your deal, Eliza?" Len passes me the ball, and, to my surprise, I catch it. "You really care that much about the *Bugle*?"

"What do you mean? Of course I care."

"I thought you were just trying to get into Harvard or something."

"Well, yes, I'm trying to get into Harvard. But I also care about the *Bugle*."

"Do you actually want to be a journalist when you grow up?"

"I *am* a journalist."

"Okay, Lois Lane." Len riffles his hair with both hands—an abrupt, more hassled move than his usual tic. Then he recovers with an easy smile. "Forget I asked." He starts to get up from the bed, and then I change my mind.

"The truth," I blurt out. "I like the idea of truth conquering all."

Len sits back down. "Do you think it does?"

"Yeah, of course."

"People believe lies, though. Especially if they want to."

"That just makes fact-based journalism even more important."

"So your commitment to the *Bugle*, that's based purely on altruistic ideals."

I sit up tall. "Yeah."

Len tilts his head back against the wall, but his gaze is still on me, just half shrouded by those eyelashes. Today he's wearing a button-down in navy plaid flecked with gold. "I see."

"Well . . . okay, maybe not entirely." Now I slouch a little bit. "It's also because I like the idea of doing something important. I guess that part is about me." I jut my chin out. "I don't think there's necessarily anything wrong with that, though."

"I never said there was."

The way he chucks this at me—as if over a fence, from some

place I can't reach—is maddening. Even more so is my con-founding compulsion to tear down whatever's between us, to spoil the distance he likes so much.

"Do you remember our first student-council election?" I say before I can stop myself. "The one at the beginning of fresh-man year?"

"Sure."

"That's why I became a Bugler."

"What, you wrote a story about it and James gave you a compliment?"

"*No*, for your information, I couldn't write that story because I was in it. I was one of the candidates."

I spy a rare glimmer of surprise on his face. "You were?"

"I thought that being freshman-class president was about solving real problems."

He turns this over in his head. "You thought it would be something important."

"Right, exactly. I did all this research and put together a platform based on concrete, actionable issues, like restructur-ing the freshman math curriculum and fixing the Willoughby online student portal—"

"Wow, I can't believe I didn't vote for you." His unwelcome grin is back.

"Look, you don't have to tell me about it, okay? You thought I was boring. So did everyone else. I knew I'd made a mistake as soon as I stepped onto the amphitheater stage."

I remember hearing my voice through the microphone, the

first time it had ever been amplified like that, out over the rows of vacant faces in wooden seats. I was unprepared for how thin my words sounded. How weak, and not like me at all. I grasped then that my ideas, earthbound and miniature in scale, couldn't fill all that empty air. They were no match for everyone else's pom-pomming and grandstanding about school spirit and all that other nonsense. Which is an extremely difficult thing to realize when you're standing in front of almost three hundred people, hoping for their approval. I've tried to explain this to Kim, but she has never understood. I thought they were all fools, and even so, I felt small.

Len studies the ceiling, like he's not really listening, but he is. "What's all that got to do with the *Bugle*?"

"Well, James was covering the election, and when the ordeal was over, he came up to me and said that he could tell I was a thinker, that student council was a waste of time and I should come join the *Bugle* instead."

"So it *was* about James." He's relentless.

"No, it was *not* about James. It was about finding a place where I didn't have to change anything about myself to do a good job. Where I could *belong*." I give him a pointed look.

"Guess some jerk ruined that by putting your manifesto on the front page."

Len's voice dips into that inscrutable register, the one that I've just discovered is a DiMartile family specialty, and I can't tell whether the barb is for me or whether there is even a barb at all. I throw the basketball back at him. "What's *your* deal?"

He doesn't answer right away, just presses the ball between his hands, elbows out, as if trying to crush it.

"Well?"

He starts shooting the basketball at the hoop, over and over. Most of the time, he makes it in. "I don't care about the *Bugle* as much as you," he says, finally.

"I knew it!" I almost jump out of the chair. "I knew that schmaltzy story you told in your speech wasn't even true."

Len avoids my eyes and takes another shot at the basket. "It wasn't *untrue*," he says, in the exact way you might explain how Kraft singles aren't *not* cheese.

I've had just about enough of his slipperiness. "If you don't actually care, why'd you bother running for editor in chief?"

Again, a long silence, like he's pulling the old reporter's trick of pausing a bit longer than is comfortable in order to get the interviewee to say more. Except I'm the one asking the questions, not him.

Eventually, he sits up. "I overheard my mom telling my dad that she was worried about me," he says, studying his socks. "She was worried that, without baseball, I was getting to be like him. Unambitious."

"What's your dad do?"

"He works in market research at a big pharma company. But he was supposed to be an academic. Or that's what he wanted, anyway. He got his PhD in comparative literature." He holds the ball still for a moment. "He doesn't really seem to mind what he does now, but my mom always says it was a magnificent act of settling."

Now he throws the basketball against the wall, and each time, it hits with a loud thump.

"So that night, with the *Bugle* thing, I thought, what the hell. What's more ambitious than trying to be editor in chief of a paper you've barely written for?"

That's how he decided? With less thought than Kim puts into picking a lip gloss? I suddenly don't feel so bad about the fact that I'm planning a walkout against him. Not one bit.

"Afterward, though, I didn't like why I'd done it. For various reasons." He looks at me out of the corner of his eye. "But mostly because it was like I was agreeing with my mom—when I don't, really."

"That you're unambitious? Or that you're like your dad?"

"That there's something wrong with having no ambition."

I watch him bounce that stupid basketball off a wall that he shares with no one else, in a room that contains nothing less than probable Princeton legacy status in chair form, as he contemplates a philosophical quandary about the necessity of ambition.

"Maybe there isn't," I tell him, and he drops the ball, surprised. "For you. But if I had no ambition, I'd just end up like my sister, studying whatever my parents tell me to, biding time until some nice Chinese boy comes along to marry me."

Len considers me for a minute. "That's how it is, huh?"

My phone rings then, and I pick it up. "Hi, Mom."

"I am outside. Whose house is this?"

I start to say that it's a friend's, but I stop when I see Len get up to dunk the basketball without having to stand on his toes. He is trying to act as if he isn't eavesdropping, even though it's not like he understands Cantonese anyway.

"A classmate's. We had a group project."

"Okay. I have bad news."

My chest tightens at this pronouncement, even though it could realistically be anything on a spectrum from an overdue library book fine to someone dying. Mom's negative expressions have no gradation.

"I'll come down now."

I stuff my calculus book into my backpack and haul it over my shoulders. "Is everything okay?" Len asks, leaning on his dresser.

"I don't know. I guess I'd better find out." I flap my elbows absentmindedly. "Thanks for, uh . . ." I'm not quite sure what to say. "Thanks for letting me hang out here."

"Anytime." He moves out of the way as I bustle past him. "Tell your mom I said hi."

I'm in the hallway before I register his comment, and when I glance back over my shoulder, he gives me a small smile that makes me forget, just for a moment, that I have anything to worry about at all.

17

UNFORTUNATELY, THE BAD NEWS IS THAT THE restaurant where Dad works is closing. As bad news goes, this is pretty legitimate.

Mom frets about it all the way home, through dinner and the dishes, while Kim and I listen solemnly, without speaking to each other.

"Your dad always has such bad luck," Mom says, scrubbing a saucepan with a worn-out sponge. "Always facing so many difficulties."

When Dad gets home that night, he seems stoic, not like a man whose job is about to dissolve into the whims of Little Saigon restaurant economics.

"How much longer do you have?" asks Mom.

"A week," says Dad.

"That's all?"

"That's fate."

Mom tries to convince Dad that he should take this opportunity to get out of the restaurant business. She has been trying to get him to do this for years, and her reasons have been fairly logical: switching to a job at a *gūng sī*, or company, means paid vacation days, weekends off, health insurance. But it's always been easier for Dad to just stay working at a restaurant. It's what he has experience doing. It's the kind of work his friends can get him. Extraordinarily, it's what pays better. But it's also why he's got calluses from handling an industrial-grade wok all day, and why some nights he goes from smelling of fried rice to Hong Hua Oil, a pungent analgesic that he rubs onto his wrist for the pain.

They argue in their bedroom for a while, Mom's voice carrying through the walls. Then the door opens, and they both emerge. Dad goes over to the coffee table, where the record-player repair has been left in mid-progress. Mom, though, comes over to me.

"Eliza," she says. "Your dad is not going to work at a restaurant anymore. Can you write him a résumé?"

I'm sitting at our dining table, trying to finish the calculus homework I didn't get around to doing at Len's. Kim, sprawled out at her desk in the living room, gives me the look that says, *You're up.*

Even though Kim, being older, is generally responsible for more child-of-immigrant duties, somewhere along the way it was decided that any task involving writing would be kicked to me. "You're always reading so many books, and working on that newspaper," Mom likes to say. "You must be good at writing."

She makes me google job listings that Dad could apply for—which, because her mind skews toward the practical rather than the imaginative, all relate to her own line of work. "Look up *assembly*," she says, as if that word alone won't be laughed off the stage by the Google algorithm.

I try *assembly jobs orange county*. This shows me that the correct search term is *assembler*, and, for the first time, I learn what my mom's job title is. Because, as you can imagine, being an "assembler" is not quite as straightforward as being a "lawyer" or an "accountant" or even a "maid." Mom's employer is a microelectronics manufacturer in Long Beach, which is essentially all I've ever known about it. The one time I read through her company's website, I found it to be pretty much gibberish, all the more confusing because the words were as recognizable as they were incomprehensible. Like, what is a *die* in this context? What is *wafer processing*? Who knows?

The ironic thing is that most of the people employed in this capacity tend to speak about as much English as Mom does, and have about as much education. Which is to say, not much on both counts. That these qualifications seem to be sufficient for performing the job makes it popular among the Chinese-Vietnamese immigrant community, who pass along leads through friends of friends—in fact, that's how Mom got her foot in the door.

After I finish my homework, I go over to the couch with my laptop and open up a blank résumé template. I type Dad's name and contact info at the top, which is easy enough. Then there's the Experience section.

As I watch Dad bend over the turntable, I'm pretty sure he can do whatever assemblers are expected to do. The tricky part is figuring out how to make his skills from the restaurant seem remotely applicable. I'm not even sure what to put as his job title. In Cantonese, he is called a *sī fú*, or master, which is both appropriate and inappropriate. It's not easy to make good Chinese food, but it's also not glamorous work. But *cook* makes it sound like he flips burgers in a diner, and *chef* makes him sound like he wears a white hat and obsesses over things with only French names.

In the end, I decide to go with *chef* because it sounds more accomplished, and because the embellishment seems necessary to balance out the amount of white space left on the page. The emptiness saddens me.

"See, it works now," he says, showing me how he's gotten the turntable platter to spin smoothly. Dad gets up to plug the record player into a pair of speakers, another dumpster find from a few years ago. We normally use them now with our TV, even though it already has built-in speakers. "Surround sound," Dad joked.

I flip through the small collection of Chinese records that Dad has laid out on the floor. "Where'd you get these?" I say, handing one to him.

"When I first moved to America, my cousin brought them over here from Hong Kong." Dad slips the vinyl disc from its cover. "This singer, Sam Hui, is very funny. From the 1970s and '80s. He sang political satire for working-class people."

Kim, whose curiosity has gotten the better of her, takes a break from her own problem set to kneel on the floor next to me.

Dad positions the record onto the turntable and hits the power button. Then, carefully, he lifts the arm and sets the needle onto the spinning vinyl. At first there is just a crackly silence that is filled with equal parts skepticism and suspense. A few seconds later, Sam Hui's voice splits the air, wasting no time as he zeroes in on the beating heart of the common man: *Chin Chin Chin Chin, Chin Chin Chin Chin,* which translates roughly into "cash cash cash cash, cash cash cash cash."

Kim and I look at each other. Neither of us has ever seen a record player in action before, and it feels almost like magic that music can be so mechanical. Sam Hui's crooning, unspooling from that piece of grooved vinyl? I thought I had seen everything.

Mom comes out of the bedroom to see what all the noise is. In the background, Sam Hui has woven in a riff in English between all the *Chin*s: "No money no talk . . . no money no talk."

"Isn't it cool, Mom?" I say. "Dad fixed the record player."

Mom's interest in the turntable has not increased with its extended presence in the apartment, but she tries her best to join in the enthusiasm. "Yes, it's cool," she says, giving us a tired smile. "But it's late, and the neighbors might complain. You'd better turn it down."

And just like that, it's over. Dad turns off the record player, Kim retreats to her desk, and I crawl back up on the couch. I open up my laptop again to finish Dad's résumé.

Under the Education section, where I list the machine-shop courses Dad took at community college long before I was born, I add in a Skills and Hobbies section. Underneath the bullet point about Dad being trilingual (English, Vietnamese, and Chinese), I type: *Repaired a variety of home appliances and electronics, including a vintage record player.* I delete the sentence and rewrite it again and again, but I end up leaving it the way it was originally, because I can't seem to find the right words.

18

THE NEXT DAY, RIGHT BEFORE FIFTH PERIOD IS about to start, I walk up to my desk to find a book on my chair. I look around out of instinct, as if I'm checking to see who left it. Even though I already know exactly who it was.

I slide into my seat and open this copy of *Life: A User's Manual*. Inside, there's a Post-it with a message in neat, slanted handwriting: *Thanks for the recommendation.*

Across the room, Len appears to be ignoring me, busy reading *Macbeth*, but at the last second, he glances over. When he catches my gaze, he gives me half a grin, and then turns back to *Macbeth*, as if our eyes met only in passing.

I feel suddenly gobsmacked.

"Hey, Eliza." Serena has appeared, taking the seat in front of me, even though it's not her desk. She eyes my sweater, a striped pullover that I haven't worn since seventh grade. "Is that new?"

The loss of my trusty gray cardigan has meant I've fallen off my uniform game, since I've been forced to go through a number of alternative garments to fill the sweater-shaped hole in my heart. Unsuccessfully, I should add.

"No," I say, tugging absently at my sleeves.

Serena's holding a copy of Rebecca Solnit's *Men Explain Things to Me*, which has featured prominently in her latest Insta posts. She starts talking about something she read in one of the essays, something about silence, or violence. I have no idea because I'm not listening.

Instead, I'm thinking about Len and all the things he said to me yesterday while we were alone in his room—how it seemed like a lot and not enough at the same time. Since then, a kind of guilty curiosity has come over me, and I realize, fingering the cover of *Life: A User's Manual*, that I feel compelled to read it immediately, not just to prevent him from one-upping me intellectually, but also because I sense that maybe the book contains answers to questions I feel like I can't ask. Answers that, all of a sudden, I'm dying to know.

That's when I realize that Serena is still talking. She hasn't noticed that I haven't heard a word she's said, but in that moment I feel, despite my very short tenure as a public feminist, the weight of being a bad one.

Life: A User's Manual is a thick book, and I'm aware of its heft in my backpack all day. After school, when Winona is late meeting me by her locker, I consider taking it out to read. It's a book, after all—isn't that what it's for? But I have an irrational aversion to being seen with it, I realize. As if someone who saw me would be able to tell, just by looking at it, that I got it from Len.

Before I can make up my mind, Serena comes rounding the corner.

"Heyyyyy." Serena rarely just says "hey," which drives Winona up the wall. "You're not doing anything, are you?"

I rearrange my expression into something that doesn't say I've been thinking very intently about Len. "I'm, ah, waiting for Winona."

"Oh, good. I'm so glad I ran into you. The junior-class committee meeting got canceled, so I figured we could do some recruiting for the walkout."

I can't tell if Serena's face glows the way it does because of her relentless enthusiasm or her flawless skin. Either way, it makes letting her down weirdly difficult. But the situation's kind of tricky. Late last night, after extensive brainstorming (and cajoling) via text, I finally got Winona to buckle down and work on the changes for *Driveways*, and we're supposed to shoot today. Her new idea is to put herself into the movie somehow, maybe as a third character, to make the story more, well, personal. It's not something she's really used to doing, especially since the last attempt felt like such a failure, but she wants to try—and I want to help, of course.

On the other hand, Serena is undoubtedly pouring a lot of energy into making this walkout a success. Can I really tell her that I don't have time to recruit people for my own protest?

Winona shows up then, looking surprised to see both Serena

and me standing there. "What's up?"

"We're recruiting for the walkout!" Serena announces. "You want to join?"

I've decided that we should go ahead with the filming, given that Winona and I made those plans first, so I shake my head. "Actually—"

But Winona interrupts me with a declaration I never thought I'd hear come out of her mouth. "Actually, Serena, that sounds like a great idea."

"What?" I squint at her. "Wait, I thought we had to film today. Didn't you finish writing a new scene?"

"Yeah." Winona is almost breezy as she dismisses my concern. "But it wasn't good, so I've decided to rewrite it. We'll talk about it later."

"Awesome!" Serena loops her arms through both of ours, and Winona has to stop herself from recoiling. But she soldiers on, because with Serena sandwiched between us, I can't exactly continue my interrogation. I remind myself to ask her, later, just what was so bad about the perfectly good scene I read last night.

Recruiting girls, as you might expect, is the easy part. When we broach the topic to a gaggle of freshmen milling around in front of their lockers, they're on board without any hesitation.

"Oh my God." One girl, sporting blunt-cut bangs and jeans that bag around her hips, fans herself. "You're all, like, so inspiring."

"I've decided to join student council next year," says another with a pixie cut and rainbow peace signs dangling from her ears. She's also wearing an *I AM A FEMINIST* button. "Maybe I can be president when I'm a senior."

"I'm so proud of you," Serena effuses, even though they've just met. The girl nearly faints from the praise, and Serena gives her shoulder a reassuring squeeze. "Now, remember, ladies, don't post anything online, okay? We don't want to get shut down before we've even gotten started." Then she winks, and with two parting air kisses for each girl, she waves us along. Winona, apparently forgetting that she signed herself up to be part of this brigade ten minutes ago, tilts her head at me, blinking in disbelief.

Serena has a different strategy when it comes to boys, which we witness when we come across some seniors sitting around a lunch table.

"Hey, Hunter," says Serena.

"Hi, Serena," he replies pleasantly.

Hunter Pak is the president of Key Club. He's not quite cool enough to be in student council, but he's too handsome to be a true nerd. His dad is a pastor, and sometimes Hunter, soft-eyed behind plastic-rimmed glasses, seems on his way down the same path.

"You know Eliza, right?" Serena slides into the seat next to him. "And Winona?"

"Not officially." He waves at us.

"We have a question for you guys." Now Serena's addressing the others, too. "What do you think about the whole *Bugle* situation?"

Calvin Vo puts his feet up on the seat. "Don't care."

Hunter directs his niceness at me. "Sorry it's been so rough for you."

"Eliza was *robbed*," says Serena. "You all know it's true."

"Still don't care," says Calvin.

Serena turns to Hunter, and her voice gets earnest. "Don't you think it's *so* unfair? Eliza is so much more qualified than Len to be editor in chief. He's just a jock."

"So's your boyfriend," Gabriel Evangelista butts in, sniggering.

"Yeah," says Serena. "And I wouldn't want him to be editor in chief either."

This makes even Calvin laugh.

"Len *is* smarter than Jason," Hunter points out.

"Maybe," Serena allows. "But he wasn't picked because he's smart. I mean, you tell me." She homes in on Gabriel. "Who would you have voted for, Len or Eliza?"

He hesitates for just a beat too long. "Eliza, if you say she's more qualified."

Serena gives Hunter a confiding look, one that says, *What did I tell you?* He, of course, interprets it to mean, *You're special.* You can tell it's over for him.

"Well, what can we do about it?" Hunter asks.

"We're planning something." Serena pushes her phone over to Hunter. "To get Len to step down. I'll text you the details if you want to join."

Only Serena can make signing up for a feminist walkout seem flirtatious—and also, at the same time, have it mean nothing at all. Because Hunter must know that there's no way Serena likes him, yet there he is, tapping his number into her phone like he's just agreed to sign over his dad's entire congregation to the cause.

"Aren't you going to ask for my number?" says Calvin.

"Are you offering it?" Serena smiles slyly.

In the end, she gets all three of them not only to sign up for the walkout, but also to swear that they won't tell a soul about it.

"That was impressive," I say, as we walk away.

Winona, now utterly flabbergasted, is no longer linking arms with Serena. "That's one way to put it!"

Our next stop is the art studio, which is in one of those permanent portable classrooms on the edge of campus. It's perched on a slightly elevated foundation, so there's a ramp leading up to the door. As we make our way up, Serena grabs Winona by the arm and pulls her in front of us.

"What are you doing?" Winona demands.

Serena gestures at the building as if it's obvious. "This is where the 'alternative' kids hang out."

Winona scratches her head. "What's 'alternative' supposed to mean?"

"It means," says Serena, pushing us through the door, "they'll respect *you* more than me."

The studio is quiet when we stumble inside. There are a few kids at the easels, each focusing on a display of plastic fruit strewn over red drapes. They all notice us, but only one doesn't turn his attention right back to painting.

"Hey, Winona," says Ethan Fiore, who's a junior, like us. He's got an aquiline nose and serious eyes, plus a head of curly hair that falls over his eyes.

To us, Serena telegraphs a self-satisfied *See?* She nudges Winona, who is waving back awkwardly. "That's your opening," she whispers. "I'm definitely feeling some potential there."

Winona, lasering Serena with an incredulous look, shoves us all back outside.

"What's up?" says Serena, amiably enough, but with the thinnest layer of exasperation.

"I thought this was supposed to be about feminism," says Winona.

"It is," says Serena.

Winona crosses her arms. "So what's with your backward-ass heteronormative bull—"

I try to intervene. "I think what Winona is trying to say is . . . she's not sure that flirting with Ethan Fiore is really the best tactic for her."

"Or for anyone," adds Winona.

"It's not flirting," says Serena. "It's just being strategically persuasive. The point of a walkout is to have *a lot* of people walk out. What's wrong with appealing to people in whatever way will connect most with them?"

Winona stares at Serena like she is an extraterrestrial life form, then appeals to me for help.

"You don't have to talk to Ethan," I offer.

Winona is disgusted. "Why bother with Ethan, or even this walkout?" She flutters her hands around in scorn. "Why not just cut straight to the source? Eliza, go show Len a little leg and then ask if he'll resign."

I'm not sure what horrifies me more, the suggestion itself, or the way everything tumbles around inside me when I catch myself imagining it.

Serena, too, is momentarily disarmed, and—amazingly—appears to contemplate the idea, though only for a second. "Oh, Winona," she says, her smile indulgent. "That's totally different."

"No, it's not. It's a hundred percent the same. It just *seems* different."

At this, Serena regards Winona with a sudden gravitas. "But that *always* matters."

There's a pause, which means Winona is thinking this over. Her only response, however, is a mutter. "I need a break."

"No problem." Serena leans over to inspect her reflection in the window. "Ethan will just have to make do with me." She smooths her hair back, adjusts her earrings, and dons that smile again, partly for practice and partly for us, and somehow I doubt she'll have any issues with Ethan or anyone else.

As soon as Serena disappears into the classroom, Winona unleashes her fury. "God, what is even her deal?" She paces up and down the ramp. "I was totally right about her. She's not a feminist at all!"

In my mind, yesterday's conversation with Serena, about how much work goes into the Hwangbo effect, wrestles for space next to Winona's claim. "Maybe," I posit, "she comes at it from a different place?"

We watch through the glass as Serena laughs at something, her fingertips lightly brushing Ethan's elbow. We don't need an update to figure out whether he's signed up for the walkout.

"You're going soft," Winona harrumphs.

This pinches in an unfamiliar way, and I can't help worrying that Winona, despite knowing me so well (or maybe because of it), would be my harshest critic if that were really true—if I really *have* gone soft. I just wish I could explain to her how unwieldy all this feminism stuff is starting to feel.

"Look," I say, "I get that Serena is . . . something else. But we need her." As she heads back toward the door, facing away from Ethan and the rest of them, I catch her letting out a small, private exhale. Winona, in spite of herself, also notices. "And, more importantly, I think she needs us, too," I add, nodding at the window. "Which is the point of feminism, right? All of us sticking together?"

Sighing, Winona hoists herself onto the ramp railing and dangles her boots in midair. "Yeah, I know," she grumbles finally. "Just wish we could all agree on the details."

19

THAT FRIDAY, DUE TO TIM O'CALLAHAN'S UNEX-
pected absence from school, James has a last-minute *Bugle*
assignment for Len. "Or, I guess it's for you, too, Eliza," he
adds, waving at me.

I saunter reluctantly over to Len's corner.

"Okay," says James. "Since Tim was out sick today, I'm
wondering if you two could cover for him."

"What's the story?" I ask.

"Well, you're not going to like this, Eliza, but . . . it involves
a baseball game."

I make a face. "How is a baseball game news?" I'm kidding,
but only a little.

"It's going in the Sports section," says James. "You know we
have one of those, right?"

"Yeah, yeah."

"Plus, it's not just any baseball game," Len explains. He's
sitting cross-legged, as usual, on top of a desk. "It's a possibly
historic baseball game."

I assume that this is just Len's jock bias surfacing, but now James is also nodding along with enthusiasm. "Right," he says. "Willoughby is playing Hargis High, and Jason Lee is expected to break the single-season home-run record."

They both wait expectantly, like I am now supposed to understand why this game is a big deal. I give James an *et tu* look.

"You mean the Jason Lee who is dating Serena Hwangbo?" I say.

"One and the same," James answers. "Center fielder."

"He's actually really good." Len offers this more seriously than most things he's uttered.

"So, can you both make it?" says James.

"Hold on." I grab my phone and text Winona, willing her to reply that we absolutely, a hundred percent need to work on filming *Driveways* today.

Winona: Nah, we don't have to film today.

Me: Are you rewriting again?

Winona: I just need this to be good. You get it.

Me: You also need to finish?!

No immediate response from Winona after that, and I suspect that none is coming. I'm about to prod her again when I notice that Len has vacated his perch on the desk and is now standing next to me, close enough for a peek at my screen. Which is to say, *rudely* close. Flustered, I swat him away.

"Well?" Len's grin can't quite contain itself. "Were you able to reschedule your Friday cocktail hour with the county assessor?"

I glower at James, who seems awfully entertained by all this, and then back at my phone. But there still hasn't been a further peep from Winona.

"I had to shuffle some things around." I square my shoulders at Len. "But lucky for you, I can make it."

"What can I say? I've always been a lucky guy."

It takes a lot of effort not to smack him on our way out.

The afternoon is unusually windy, with a heat that is incongruous with the brute force of the gales, and a dryness that creeps over your hands and cheeks. The discomfort, along with the accompanying sense of feeling like a stranger to yourself, is vague, kind of like premenstrual sadness. The dust that you feel coated in, that lines the inside of your nostrils and fuzzes up your mind, is there and not there at the same time. It seems all in your head until you realize the source is a perennial visitor that, for some reason, you never see coming: the Santa Ana winds.

"Seems like bad weather for a baseball game," I say, shouting to be heard as I fight my way around to the passenger side of Len's car.

"It's not great," Len yells back.

We're headed to Hargis High, and Len has offered to drive, mostly because I would otherwise have no way of getting there. When I try to get into his car, the door flings itself open with abandon. Tumbling into the seat, I brush aside my hair, which has whipped itself into a tangle over my face and, curiously, smells foreign and coppery—neither like my shampoo nor myself. Pulling the car door shut against the violent air, insulating myself against the now muffled howls, feels in itself like an act of triumph.

"Santa Ana winds." Len rubs his eyes with his arm before he turns on the ignition. "They're no joke."

His hair is windswept, and I almost consider reaching over to touch it—but whether to smooth it down or make it worse, I really couldn't say.

I sit on my hands and try to think of something normal to talk about. "I read an essay about the Santa Ana winds the other day. By Joan Didion."

Len starts the car. "Yeah? What's she got to say about them?"

"Mostly she talked about how unsettling they are. How the air itself makes people do strange things, like kill themselves or get into accidents." God, I'm really doing a top-notch job with the direction of this conversation. But Len seems intrigued, so I keep going.

"She also talked about how people who aren't from Southern California think we don't have any weather here, but actually we do. There's a line that I remember, something about how Los Angeles's weather is the weather of apocalypse. Because the winds can make the city go up in flames, just like that."

"Hmm, yeah." For a second, as we are waiting to turn out of the parking lot, Len gives me a look that makes me feel as if I'm the one who came up with the line, not Joan Didion. Turning away, I look out the window at the trees, their leaves frantic.

"I just liked the way she wrote about it, I guess. Like, she took this thing that I've experienced in such a mundane way, and she made it into something else. For the first time, I felt like someone was writing about a place that I knew, in a way that felt like literature." Suddenly, I'm not sure why I've gone on about this for so long. "Anyway."

Len, though, picks up the thought like I didn't mean to drop it. "Yeah, I know what you mean. It was like her writing made this place seem . . . worthy, somehow."

"Yeah, exactly." I'm surprised that he understands. "Anyway, you should read it. It's in our AP reader, actually. That's where I found it."

"Maybe I'll check it out."

The parking lot is on the north side of campus, so we're just now turning onto the main drag. "I wonder how Boba Bros is doing," I say, as we pass it. "Some bubble tea sounds good right now."

Without any warning, Len veers into the strip-mall parking lot, scraping the bottom of his car against the curb.

"What on earth?" I exclaim.

Len pulls into an empty spot, then flashes his trademark grin. "You made a good case."

I get my usual lavender tea, but Len tries something new— matcha with oat milk. Once again, however, his boba game is pathetic. Back in the car, when he puts his tea in the cup holder between us, I see that he's already consumed about a third of the liquid.

"You're drinking it too fast," I say, examining his cup. The straw is already chewed up. "You still have all these tapioca balls left."

"I know. It's hard to get the balance right."

"It *is* an art," I concede, and take a measured sip from my own drink.

While we continue on our way to Hargis, I sneak a better look around his car. It's as clean as his bedroom was, but otherwise, not what I was expecting. I'd assumed he'd drive a boxy monstrosity of a car, so high off the ground that even humdrum trips make you feel like you're riding a float in your own parade. Instead, he's got this little old Toyota. Even with the seat pushed all the way back, Len is somewhat hunched over with his elbows and knees bent, a bit like he's driving a clown car.

"What's so funny?" he asks, ducking his head to peer at the stoplight.

"Your car is smaller than I expected," I say.

He laughs. "What, you're not impressed by my sweet ride?"

"I'm not saying it's a bad car. I'm just saying, it's a car that my mom would drive."

"This *was* the car that *my* mom drove."

For some reason I find this hilarious, which amuses him, and for a few minutes, it really does feel like we're friends.

"By the way," he says after a moment. "Did everything turn out okay with your mom?"

It takes me a second to remember that Mom called me while I was at Len's house. "Oh," I say. "It is what it is, I guess." I tell him about Dad's job situation, and how I'm trying to help him with his job applications. Sometimes, when people find out that Kim and I do stuff like this, they seem appalled, like I've just told them that in our house, we have to scrub the floors with a toothbrush. "Why?" they ask, incredulous, and I never know how to answer.

But Len doesn't ask why. "That's nice of you," he says.

I prop my elbow up against the door. "Not really. I mean, I have to do it."

"Still. I don't have to do anything like that for my parents."

"You *do* carry the groceries for your mom."

"That's right, I have manual labor. My dad makes me mow the lawn, too."

"The burdens of being a male child."

"I knew you'd understand."

As we near Hargis High, I roll down the window to scope out the campus. And for a split second, it seems like I'm seeing an alternate-universe Willoughby. Everything is the same: the circular driveway, the stucco facade and cinder-block walls, the placement of the windows. The only differences are the paint job (navy instead of maroon) and the collegiate lettering spelling out *HARGIS HIGH*.

"This is so weird," I say, after Len has parked. "I feel like we're gonna run into the alternate-universe versions of ourselves here."

"Oh yeah?" Len's got the camera around his neck again, this time with a long zoom lens. Walking backward, he holds it up and snaps a photo of the Hargis quad. "What would they be like?"

"Well, alternate-universe Len would be . . ." I study him as he takes a second photo. "Chatty. Direct. Very serious." Another click. "And a feminist, of course."

Len lowers the camera and grins at me. "I see."

"What about alternate-universe Eliza?"

Len thinks about it for a moment. "She'd probably be . . . easygoing, humble, and *totally* obsessed with boys."

I snort. "What does she think of alternate-universe Len?"

"Oh, she likes him."

"Does he like her?"

"Sure. They get along pretty well."

He's standing close enough now that the only distance separating us is the camera, with its extended lens, held level at his chest. If, for whatever reason, I were to lean forward too abruptly, I could break one of the most expensive pieces of photographic equipment the *Bugle* owns. It makes me strangely nervous.

"They both sound like a drag," I say, slipping away.

20

AT THE FIELD, LEN AND I SIT DOWN IN THE bleachers, where we've got a pretty good view of home plate through the chain-link fence. We're on the side that's closer to the visiting-team dugout, and I can see a few of the Willoughby guys, clad in maroon and white, playing catch.

"It's called warming up," says Len.

"Sure," I say.

One of the juniors, Luis Higuera, notices Len and waves. "Len-*chan*!" he yells, which is probably the only Japanese he knows. He and a senior, Adam Gibson, jog over to the fence.

"How's it going?" Len calls out, grinning wide.

"You gonna pitch for us today?" says Adam. "I'll let you start."

"Nah, man, still recovering." Len points at his elbow.

"Yeah, yeah," says Luis. "That's why we're stuck with this guy."

"Go fuck yourself, Higuera," Adam says cheerfully.

Len surveys the blustery sky, which is cloudless and unnaturally bright. "You guys gonna be all right in this wind?"

"Dude, it sucks." Adam pulls his cap down while Luis shakes his head and makes the sign of the cross. Then Adam nods at the camera. "You're documenting this?"

"Yeah, Eliza and I are covering the game for the *Bugle*." Here Len gestures at me.

"Hey, aren't you that feminazi girl?" asks Adam, acknowledging me for the first time. Luis elbows him, as if trying to keep him civilized, but Adam looks from Len to me and then winks. "Guess you guys made up, huh?"

I feign innocence. "About what?"

"All right," the umpire hollers. "Let's go!"

As the guys take their places—Hargis out on the field, Willoughby in the dugout except for Luis, who's the first one up to bat—the wind picks up, swirling the dirt into a Dust Bowl situation that takes a solid minute to settle down. Len and I have to hitch our collars up over our faces to avoid breathing it in.

Finally, the umpire gives a signal to start. The Hargis pitcher, a pale redhead with gangly legs, winds his arm up and sends the ball hurtling over home plate.

"Strike!" the umpire barks.

I've barely had time to blink. "But Luis didn't even swing."

"Doesn't matter," says Len. He studies the pitcher for a second. "That McIntyre kid seems good."

Luis makes it to first base, though McIntyre proceeds to eviscerate our next two hitters like the Santa Anas are barely a light breeze. But then it's time for Jason Lee to step up to the plate.

The crowd knows exactly who he is, and its collective attention fuses into a jolt that is perceptible even through the static of the winds. All around me, backs straighten, necks crane, breaths stop—everyone is focused on this round-shouldered kid with a boxer's swagger and a baseball bat. Even I am curious to see what he'll do.

Unlike the other Willoughby guys, Jason appears to be a left-handed hitter. He twists one foot into the dirt, taps the same spot with his bat, then repeats on the other side. It occurs to me, as I watch him twirl the bat forward and backward before sinking into his batting stance, that Jason makes that stick of aluminum seem like it's weightless.

McIntyre throws the first pitch, a fast one that goes right at Jason, who is forced to jump out of the way.

"Ball," calls the umpire.

"That almost hit Jason!" I exclaim. "McIntyre was doing so well."

Len squints an eye at the pitcher's mound. "He might have done that on purpose," he says. "Just to throw Jason off his game."

"He's allowed to do that?"

"Can't stop him."

"Did *you* used to do that?"

"If I had to." He starts to turn toward me, but his eyes linger on the field until he registers my mute disapproval. "What?" he says, laughing. "You thought I'd play it straight?"

I feel an inexplicable tickle of a smile come on—and I squelch it in a hurry. "Guess not."

Len's hypothesis about McIntyre, however, seems shaky when the next pitch turns out to be, once again, a ball. The Hargis fans realize this, too, and their distaste awakens like a beast. "Come on, McIntyre, get it together!" a voice thunders from the bleachers.

The Willoughby contingent, for its part, is also unhappy. Their protests are just as loud, and it's clear what they're thinking: Our boy Jason is better than this—how's he gonna break the record without getting anything to hit?

But the next pitch is yet another ball, and now McIntyre's really done it. The wind whips up another round of dirt, and the subsequent delay becomes his fault. "Hurry up and do it already, Georgie!" someone yowls. "Quit throwing like a girl!"

I look around, but no one besides me seems rankled by this comment. I slowly begin to realize that I am in the middle of a mob, goaded on by misplaced fanaticism and the Santa Anas, and it's only the first inning.

McIntyre's fourth pitch is, at long last, acceptable, and Jason swings, hitting the ball with a satisfying whack. Up it goes, rocketing toward the outfield, tracing an elegant parabola that seems destined to become a home run—but no, the devil winds have their own calculus, and at the last second, the shift happens. We all see it: one moment it's headed over the fence, and the next it's blown off course, falling into the waiting glove of the Hargis outfielder who, bless him, never took his eye off the ball.

The crowd is stunned. The Hargis fans react first, erupting in cheers as the umpire calls the inning. McIntyre, vindicated, is now a hero, and he practically skips toward the Hargis dugout, clearing the foul line with a jubilant hop.

"Everyone is so . . . emotional," I remark to Len as Willoughby takes the field.

He doesn't respond right away, because he too is focused on the first Hargis batter—who, from the sound of it, has made contact with Adam Gibson's first pitch. I turn just in time to see our right fielder stumble and drop the ball.

Len utters a noise that sounds like someone has just broken his finger. "What was that?" he demands. He throws his hands in the air, and his neighbor, a middle-aged man in a nylon windbreaker, agrees wholeheartedly.

I stare at Len, not quite believing that he's the same boy who reads semi-obscure French literature for fun.

"I guess I don't really see the point of watching sports," I say, once he's returned to normal.

"No?" Len leans both elbows on the bleacher behind him. "You're telling me that when Jason Lee hit that ball, the suspense of where it would land didn't thrill you even a little bit?"

"If you're trying to argue that it's not always totally boring, then sure. But I've never understood all this devotion." I gesture around us. "People get so excited when their team does well, and so angry when they don't. Including you."

Len ruffles the back of his hair, smirking. "That doesn't seem reasonable to you?"

"No, I think it seems like a form of tribalism. It's one of those things that everyone accepts is normal, but is kind of weird when you think about it. Because what do you or I really get if Willoughby wins this game?"

"A good story."

"I disagree. It could still be a good story even if Hargis won."

Len doesn't say anything for a minute, but this time it's because he's thinking. Meanwhile, Hargis scores a run and the bleachers explode in elation.

"There is something arbitrary about it," Len agrees, leaning in so that only I can hear him. "I want Willoughby to win because it's my school. And that means I have to hate Hargis, just because they're not my school. So, in that sense, yeah, I see what you mean." He shrugs. "But it can also be more than that, I think."

We watch the next Hargis batter walk up to the plate.

"You know, my grandpa's dad—my great-grandpa—played baseball while living in one of those World War Two Japanese internment camps."

"Really?"

Len takes his phone from his pocket and pulls up a photo to show me. Angling it away from the sun, I can see that it's a picture of a baseball team: two rows of young men in white uniforms, posing in front of the backstop while the desert recedes beyond them. At the bottom, a few of the neat, elegant

Japanese characters are similar enough to Chinese that I can make out that the photo was taken in 1945.

"Which one is he?"

"Can you guess?"

I zoom in closer. One guy, kneeling in the front row, has a knowing grin and familiar eyes. "That one."

Len laughs. "You're good."

I hand the phone back to him. "It's pretty incredible that your great-grandpa went through that." My family, with its history of fleeing war in Southeast Asia, has obviously spent its share of time in detention centers, but they were refugees trying to get to America. Len's family was already American. This stuff wasn't supposed to happen to Americans.

"Yeah, it was definitely messed up. But I think that's part of the reason why baseball was so huge in the camps. It was a way to be Japanese American when the rest of the country didn't see them as American at all. They built up these fields from basically nothing, and sometimes even teams from outside—people who weren't incarcerated—would come into the camps to play against them."

Out on the field, the Hargis batter hits the ball with a crack, and we both look over to see it veer off the diamond.

"My grandpa said his dad always thought baseball was a way to bring people together, despite their differences."

"Do you think that's still true?"

"I don't know." He glances at me, then contemplates the field. "Maybe sometimes."

The wind picks up again, throwing us all into a haze of dust, but sitting so close to Len that our knees almost touch, I wonder if maybe baseball isn't so boring after all.

Unfortunately, by the time the ninth inning rolls around, the score is still 1–0, with Hargis in the lead. Jason still hasn't hit a home run, which means the whole point of our article may not, in fact, actually be happening.

"He had one job." I shake my head sadly.

"Hey, don't doubt Jason Lee," Len says.

We're down by the side of the field now, and I've convinced Len to let me fiddle with the camera. He's spent the entire eighth inning teaching me how to use it, but I still don't quite know what I'm doing.

"When do you think you'll go back to playing baseball?" I ask, snapping a photo of Isaac Furukawa, the current Willoughby batter.

"What?" Len is watching Isaac, too.

"Baseball. Pitching." I look at my photo of Isaac, but the whole thing is just a blur, and not in a cool way. "When are you going back?"

"Oh," says Len. "I'm not."

In my surprise, I almost bang the camera up against the fence. "What? What about all that stuff about your great-grandpa? And baseball bringing people together?"

"I still appreciate baseball. I just don't know if I want to play anymore."

I turn the camera on him, but I have to step backward because the zoom lens is so long. "I don't understand."

Len puts up a hand to block the camera view. "Can I have that back now?"

"Move your hand."

"I think I prefer taking the photos."

"Come on."

He finally acquiesces, and I manage to snap a picture of him grinning, but in an embarrassed way.

"How come you don't want to go back?" I ask, admiring the photo. It's a good one, but I couldn't tell you how I managed it.

"I just don't."

I aim the camera back out at the field and capture a photo of the latest Hargis pitcher, a stocky blond kid named Walnes. "Are you afraid you won't be as good as you were?"

He still hasn't answered by the time I lower the camera, so I suspect I've lost his attention to the game. But he's looking down at the grass.

"My doctor actually said I could go back this season." He traces a line with the toe of his sneaker. "He said if I'm careful, and I work hard, I could eventually pitch the way I used to. Probably."

"That's good, isn't it?"

"Maybe. I'm just not sure it's worth all the effort."

He tries to say this carelessly, like throwing keys on a table, but some syllable of it makes me sad.

"Sure it is," I find myself saying. "I've never seen you pitch, but if you were half as good as McIntyre"—here his mouth twitches—"then I'd say you were probably pretty good." He pretends to roll his eyes at me. "And if you can do something that well, I mean, I think it's like what you were saying about Jason's hitting. There is something kind of thrilling about it."

Now a big grin, which I don't like one bit, slowly takes over his face. "Wait, are you saying you *are* thrilled by baseball?"

"*No.* God, Len." My face has gone totally warm for no reason. "I'm just saying, I think it's always worth trying to be good at something."

"I'm good at lots of things without trying," he jokes, and I wish I had a baseball to throw at his head.

But then his grin fades a little bit, and his eyes rove over the field. "You want to know the truth?"

"Sure."

He rubs his left shoulder, and then the thin crescent of a scar that stretches along the inside of his elbow. "Ever since I discovered I could throw a baseball better than the average kid," he says, "I've been a pitcher. It was a big part of how I thought about myself. And it's true. Part of me doesn't want to go back now because I'm afraid that I won't be able to do it again." He leans against the fence. "Especially because this time, it feels like I'm making this big commitment. It's like I'm saying, I *want* this. I want to be the star pitcher."

He doesn't look at me, but I suddenly understand. "And that's what you're most afraid of. Failing at something you actually want."

"Yeah." He runs his finger along the metal links of the fence. "But here's the other thing. When I tore my elbow—which hurt like fuck, by the way—the first thing everybody wanted to know was how to save it. So I could keep on being a pitcher. It was like they all thought my life would be over if I couldn't pitch anymore. But as I was lying there, about to go under for the surgery, I had this thought."

Now he sweeps his gaze back to me, as if to see whether I'm still listening. I've let the camera hang slack over my stomach, and I've long ago stopped following the game.

"It was the pitching itself—too much of it—that made me *not* a pitcher anymore. I thought that was so bizarre. It was like my identity was eating itself."

He puts his hands in his hoodie pockets, drawing himself inward like it's gotten cold, even though the wind has been blowing just the same as it always has.

I think about putting a hand on his arm, but I don't. "You wanted a new identity."

"Maybe."

"And you're afraid that if you go back, you'll *really* be going back. Maybe you'll get as good as you were, or even better. And then you'll be stuck. Len DiMartile, star pitcher. Until it all goes away again."

"I guess so."

"So you're afraid you'll fail, and you're afraid you won't."

"Yeah." His laugh is sheepish. "I guess it's just easier not to go back."

"Right, it's easier to just walk on to being editor in chief of the *Bugle*."

He studies my face, like he's trying to figure out if I'm upset or not. "I'm only telling you this because you already think I'm a dick," he says lightly.

"I never said that."

"True. The things you said were both worse and more specific."

"Were they really?"

"I'm kidding, Eliza."

I cradle the camera in my hands, feeling its unfamiliar weight. "Well, I just have one more thing to say."

"Just one, huh?"

"I don't think being afraid is a good reason for anything."

Len doesn't have a response to this, and for a while, we both watch the field in silence.

Eventually, when it's Jason's turn to bat again, Len elbows me. "He's back up," he says. "Are you ready to shoot?"

"Here." I stand on my toes to loop the camera back over his head. "I don't want to be the reason the *Bugle* has no good pictures of Jason Lee making history." Then I put my hands on my hips and focus on this final face-off, along with everyone else.

Jason, like many baseball greats (I'm told), is a man of many superstitions, and he repeats his batting routine, motion for motion. Then Walnes hurls the ball straight toward home plate with spectacular speed.

But Jason comes through, just as Len promised, with an expert swing that sends that little sphere of leather soaring, once again, over the outfield. This time the winds, out of either mercy or indifference, wave the ball onward, allowing it to complete its rightful arc over the fence.

The crowd jumps to its feet, and even the sounds of disappointment blend into the cheers so that all I can hear is great, thunderous applause. Luis and then Jason round the diamond toward home, waving like war heroes.

Len whoops and grabs my shoulders, yelling, "He did it!"

I am, uncharacteristically, also hopping up and down, clapping and laughing, and it's only when the camera lens brushes up against me that I realize what is happening: I'm at a baseball game, and I am happy for no other reason than the fact that someone hit a home run.

I am so mystified by myself that I hardly pay any attention to the end of the game, and it's over before I know it. Hargis fails to come back in the bottom of the ninth inning, and they're done—we've won.

As the teams meet in the middle of the field for a handshake line, Len notices my silence and gives me a bro-ish clap on the back. "Come on," he says, walking down to the Willoughby dugout. "Time for something in your wheelhouse."

"What's that?"

"Asking questions."

We spend a while talking to the guys, and Len lets me lead most of the interviews. They have jokes I don't understand, stories about something one or another of them did in years past, and Len laughs a lot, his eyes crinkling up so much that I'm not sure his face can handle another tale about hijinks from "that game against St. Agatha's last spring."

As for me, I am almost universally regarded with a deferential courtesy that baffles me. Other than Adam, whose role seems to be "the inappropriate one," nobody makes any allusions to the whole feminism thing. I get the sense that if a stranger in the bleachers were to lob an insult at me right now, I'd have the entire team pouncing on the perpetrator in a fit of chivalrous rage.

I'd be lying if I said I wasn't charmed by them, these good-looking boys and their good-natured ribbing, which is at once affectionate and protective. I wonder if they're being so nice now just because they're all still upbeat from the victory that they bagged so narrowly, or if it's an extension of their devotion to Willoughby. I'm not so full of self-importance to think that it's because of my professionalism as a *Bugle* reporter. I feel like I'm someone's kid sister, or someone's girlfriend.

A few feet away, Len is part of another conversation, but when our eyes meet, he smiles.

And that's when I understand: the reason is Len. I'm just the girl with Len. I could be Natalie, or Olivia, and it wouldn't really make a difference. It doesn't matter what kind of ruckus I've caused outside this situation, or what kind of stuff I've said about Len. The important thing is that I'm here with him, and he seems fine with it, so the respect they have for him carries over to me. It's disquieting. It makes me feel complicit in something I don't understand.

I decide then that I've had enough of the team for now. I text Len to say that I'm going to find a bathroom, and I don't wait for him to respond before I head out.

The girls' locker room is the closest possibility, but everyone else had the same idea as me, so the line is very long. It occurs to me, though, that since I have a mental map of Willoughby in my head, I should be able to find another bathroom pretty easily. And sure enough, when I wander over to the main building, I find another one there—just like at Willoughby.

Len texts me while I'm washing my hands:

Which one?

I message back:

The breezeway

Before I head out, I glance in the mirror, and dismay creeps up under the fluorescent light. My hair is frizzled and full of static, my cheeks are whipped pink from the winds, and the overall effect is not great. I dig into my backpack, remembering that Kim gifted me a small tube of fancy moisturizer a couple of months ago, which I wrote off as a pretty lousy birthday present and tossed in here without a second thought. But now, with my skin the consistency of sandpaper, I'm kind of glad to have it.

As I dab on the cream, however, my reflection—the way I'm leaning over the sink, inspecting my face with hopeful, anxious concentration—makes me pause. I'm not sure why, until I realize it's because I remind myself of my sister.

And I don't like it at all.

I think back to many years ago, shortly after Kim began middle school, when we overheard Mom talking to one of our aunts.

"Kim was so pretty," A yī said, when they were in the kitchen and didn't know we were listening. "What a shame her skin turned out like this."

"We can't let it get worse," Mom agreed in a low voice. "A girl's face is very important."

Kim and I were watching TV in the living room, but this made her get up wordlessly and skulk over to the bathroom mirror, where she proceeded to brood over the constellation of acne that had recently spread across her forehead.

"It's really not that bad," I tried to tell her, but she shut the door in my face.

I questioned then, standing alone in the dark corridor, whether there was any point in being pretty if it could so easily, and arbitrarily, be lost. Even when you got it back (as Kim did, thanks to the dermatologist daughter of A yī's coworker and, if you ask Mom, excessive prayer to the Guanyin Buddha), keeping such a fickle thing around seemed to require constant obsession. That's how I decided I would never get caught up in such a raw deal. Everyone was always saying I was smarter than Kim, and so I would be.

Now, though, *I'm* standing in front of a mirror, cheeks

smudged with Kim's eucalyptus-scented moisturizer, wondering a little bit what somebody else sees when he looks at me.

Geez, I need to snap out of this. I shake my head, then rub the cream into my skin vigorously, until every last trace disappears.

When I emerge back outside, I see Len leaning against a pillar over by the cafeteria windows, reading something. As I get closer, I notice the book is our AP English reader and decide to send him another text:

Catching up on Didion?

He pulls his phone out of his pocket when it buzzes and, for just a second, I catch a flicker of a private grin. Then he raises his head. But before he notices me, I can tell from his face—even in the distance—that he's seen something else. First there's puzzlement, and then chagrin. Curious, I take a few more steps forward and follow his gaze.

There, under the stairwell, is Jason Lee, unmistakable in his maroon-and-white jersey with the number 18 on his back, standing awfully close to a girl who definitely isn't Serena Hwangbo. She's up against the wall, and he's leaning over her, propping himself up with an extended arm.

I'm far away enough that neither of them can see me, so I skedaddle toward Len, who is gesturing at me to follow him. Then we both hightail it to the parking lot.

Len and I stumble into the shadow of a shipping container, the kind that we also have sitting in the Willoughby parking lot, mostly for storage. For a moment, sheltered from the fading light of the sunset, we exchange a silent glance of horror. Then we burst into the hopped-up laughter of people who have witnessed something they would prefer to unsee.

"What was *that*?" I fall back against the side of the container. "Did you see?"

"I saw," says Len.

A million questions fly through my mind. Who was that girl? Why wasn't Serena at the game? Isn't that what girlfriends are supposed to do, go to their boyfriends' baseball games? Especially if the boyfriend is Jason Lee, breaker of league home-run records?

Then I catch myself. Why does it matter whether Serena was here or not? The real question is, why is Jason such an asshole?

"We have to tell Serena," I say.

Len rubs the back of his neck and grimaces in Jason's direction. "Do we?"

I glare at him in disbelief. "Um, yeah. It's the right thing to do."

"Is it, though?" Len tries to cross his arms but remembers that he's still wearing the camera. He takes it off and starts to pack it into its case. "Maybe it's not our place."

The wind lets loose an angry gust in response, and Len's flannel button-down flaps like it's about to fly off his back. I try to keep my own shirt pinned down by wrapping my sweater—a brown and chunky knit, still a substitute—more tightly around me.

"Okay, how about you suggest to Jason that he tell Serena

himself." I brush my hair out of the way as it whips around my face.

Len looks at me like he thinks I should know better. "Have you met Jason Lee?"

A suspicion illuminates in my head. "Is this because you used to be on the team together?" I say. "Is this a 'bros before hos' thing?"

Len seems offended. "First, let the record show that you're the one who brought up hos, and second, no." He kicks a rock across the asphalt. "I just don't know if it's any of our business."

"But don't you think Serena deserves to know?" It feels wrong to keep it from her, especially now that she and I are . . . well, friends. And the girl is also planning a walkout on my behalf, so there's that.

Len, however, does not have similar qualms. "What exactly does she deserve to know, though? Like, what's the situation, really?"

"Are you joking? We know what the situation is. We both saw it."

"We don't know what it *means*."

Now it's my turn to look at him like he should know better. "No guy leans into a girl like that without being into her," I say, with an authority that is not based on personal experience.

"That seems like conjecture."

"No, it's definitely true."

"Are you sure?" Len takes a few steps closer and unexpectedly pulls the move on me, putting out a hand to support his weight against the shipping container wall. "Still?"

He's grinning, like he's sure this little maneuver will force me to concede that I could be wrong about Jason—because, in his mind, he's clearly disproving my claim in this very situation, at this very moment. He thinks he's being so provocative, getting under my skin like this. And I admit it, I stop breathing for a full three seconds before a realization begins to slink into my consciousness. He seems a bit too pleased with himself, a bit too smug about this victory. When I understand what he doesn't, I lean up and kiss him.

His very obvious surprise doesn't stop him from kissing me back, and it throws me off a little, how much he is kissing me back. It's not very long before we're *really* kissing, and I feel like I'm dissolving, like it's goodbye to Eliza and all that's left is this other liquid, diaphanous self that collects in a pool inside me. It's when this unmoored sensation gets to be too much that I remember to break away, pushing him off like I've made my point.

"Why don't you tell me," I say, brushing past him.

Later, long after Len has given me a ride home and we've parted ways for the night—both committed with assiduous cheerfulness to the falsehood that nothing out of the ordinary has happened—when I'm already in bed with the lights out because it's past one a.m., I get a text message that sends a thrill down past my stomach. Especially when I imagine Len in his room, typing it out while he lies there in the dark:

You were right.

I've never failed to appreciate those three words from anyone, but this time, coming from Len, they buzz around my mind for hours, like mosquitoes gorging on warm weather. I toss and turn and don't quite know what to do with myself.

21

THE BECHDEL TEST, I'VE LEARNED FROM WINONA, measures whether at least two women in a work of fiction—say, a movie—have a conversation about something other than a man. The implication, I've always reasoned, is that there is something inherently unfeminist about women who concern themselves primarily with men. A feminist should have hopes, dreams, and wants that are completely independent of male needs and desires. A feminist should not require the affections of a man to make her complete. A feminist should not, in other words, spend the majority of her time thinking about a boy.

The problem is that I have been spending a lot of time thinking about Len.

I do my homework, I help Dad apply for jobs, I edit *Bugle* articles, and in between all that, I replay the kiss and every interaction and conversation we've ever had. That Monday right after the game, it's especially bad. Whenever I enter a room where Len might be, like the *Bugle* newsroom or fifth-period English, my heart starts up like nobody's business, and I scan around casually, as though I'm looking for no one in particular—but of course I'm looking for him. And every time I see him, it hits me like I'm realizing it for the first time: goddamn, he *is* good-looking.

But then I turn back to whatever I'm doing and act like everything is totally chill.

Len, for his part, could teach a master class in chill, and other than a curious glance the first time he saw me (which I ignored), he also betrays nothing. He is so stoic that sometimes I even feel like I might have imagined everything that happened.

But then I check my phone, and there's that last text he sent, still waiting for a response.

The next morning, I see him and Natalie arrive for zero period at the same time. They've clearly walked over from the parking lot together, and Natalie is doing most of the talking.

"How fast were you pitching before the surgery?" I overhear Natalie saying. She looks pretty today, with her hair in a side ponytail. Maybe too pretty.

"Like in the nineties," says Len, setting his backpack down in his usual corner.

"Miles per hour?" Natalie's eyes grow large. "That's really good."

"It wasn't bad," says Len, laughing. He climbs up on the desks and opens his laptop, just like he does every day. What kills me is that Natalie puts her stuff down and takes a seat, too, like she's been invited, and Len doesn't say anything about it.

"I heard you had more strikeouts than anyone else on the team," says Natalie, who is apparently now a fount of Willoughby baseball statistics.

"You heard that, huh?" Len grins at her.

"Well, I read it in the *Bugle*," says Natalie. "How'd you get to be so good at pitching?"

Len shrugs. "Probably practice," he says. "Who knows?"

"Maybe it's because you're so tall." Natalie rests her chin on both hands. "How tall are you, anyway?"

"Six three," says Len. "How tall are you?"

"I'm five three!" Natalie laughs like this is the most hilarious thing in the world.

"Hey, Natalie," I say, because I don't want to vomit in my mouth. Why is she acting so stupid? Her one redeeming factor has always been that she isn't dumb.

Both Len and Natalie turn to me.

"Can I see your draft, please?" I say.

"Sure," says Natalie. But my interruption apparently isn't enough to kill off this scintillating exchange, because then she turns back to Len. "It's too bad you're not pitching anymore," she says. "It would have been cool to see you play."

"Maybe you will," says Len. "Maybe I'll get back into it."

And Natalie looks so pleased that I call out, "Anytime today, Natalie."

◆◆◆

Afterward, when I see Len at his locker, I can't help myself. I walk over and, unable to keep the irritation out of my voice, say, "Why do you keep telling everyone you're going back to baseball if you're not planning to?"

Len, rummaging through the books in his locker, takes his time answering. When he finally does, the response is so cool, it's practically served on ice. "You mean, why did I tell Natalie?"

"Yeah, sure."

"Maybe I've changed my mind since we last talked." He shuts his locker door with a controlled clang. Then he gives me a smile, too polite to mean anything, and strides away.

I trail after him. "I don't know how you stand her," I say, hating how peeved I sound. "She's the worst."

"Well," he says, "she's nice to me."

"She's obviously flirting with you," I argue. "She's always flirting."

"What's wrong with that?" He stops to face me when he says this, and I almost fall over his toes. "She knows what she wants, and she lets people know."

He doesn't seem angry, but the remark is a blow for sure. When I can't decide how to respond, he starts to turn away.

"But do you even like her?" I blurt out. "Because if you don't, then you shouldn't encourage her."

Len looks at me for a long moment. "Sometimes, things aren't always so black-and-white," he says. "I think you know how it is." And he walks off without another word.

I let him go. I know I'm being terrible, but what else can I do? I should tell him I'm sorry, I was just messing with you when I kissed you, it didn't mean anything to me, I don't like you.

But I can't bring myself to say all that because I'm not sure it's really true.

The realization unsettles me. My first reaction is the vague sense of having let myself down. How conventional, to have a crush on someone like Len. How unimaginative. The guy is one semester removed from walking around in a varsity jacket. Why couldn't I have fallen for someone like James, who at least has progressive politics and an ex-girlfriend who smokes?

My second reaction is panic. In two days, I'm supposed to be leading a walkout to protest the fact that Len is the incoming editor in chief of the *Bugle*. I'm not supposed to *like* him. I imagine Winona's lip curling the way it does when she's repulsed by something. Or Serena hurling her latest feminist book in my face, shouting, "You like him? You *like* the patriarchy?"

If this gets out, everything I've ever said about feminism will be a complete joke. Which would be fine, except that now other people seem to have a stake in whether or not the things I say are a joke. Sixty-four other people, to be exact, according to Serena's latest numbers. That doesn't sound like a lot, until you think about the fact that it's six percent of the student body walking out of school because *you* told them it would mean something.

Maybe I should just call it off? Except that feels like it would be the *least* feminist thing I could do. I already know how the story would go: Eliza backed down because of a boy. Of all the boys, too.

I let out a long sigh. Suddenly, I seem to want such complicated things. I still want to be editor in chief of the *Bugle* and I still want to be a feminist. I want others to be feminists, too. But I also want something from Len that I understand only in fragments. I think back to the night of the baseball game. Why did I kiss him? Why did I kiss him *first*? It feels like I've lost something, somehow, even though I haven't. I mean, I know he kissed me right back—God, how he kissed back—but what is a boy's want really worth, anyway? And is a feminist supposed to want it? Is a feminist supposed to feel bad about wanting it?

And then I remember the first day this whole mess got started, when Len sat on top of his desk and read out loud what I'd written about him, his tone flippant in a way that I now understand was not fully sincere. He pretended that what I'd said didn't matter to him, but it wasn't true. And for some reason, it's that pretending that gets me.

I feel like garbage.

22

"SO I'M THINKING WHITE FOR SURE," SAYS SERENA, as she flips through the dress rack at the back of the Goodwill store. "That definitely says 'Greek' to me."

I follow behind her, carrying a bunch of dresses that she's already handed to me. "Actually, Lady Justice is based on a sixteenth-century imagining of Justitia, a Roman goddess," I say.

"The Romans probably ripped off the idea from the Greeks." Serena dismisses an entire empire change with the flick of her wrist. "They're always doing that, aren't they?"

For my Lady Justice getup, we've already got the scales (from a console table in Serena's foyer) and the sword (lent to us by Doug, who went as King Arthur last Halloween), so now all we need is the dress. Serena has enthusiastically volunteered to help me pick out the perfect one.

As she hands me yet another ivory ballgown, I decide not to point out that scholars have recently discovered that ancient Greek and Roman statues weren't actually white to begin with—that it's likely the marble we see was once painted over in bright, maybe even garish colors. Ms. Perez, my world-history teacher from last year, told Winona and me about it one rainy day while we ate lunch in her classroom. The idea of pure white as the paradigm for classical perfection, Ms. Perez had said, is a modern myth.

But Serena seems pretty set on it, so I don't argue. Besides, I've been preoccupied with a somewhat more delicate matter— namely, how to not betray the fact that every other minute, I'm wondering how Len is going to react to this walkout. It's T minus two days at this point, and the closer it gets, the worse I feel about it. He'll act like it's fine, but I know it won't be. He's going to give me that polite smile, that kiss of death, and I'm never going to get the real thing again.

Should I tell him about it? Should I tell him it's not really about him . . . even though it kind of is?

And that's when I realize I don't want to hurt him. Even more unnerving: I don't want him to hate me. I'm *afraid* that he'll hate me.

"Okay, why don't you go try those on," says Serena, saddling me with one more.

The fitting room is just big enough for me and my pile of dresses, which I unload onto the chair in the corner. Someone has scratched *You look beautiful* into the wall with a ballpoint pen.

I try on dress after dress, and Serena finds them all unsatisfactory. A line has started to form for the fitting room, but instead of taking this as a sign that we should speed things up so these good people can get on with their lives, Serena responds by looping them all into her judgment process.

"The chest area is too big, isn't it," she says, turning to a diminutive woman holding a pair of boot-cut jeans.

"*Sí, sí,*" says the woman, while her husband waits next to her silently.

About another dress: "Those sequins don't look as good as I thought they would."

"Yeah, totally," agrees a girl wearing a prairie skirt with sneakers.

Finally, though, when I try on a simple sleeveless gown that's gathered at the waist, Serena squeals.

"Oh my God," she says. "It's perfect."

I twirl around to demonstrate the flowy skirt, but I can't really see what's so special about this dress. "It's good?"

"It's the one," declares Serena. Everyone in line behind us nods in agreement, and I don't think I'm the only one who's relieved that she's made up her mind.

While we are waiting to check out, Serena gets a phone call.

"Hi, babe," she says, her voice turning into a purr.

It's Jason. My stomach does a flip. I completely forgot about that whole thing.

"I'm at Goodwill," she says into the phone. Then she giggles. "With *Eliza*."

It's my turn at the cash register, and the whole time I'm paying for the dress, I am dreading what I should say once she hangs up. Suddenly, the thrift-store smell of disinfectant and ancient perspiration feels like too much, and even the change that I'm handed feels grimy as soon as I touch it.

"Yeah," says Serena, still on the phone. "Okay, well, I'll call you later?"

At the door, there's a donation box, and I drop the coins into the slot, anxious to be rid of them. I consider not telling Serena about Jason after all, because maybe what I saw was nothing. Maybe it's better if I don't get involved.

"Love you," Serena tells Jason, which makes me cringe. As she hangs up, she says to me, "You're so nice, Eliza."

"What?" This is not something I get told often.

Serena pauses in front of her car door and nods back toward the donation box. "My pastor always says to remember the needy, but, like, I never have any change, you know?"

She is so absurd. And that's when I realize I can't chicken out.

We both get into the car, but before she can put the key in the ignition, I stop her. "Wait," I say. "There's something I have to tell you about Jason."

Serena stares at me in silence as I relay the whole sorry incident. When I'm done, the first thing she says is "Who was she?"

I shake my head. "I don't know."

"Does she go to Hargis?"

"I don't know. Probably?"

"You saw them kissing?"

For a second, I worry she'll go into denial if I say that, technically, I didn't see them doing anything besides standing very close.

"No," I say. "Not exactly."

"What were they doing?"

"Maybe you should just talk to Jason about it."

I mean, of course, that she should discuss it with him later, privately, once I'm out of the car. But Serena calmly nods and picks up her phone. "You're right," she says, and calls Jason. I hope that he isn't smart enough to make the connection between the mention of my name in their earlier conversation and the source for Serena's new intel.

"I know about her," she says, as soon as he picks up.

Incoherent sounds spill out of the phone.

"Tell me the truth," Serena demands. "I want to hear it from you."

Jason, however, apparently refuses. "Don't pull that bullshit on me," says Serena. "Do *not* call me crazy."

The conversation swiftly escalates from there, and at one point, Serena screams, "Eliza wouldn't lie! Not like you and your skank!"

I seriously need to stop accepting rides from Serena.

Eventually, many expletives later, something shifts on the other end of the line, and tears start rolling down her cheeks. "Don't ever talk to me again!" she cries, and hangs up the phone with contempt. Then she breaks into a sob. "It's over," she says. "He admitted it."

I have no idea what to do. Cautiously, I reach out and put a hand on her shoulder. "I'm sorry, Serena."

"It's over," she says again. "It's over."

I confess that I'm somewhat taken aback by the depth of Serena's despair. I didn't know she actually liked Jason that much.

"I'm gonna have to go to prom *alone*," she says, practically hysterical.

And then, sometimes, I forget that Serena is a cool girl, with specific cool-girl concerns.

"Hey," I say. "It's ages away, and you're Serena Hwangbo. You'll get a date if you want a date."

"It's *four weeks* away," she wheezes, fumbling to open the compartment between our seats. She pulls out a box of tissues and begins to wipe her eyes.

"Okay, well, it can't be that bad, right?" I say. "I'm gonna have to go alone, too." I've never been asked to a dance of any kind, and the way things are going, it doesn't seem like it's going to happen anytime soon.

Serena responds by blowing her nose.

"Hey," I try again. "We're feminists, remember? We don't need prom dates."

Serena looks over at me, her eyes red. It seems like she uses waterproof mascara, though, because none of it drips.

"It's not just that," she says in a small voice. "I . . ."

I'm too busy hoping that she won't claim something absurd—like *I thought Jason was the one*—that I almost miss what she actually says.

"I'm afraid of being alone."

She pronounces this so seriously, leaning forward as if it is very important for me to understand, that all I can think to say is "Oh."

"I was a nobody before Willoughby," Serena explains. "I went to junior high in a different district, so you wouldn't know. But the first month of freshman year, my brother's friend Matt Cho asked me out. You remember Matt?"

Who could forget? Matt was a senior then, so it was a big deal that he had noticed Serena. That, come to think of it, was the first time I'd heard of her.

"That changed everything," says Serena. "That's how I got into student council, because Matt was involved." She blinks back some tears. "And ever since then, I've always had a boyfriend. I don't know what it's like to be in high school and *not* have a boyfriend."

We sit in silence for a while, except for the crinkling from the plastic bag that contains my dress, which moves when I squirm in my seat.

"You probably think I'm totally failing as a feminist right now." Serena sounds like she's on the verge of fresh tears.

"No, definitely not." I rush to say something that will make her feel better. "Just because you always had a boyfriend doesn't mean you always needed one. You didn't. And you don't need one now. You're the reason why everyone's wearing *I AM A FEMINIST* buttons. You're the one who's making this walkout happen. You've done it all, not Jason."

Serena looks a little less despondent. "I guess you're right."

"You're a good feminist, Serena," I say. "If anything, not

dating Jason probably makes you a better one. He didn't seem that concerned with sexism."

"He wasn't," she agrees.

"Right. Anyway, now you won't have to be defined by your relationship to him, or to any guy." I'm on a roll now. "You can be your own person."

Serena's phone buzzes then, and she holds it up to show me the selfie of Jason that has appeared on the screen. "It's hard not to pick up," she admits.

"What do you think he's going to say?"

She cradles the phone in her lap. "He probably wants me to take him back."

"Is that what you want?"

Serena reconsiders the photo, and I think she's about to cry again, but she shakes her head. "No."

She lets the call go to voice mail, staring at the screen until it fades out. Then, as I offer an encouraging smile, she leans over and startles me with a hug.

"Thank you, Eliza," she whispers. "You always know what to do."

I blanch at how false that seems, horror-struck that I once believed—and perpetuated—such a delusion. Now, with Serena's arms wrapped tight around my neck, it's all I can manage to pat her on the back, trying not to feel like I'm choking.

23

"ELIZA," SAYS WINONA, AFTER I HIT DOUG WITH the boom mic for the fifth time this afternoon. "Is something up with you?"

"What?" I swing the mic around, and Sai has to duck down to avoid being swatted. "Sorry," I tell him, wiping a sweaty palm on my jeans. We're at less than twenty-four hours before the walkout now, and I'm definitely feeling it.

"You know the boom mic isn't supposed to appear in the frame, right." Winona taps the metal pole impatiently.

We're finally shooting again for *Driveways*, which is due in precisely one week, and everyone's nerves are a bit frayed. Winona is anxious for the scene to turn out just right, Doug and Sai are tired of being ordered around, and I'm distracted by the Len situation. I really wish I could come clean to Winona, but I just can't bring myself to do it. Maybe I don't want to hear her say that the old Eliza would never have let a boy get to her like this. That making out with Len, given the circumstances, was unusually obtuse for a number of reasons, and frankly, she doesn't even know who I am anymore. Winona wouldn't hesitate to assert any of these things if they were true, and I guess that's just it—I'm not sure I'd like the truth right now. *Especially* not the way I've been thinking about that kiss.

"Eliza! Seriously?"

"Sorry!" I flush bright red and straighten my arms so that the mic isn't grazing the top of Doug's head.

The scene we're filming today is a reworking of one that was in the original screenplay: the moment when Doug's character is accused of stealing the gum. Winona's character hasn't shown up yet, so it's just Doug and Sai in the frame, and my voice off-camera as the clerk who makes the allegation. We hole up at a nearby 7-Eleven for the next three excruciating hours, shooting and reshooting, before Winona lets us play back some of the footage.

Twenty seconds in, she asks, "Do you think—"

"No," Doug and Sai say together.

"It's fine the way it is," adds Doug.

"Should there be another beat where Sai confesses to stealing the gum?" Winona turns to address me pointedly, as though the boys aren't even there. "Do you think Sai stole the gum?"

Behind her, both Doug and Sai gesticulate at me to shut this down. "Hmm," I mumble, peering into the camera display. "Maybe it's more impactful if you leave it ambiguous? Like the question of who actually did it."

"Plus, Sai would never confess something like that," Doug contends. "He'd hide it forever."

"Nuh-uh!" Sai protests.

"Okay, first, this isn't really Sai we're talking about." Winona holds up a finger, which she then points at Sai. "And second, Sai, you should always admit it when you've done something you shouldn't have. *Always*."

I busy myself with the boom mic.

Sai scowls, but Winona responds by producing a pack of gum from her back pocket. "Here, let's go inside," she announces. "I want to do another version. Maybe my character *could* appear at this point, and she's the one who sees Sai stealing."

Doug, however, immediately swipes the gum out of her hand. "No, Winona," he declares. "We quit. We don't have time for more baloney."

"*Baloney?*" Winona towers over Doug. "This isn't baloney. This is *art*. There are no shortcuts to greatness."

"We just did fourteen takes of this one shot *alone*!"

"And whose fault was that?"

The brawl is about to escalate even further when my phone vibrates with a message:

Can you talk? Jason keeps texting me . . . 😶

Ever since I served as a witness to her breakup with Jason, Serena has been religious about providing me with real-time updates on the carcass of their relationship. "I don't want everyone else to think that I'm obsessing over it," she says, as she obsesses over it to me, for hours.

"Ugh, it's Serena." Without thinking, I hand the mic to Doug so I can text her back. He, of course, leaps to take advantage of the moment.

"See, even Eliza is sick of this!" he crows.

"Okay, wait," I argue. "I didn't say that—"

My phone, however, continues to buzz with texts from Serena, because apparently not having a chance to respond to one of her messages sends a signal that she should absolutely write more.

"Fine!" Winona throws her hands up in the air. "We'll call it a day." In response, both Doug and Sai dance around joyfully. "For *now*."

As we trudge along Palermo Avenue, back toward the Wilsons' house, I struggle to keep up with Serena's messages.

"Is she still going on about Jason?" Winona's disapproval is palpable.

"Yeah," I admit, half as apology and half as defense. "I mean, she did just break up with him."

Winona sends a pebble skidding along the sidewalk, each clink more dismissive than the last. "Why is she getting so hung up on such a useless thing?"

I shrug, like I don't understand either, but my cheeks burn up like she's talking about me.

24

ON THE MORNING OF THE WALKOUT, I WAKE UP
with a dull ache in my stomach. As I sit at the dining table,
biting absently into a steamed lotus-paste bun, Mom walks
into the kitchen.

"Are you getting sick?" She seems perturbed. "You look like
a *behng māau*." A sick cat, as they say in Cantonese.

"Nope." I quickly stuff the rest of the bun into my mouth.
The only way to convince Mom I'm fine is by eating, preferably a large amount.

"Are you sure?" Mom pulls the metal rice pot from the
fridge and plunks it on the counter, spooning a mound into
her Tupperware. "You don't seem like yourself."

Her observation makes me pause, my cheeks full of lotus
paste. The truth is, I don't *feel* like myself.

It makes me think of this one time in first grade, when my
teacher, Ms. Beaumont, sent a letter home informing Mom
and Dad that she'd recommended I get assessed for the gifted-
and-talented program.

"What is 'assessed'?" Mom muttered, poking out the letters on her portable electronic English-Chinese dictionary. Kim was already in third grade and no teacher had ever sent home a letter like this about *her*.

The test itself was in a windowless room next to the principal's office. I sat at a round table next to a large woman with blond hair. She smelled like the home-decor aisle at Big Lots, but she smiled a lot and asked me a bunch of easy questions, so I liked her. But then, right near the end, she stumped me.

"Okay, Eliza, imagine you have ten pieces of candy, and you want to share them with five friends. How many pieces of candy would each friend get?"

Shoot. I didn't know. I looked around and imagined Kim and four of my cousins sitting at the table, and then, in my head, I started passing out candy to them. One for Kim, one for Tommy, one for . . .

"Eliza?" said the woman. "It's okay if you don't know."

"Two," I said. "Each person gets two."

Afterward, when I told Kim about this question, she guffawed. "That was a division problem, dummy," she said. "If you don't know division, you totally cheated to answer that question."

"What's division?" I asked, somewhat shaken.

"It's like the opposite of the times tables," said Kim. "You know, the stuff I had to memorize?" She waved away my ignorance. "How can they let you in the gifted program if you don't even know what division is?"

When they did in fact let me in, my stomach didn't feel so

good that time either. Kim had already forgotten what she'd said to me about division, but I hadn't.

"Eliza is so smart," Mom boasted to A Pòh on the phone. "She got into this special program for kids who do well in school. Kim needs to work harder so she can get in it, too."

I tried to explain to Mom that the school had made a mistake.

"What? But of course you're smart." She did not understand the problem. "Anyway, even if they did make a mistake, it'd be stupid to *tell* them. Your dad and I don't know anything. We're immigrants. You need every chance you can get!"

But the next day, I went up to Ms. Beaumont anyway. "I cheated on the gifted test," I said.

Ms. Beaumont listened carefully as I explained the situation, but at the end of it, she only smiled.

"Thanks for telling me, Eliza," she said. "But what you did was fine." She told me that I had done the division correctly, even if I didn't know what it was called, and actually it was a good sign that I had been able to reason through it.

"You're a bright girl," Ms. Beaumont said after a moment. "What really makes you special, though, is that you're not afraid to do the right thing." She patted my arm with a wrinkled hand. Her palm was surprisingly soft. "You, my dear, have a code. And one must always have a code."

I've never forgotten that incident, because it was the day I learned about division, and also the day I learned the best thing about myself: I had a code.

But where has it gone? Suddenly, in its place, I have so many secrets.

Keeping things from Mom is one thing. That's just basic Asian-kid survival. But from Winona? From Serena and everyone she's turned into a feminist?

From Len?

I haven't talked to him in days, but it seems like forever. When no one is looking, I still find myself watching him from across the room. The other day, he walked into English class carrying a nearly finished boba tea, and my first thought was, completely unreasonably, *He went without me?* He took a long sip before setting it down on his desk, and I could see that the end of the straw was all chewed up. The cup had no tea left, but it was still filled with ice cubes and tapioca balls. It reminded me of the drive to Hargis that day— how, for one fleeting afternoon, we were friends. And it's the loss of that delicate thread between us, almost too faint to see, that really guts me. I wish I'd appreciated its improbable existence before we ravaged it with one complicating kiss.

I stare at the plywood tabletop in front of me, swallowing the remains of what has to be the driest, thickest rendition of a lotus-paste bun I've ever consumed. Even after I've forced it down, I feel a lump lodged in my throat. But I know that it's not really the bun. It's me.

And that's when I decide I should tell Len about the walkout.

◆◆◆

At school, it's difficult to catch him alone, which makes me realize—with a perverse disappointment—that he is avoiding me as much as I have been avoiding him. I ultimately manage to corner him at lunch, with less than an hour before the walk-out, when it's just the two of us and Johnny Cash in the *Bugle* newsroom.

"If I were a betting man," he says, without looking up from his computer, "I'd say you were following me."

I draw in a deep breath. "I need to talk to you."

He's still glued to his laptop screen, but I can tell he isn't reading anything.

"You know," he says, "there's this thing called texting? I'm pretty sure you have my number, so you could've just done that."

I blush in spite of myself. I thought of texting, but I didn't want to face the fact that I'd ghosted him. Before this, I always believed I was someone who most definitely did not ghost. I was wrong. And now, to make it worse, Len is clearly making a dig about it—but pleasantly, like it's only for sport. Lately, he's demonstrated an astounding gift for making digs that are supposedly only for sport, and I'm sick of it.

I walk over and snatch his computer out of his lap. The move surprises him.

"Look, I'm sorry," I say. "I don't know what you want from me."

"I don't want anything." He shrugs, as if it's absurd that I'd think anything I did could possibly bother him. Even though I'm trying to apologize, it pisses me off.

"What do you want me to say, Len?" I wave his laptop like I'm about to throw it across the room.

"Nothing." He eyes the computer as it dangles from my hand, but he doesn't break his calm. "Say whatever you want, I don't care."

"Don't lie," I say. "You want me to say that I like you." The words come out before I can stop them. "You want me to say that every time I have a bubble tea now, I can't help thinking of *your* sad boba-drinking technique. That I sped through three hundred pages of *Life: A User's Manual* with a confusing sense of urgency because *you* lent it to me. That I've read all about Tommy John surgery even though I don't give two shits about baseball because I wanted to know if *you* would be okay."

This is *not* how I envisioned this conversation going, but it's too late. I've lost it. Len is staring at me—unable, for once, to conjure a quip. Time to cut to the chase and get out.

"But things are . . . complicated," I say. "And that's what I wanted to talk to you about."

I tell him about the walkout, the explanation rushing out in a jumble because I'm in such a hurry to get it over with. He listens the whole time without reacting, which is nerve-racking and also, at the same time, a relief.

"I just thought you should know," I say when I'm done.

Without his laptop, Len doesn't have anything to do with his hands, so he rubs the top of his knees as he contemplates the wood grain of the desk. Finally, he gives me a small grin, the first real one I've gotten since the baseball game.

"You really want to be editor in chief that badly?" he asks.

"No," I say, because at this point, it's true. I'm feeling pretty conflicted about a lot of things right now, but at least I can hold on to this: the walkout, and what it's supposed to symbolize, is still important. It was the right thing to tell Len about it, but it's also the right thing to go on with it. "No," I say again. "It's the principle of it."

He drags his hands over his face, like I exasperate him. Then he kind of chuckles as he rubs his eyes. "It's always about the principle with you, isn't it?"

"A girl's gotta have a code."

Before Len can respond to this, James enters the room. "Hey," he says. His eyes ping from me to Len. "What's going on in here?"

James knows about the walkout because I told him, thinking that it should probably be a *Bugle* article. He seemed almost disappointed to have been left out of the planning, but he agreed to assign the story to Olivia, the News section writer with probably the least animosity toward me (a feat), and Cassie, who would take photos.

Now he gives me an inquiring look, which I ignore. "Nothing," I say to him, shoving the computer back into Len's lap. "I'll see you guys around."

It's later than I thought, so I have to run to the girls' locker room, where Serena and Winona are already waiting. Like everyone else who's planning to participate in the walkout, they're both wearing all black and *I AM A FEMINIST* buttons.

I, of course, will be wearing white.

"Where have you been?" asks Winona, as I pull my Lady Justice dress out of my locker.

"Sorry," I say. "I, uh, got sidetracked at the *Bugle*."

"It's fine—we still have fifteen minutes before lunch is over," says Serena. "Hurry and get changed!"

After I put on the dress, Serena makes me sit down on a bench as she stands over me, running a comb through my hair. "You need a haircut, Eliza," she says, studying my ends.

"Do we have time for one?"

"Very funny."

In the end, Serena decides to plait my hair into a crown braid. Then she brandishes a tube of lipstick.

"What is that?" I jerk backward.

Serena turns to Winona, confused. "Eliza doesn't do lipstick," Winona explains.

"It'll look good, I promise," says Serena. "Besides, you're dressing as Lady Justice, not Eliza Quan. You could use a little glamour."

"Why couldn't Lady Justice just wear jeans and a T-shirt?" I complain. "I mean, if she had a choice."

"Good question," says Winona.

"Because," says Serena, swiping on the lipstick in two expert strokes. She grabs my arm and shepherds me over to the full-length mirror. "Maybe she liked the way she looked in a dress."

My reflection surprises me. Not that much is out of the

ordinary, and everything that is different is also simple. The dress is minimalist, my hair is up but unadorned. Only the lipstick is bold: a bright red-orange. Yet I feel so different, seeing myself like this. Older, maybe. More assured. I look like the type of girl who isn't afraid of anything. I'm genuinely astonished.

"I look pretty good," I say.

"You look fierce," agrees Serena.

Winona drapes a black pashmina around my neck. "All right, here's your blindfold," she says. "And your sword and scale." She hands both to me. "Are you ready?"

"Let's take down the patriarchy!" I raise my sword, and both Serena and Winona high-five it.

Fifth period, my first class after lunch, goes by in a blur—I spend most of it avoiding Len and hoping Ms. Boskovic doesn't notice the sword hilt sticking out of my backpack. Before long, the bell rings for sixth period, and I'm hotfooting it to history class, amped up for showtime.

I draw some quizzical glances as I unpack my Lady Justice accoutrement, but no one comments besides Mr. Schlesinger, who studies me for a second. "Lady Justice?" he guesses, and when I nod, he seems pleased to have gotten it right.

I try to pay attention to the lecture, but it's impossible. I keep jiggling my knee under my dress, because I'm feeling jumpy, like I've had too much caffeine. At one point, Winona, who sits in front of me, turns around and signals at me to cut it out. Apparently, my nerves are getting on her nerves.

Finally, at exactly one forty-five p.m., I tie the pashmina around my eyes and stand up, holding the sword in one hand and the scale in the other. It's kind of a relief that I can't see anything, because I hear Mr. Schlesinger stop talking in mid-sentence, and then about twenty desks creak as everyone turns around.

"Eliza?" says Mr. Schlesinger. "Can I help you?"

Winona stands up, too, and according to plan, she carries a sign that says *Walkout for Gender Equality at Willoughby.* And then she leads me out of the classroom.

I experience the walkout primarily through sounds—our footsteps on the tile floor, the door opening, and then the noises of people getting up to watch where we're going. It makes the whole thing feel even more surreal than it already is. Once we're outside, I feel another hand on my other arm, and it's Serena. She's holding a sign that says *Eliza for Editor in Chief!* Or, at least, I assume she is.

Winona and Serena lead me to the center of the quad, and I manage to climb on top of one of the lunch tables while still blindfolded. Everyone else who has walked out, presumably, is standing in a giant circle, all holding signs that say things like *Ban sexism at Willoughby!* and *Down with the patriarchy!* Someone takes the scale from me and replaces it with a megaphone.

The afternoon sun warms the crown of my head. I have never given a speech while blindfolded, and it is disorienting and invigorating at the same time. "This walkout," I shout into the megaphone, "is for those of you who see that the playing field clearly isn't even—at Willoughby, and beyond." A cheer goes up around me, raucous and overwhelming, the roar in my ears more intense because I can't see anything. I swear it sounds like at least a hundred people out there—maybe more. The last time I stood in front of a crowd this big was that long-ago, ill-fated freshman election. But today, I don't feel small at all.

"This is for those of you who've been told too many times that you 'don't look like a leader.' For those of you who get called 'abrasive' or 'not a team player,' just for speaking up. For those of you who haven't pursued your biggest dreams because you haven't felt 'ready'—because you've been ignored or shut down every time you tried." I stab the sword into the air. "I'm here to tell you all that you *are* ready. *I'm* ready."

"Eliza for editor!" a girl yells in the distance, echoed by other exclamations of support all around me. I go a bit unsteady when I remember that people are probably recording me, and maybe posting it online. We expected this to happen, of course, but Serena was convinced it was a good thing. "We need to drown out all that other stuff people have said about you," she reasoned.

All the same, in the moment, it's stressful to know that your every move is being documented. But as Mom likes to say in Cantonese, "If you've already gotten your hair wet, then you need to wash it." In other words, there's no turning back now. I fill my chest up with a fortifying breath and hoist my sword again, preparing to continue with my oration.

But before I get a chance to say another word, another voice fills the quad.

"Good afternoon, everyone. Will you all please follow me into the multipurpose room?"

I feel an aftershock of silence ripple outward from my feet. Trembling slightly, I pull the pashmina back up over my head to see Dr. Guinn standing at the mouth of the breezeway, holding up his own megaphone.

25

AT THE FRONT OF THE ROOM, DR. GUINN— standing beside a bewildered Ms. Greenberg and concerned Mr. Powell—smiles at all of us.

"Thank you all for your peaceful cooperation," he says. "I commend you for your activism. It is heartening to know that so many of you are committed to ideals beyond yourself. However, I must remind you that your actions are taking place during school hours, while classes are in session, and we do have rules that need to be followed."

Dr. Guinn explains that skipping class and disrupting other students' learning environment, both offenses that we have committed by walking out, could be punishable by suspension. "But, you see," says Dr. Guinn, chuckling, "I find it extremely ironic to punish absence from class with more, enforced absence." Instead we'll all be served with detention for five days, starting today.

The room murmurs in response to this edict. Detention is obviously preferable to suspension, but a whole week's worth?

That's rough. And for what? So I can be editor in chief of the *Bugle*? Sure, everyone is here because they're in support of feminism, or maybe because they think Serena Hwangbo is cool—but when it really comes down to it, they're all here because of me. They're here because of things that I said about sexism, and about Len. But they don't know what I've *really* been thinking about him.

The nausea overwhelms me.

"Wait." I stand up so quickly, my chair totters backward.

Everyone looks at me. "Yes, Eliza?" says Dr. Guinn.

"I don't think anyone here should get detention except me," I say.

All around me, people start to whisper. Cassie lowers the camera and bulges her eyes at Olivia, who pauses in the middle of her note taking. Winona shakes her head, gesturing at me to sit down, but that only makes my stomach constrict further, because I feel terrible for having dragged her into this.

Seeing my distress, Serena leans forward. "It's fine, Eliza," she whispers, uncrossing her legs. "We're all in this together."

And that's when I remember: Serena can't get a detention, because it'll disqualify her from running for school president. No one can serve on student council if they've had a detention in the past year.

"No," I say. "I started this. I'm the only one who should be punished. It's only the first offense for everyone else. It's my second."

Dr. Guinn folds his arms over his chest. "Eliza, should I remind you that I am the principal here, not you?"

"I'm sorry." I sit back down. Serena attempts to stand up in protest, but I stop her. "I'm the one who instigated all this, and it was a mistake. I should have taken your advice and found less antagonistic ways to express my opinions." I'm feeling so shitty about the whole thing, it's not hard to lay on the mea culpa thick. "Please don't take it out on everyone. They were just trying to stand up for what they thought was right. I'm the one who should have known better, and I'd like to take responsibility for it now."

Dr. Guinn doesn't reply right away, and in the silence, Ms. Greenberg shares a glance with Mr. Powell before clearing her throat.

"Paul," she says. "I think it has already been quite the learning experience for everyone involved. Maybe it'd be best if we just let them off with a warning."

"I'd agree with that," seconds Mr. Powell. "Plus, it might be a lot to handle for whoever's on detention duty."

Finally, Dr. Guinn speaks. "Well," he says. "We have certainly heard a number of compelling arguments. It seems that Justitia"—here he gestures at me—"has brought along Clementia." He flourishes a palm toward Ms. Greenberg. "We'll defer to your recommendation, Jill. For everyone else."

This declaration arouses another round of murmuring, this time with considerably less anguish.

"As for you, Eliza," Dr. Guinn continues, "please report to my office at the start of seventh period. You can wait there until the official start of detention after school."

◆◆◆

Detention is in Ms. Perez's classroom today, and she gives me a sympathetic look when I show up, still half dressed as Lady Justice. I've lost my sword and scale, but the blindfold remains around my neck.

"Fighting the good fight out there?" she asks as I slip into a seat near the front, tucking the folds of my dress under the chair. This is where I sat every morning for world history last year. The old overhead projector, which Ms. Perez would fire up to show us paintings and political cartoons, is still parked in the middle of the room. The agenda for the day is still written on the whiteboard. It's all the same, but I feel a thousand miles away.

"Trying, I guess," I say. "It's tough, though. I kind of maybe just threw in the towel."

"I think you did it for your friends," says Ms. Perez. "Don't discount that."

A few other kids file in, and Ms. Perez marks down that they're present. Once everyone is seated, she goes over the rules of detention. We're allowed to do homework or read, but we're not allowed to talk or use any devices. "And no napping," she adds, waiting for Bruce Kwok, who's already got his head lolled over on the desk, to sit up straight.

I end up staring out the window. The blinds are only partially open, so I can't see much of what's outside, but I do manage to temporarily impair my vision by focusing too long on the bright slants of afternoon light.

Ms. Perez walks over. "I thought you might be interested in this," she says, handing me a well-worn paperback. Its title, rather provocatively, is *Well-Behaved Women Seldom Make History*.

"Thanks," I say, assuming this is just Ms. Perez's way of expressing that I shouldn't feel too discouraged about being punished for the walkout. I decide not to tell her that maybe I'm tired of trying to be the kind of woman who makes history.

But I also don't want her to feel like I'm not appreciative of her gesture, so I open it and start reading.

A few pages in, I realize that the book, written by a historian named Laurel Thatcher Ulrich, isn't what I expected.

For one, I learn that the slogan "Well-behaved women seldom make history" is originally from an academic article about Puritan women who were, in fact, very well-behaved. The book points out that large portions of history, and ways of looking at history, are lost when we don't pay attention to the lives of women who aren't necessarily fighting to be heard.

Even after everything I've been reading about feminism lately, this is the first time I've thought about this, and it blows my mind. Feminists, after all, are often seen as women who *do* act out of line. And yet, could it be that a truly feminist version of history might also be about women who aren't "feminists"?

Leave it to Ms. Perez to bring this stuff up. She's a huge fan of "complicating" things. "This thesis statement is a good start, Eliza," she always said, "but can you complicate it?" I should have known she wouldn't recommend a book that wasn't complicated.

"Eliza?" I look up to see Ms. Perez standing at the lectern. Next to her is Ms. Wilder, holding a note. "Eliza, would you come up here, please?" says Ms. Perez. "Bring your things."

For a second, I start to panic. Is there another, special detention for kids who do particularly insolent things? Have they called Mom and freaked her out? I thought that detention slips just required a parent's signature. I was obviously planning on getting Dad to sign mine.

But when I get up to the front of the room, Ms. Perez just smiles. "You're free to go," she informs me. "Ms. Wilder says that Dr. Guinn has decided you don't have to serve detention after all."

I stare at the two of them.

"You can give me your detention slip," prompts Ms. Wilder. "It's all been a misunderstanding," she tells Ms. Perez.

I hand the slip over to Ms. Wilder. "Do I have to go with you now?"

"No, Eliza." Ms. Perez laughs. "You can just go home."

I follow Ms. Wilder out of the classroom anyway, still not quite believing what's happening. At the door, however, she does in fact turn to leave me. "Have a good day, Eliza," she says, before heading back to Dr. Guinn's office.

I step forward into the quad, blinking in the sunlight. What . . . just happened?

"Free at last?"

I wheel around, and there's Len, standing behind me, his backpack hanging from one shoulder.

"You look good," he says, grinning like he's done something very clever.

I suddenly no longer have the heart rate of a normal person, so I do the first reasonable thing that comes to mind: turn around and walk away in a hurry.

He catches up to me in a few strides. "How's it going?" he asks, like we're just taking a stroll.

"Fine." I don't look at him, and I don't stop walking.

"How was the walkout?"

"It depends. Have you resigned?"

"Not yet. Still deciding."

"Then I guess we don't know, do we?" I make as if I might dive into the girls' locker room.

"Wait." He reaches out and touches my arm. He may as well have electrocuted me. "Aren't you curious about why you got released just now?"

I feel a spark of comprehension. "What did you do?" I ask, staring at him.

He scrutinizes the palm trees overhead and chooses his words carefully. "Dr. Guinn and I had a discussion."

"What *kind* of discussion?"

Now his grin gets puckish. "I told him that you'd given me a heads-up about the walkout, and that you'd made it clear it was a matter of principle, which I respected. I said we were still, as he hoped, very much collegial." He steals a sly glance at me.

My face colors a little. "And?"

"Given that, I asked him to reconsider giving you detention, on the grounds of free speech."

I'm still dubious. "What did he say to that?"

"To be honest, he took it better than I thought. He mostly seemed kind of amused. He asked me whether I was aware that you and I share a tendency to take a critical view of the way he assigns detention."

"Our one common ground."

"Apparently." Len grins again. "Anyway, then he explained in his Guinn way that I made a valid point, students are entitled to free speech, like all citizens."

"But . . . ?"

"Right, *but* schools reserve the right to discipline behavior that is disruptive."

"Does standing on a lunch table while yelling into a megaphone count as 'disruptive'?"

"Maybe if you're dressed like that."

"Get to the point, victim-blamer."

"Okay, well, I also mentioned that my mom is a lawyer, and you'd talked to her before the walkout."

"But I didn't!"

"You *did* technically talk to her. Before the walkout."

"What!"

"I said my mom is pretty familiar with the cases governing students' freedom of speech, and basically you can't be punished for the walkout any more than you'd be punished for a normal absence from class." He strokes his chin. "Of course, the fact that only you were given detention, and no one else . . ."

"Means that the punishment was for leading the walkout, not for being absent from class."

"I rest my case."

I shake my head in disbelief. "You didn't have to do that, you know. I could have survived detention." Something bitter occurs to me. "I didn't need you to *rescue* me."

"Oh, I *know*." The corner of his mouth goes up. "But isn't it nice to have the patriarchy conspire to benefit you for once?"

I mean, I would prefer if there were *no* patriarchy at all. But also, he's not wrong.

"How did Guinn react to the fact that you were low-key threatening legal action on my behalf?"

"He asked whether my mother customarily sends me to represent her clients."

"Oh my *God*." I'm dying. "He called you out."

"A little bit."

"So what'd you do?"

"I admitted something I'm sure he already suspected."

"Which was . . . ?"

"Nothing that you don't already know."

I let his cryptic remark slide, mostly because I have no idea what to do with it. "Well, then what happened?"

"He just sat back, folded his arms, and looked at me for a long time, like he was trying to figure something out."

"And then?"

"He told me that he'd let us work it out ourselves."

"That's it?"

"That's it."

We're both silent for a minute. Then Len pulls his keys out of his pants pocket, tosses them in the air, and catches them with one hand. "So . . . what do you think?" he says, giving me side-eye. "Should we try to work it out?"

26

AND THAT, FRIENDS, IS HOW LADY JUSTICE FINDS herself straddling the patriarchy atop a well-made bed, knocking a mini basketball off the plaid comforter with a sharp, mid-encounter kick. As the ball rolls across the rug, there are giggles, a bit of a head bump, and then some serious making out. It is, all in all, a pretty good time.

We're at it for a while like that, and it's only when I feel Len's hand up my thigh, pushing my skirt along so that it bunches at my hip, that I suddenly sit back. In response, he instantly pulls his hands back behind his head.

"Sorry," he says, laughing. He sounds out of breath. "Sorry, I shouldn't have."

"It's not that." To be honest, it was exciting to feel his hand under my skirt, and I'm curious to know exactly what he wanted. It'd be easy to find out, too. But the weight of what it would all *mean* stops me, and I lean back against the wall, tucking my knees to my chest.

Len props himself up on his elbows. "Are you okay?"

"Yeah," I say. "It's just . . . maybe we shouldn't be doing this."

Now he sits all the way up. "No?"

"I almost got like sixty people suspended today because of a walkout protesting you, specifically. I can't let everyone down by letting you feel me up."

He grins. "Being a feminist means you can't hook up with someone?"

"I'm saying, being *this* feminist, I shouldn't hook up with *you*." I push his legs away so that I can stretch mine out without touching him. "Especially because it's still unclear whether you're going to resign or not."

Len raises his chin up and gives me that look through his eyelashes, the one that's lethargic and challenging at the same time.

"I'll resign," he says.

His directness disarms me. "Really?"

"Sure. If that's what you want, I'll tell Mr. Powell tomorrow."

I stare at him. After all that, it's just handed to me like Thursday night's calculus homework? It's strangely anticlimactic, but I guess it means the walkout actually worked.

Or did it? I remember Winona's comment about "showing a little leg," and once again, I can't tell if I've forfeited something I didn't intend.

"Are you just agreeing because you want to keep hooking up?"

"So that *is* on the table?"

"I'm serious, Len." I lean over his knees. "Is that why?"

"It's not why."

"Okay, then tell me the real reason. The truth."

Len lies back down when I say this, gazing up at the ceiling instead of me. And even though I've been trying to needle him, it strikes me that maybe these things can be confusing for him, too.

"I've been meaning to tell you," he says, reaching for the top of the wooden headboard. His nervousness makes me feel oddly affectionate, and I relax a little.

"It's okay," I joke gently. "I already know that you like me."

That earns me a smile, one that creases up his eyes in that familiar way, but then he's quiet for a while. I'm about to ask him what's wrong when he says, "You know, I remember you from that activities fair, when I signed up for the *Bugle*."

"You do?"

"Yeah. I thought you were cute, but it seemed like you had an unpleasant personality."

He really gets me with that. "You were right!" I climb over to wrench a pillow from under the comforter and whack him with it. "You were right and you still joined anyway. You could've said 'um, no thanks' and done us both a favor."

He stretches both arms up and then crosses them over his chest, grinning. "Well, I thought I could make a real difference by running for editor in chief," he says. "You know, bring a softer touch to the *Bugle* leadership."

"I'll show you *soft*!" I batter him again with the pillow, and he tries to dodge it by sliding off the bed, but because every sense feels heightened at the same time that my brain is wrapped in gauze, we somehow end up kissing again.

This time, we make it as far as an undone zipper fly, but Len's the one who decides that it's enough. "Wait," he says, grabbing my hand. "If we're not . . . I think I need to stop."

I scoot back over to the other end of the bed, a little bit sorry it's over. "Should I go?"

"No. I mean, probably, but . . ." He rubs a hand over his face. "Let's just talk for a little while."

"Okay, what do you want to talk about?"

"Anything you want. Ask me a question."

"What's the farthest you've ever gone with a girl?"

He laughs, letting out a low whistle like I've sucker punched him. "No softballs from you, huh?"

"Just curious."

"Okay," he says. "A little farther than this. Once."

"Who was she?"

"Katie Gibson."

That doesn't sound like anyone at Willoughby. "Adam's . . . sister?"

"Cousin. It was at some party last summer."

"What about since then?"

"Dry spell."

"So you've never gone all the way."

"No. Have you?"

The reply comes at me quick, like a baseball pitch that announces itself one way and crosses over the plate another. The kind that, as Len explained to me during the Hargis game, shows you what a pitcher's really made of.

"No," I answer slowly. "The last boy I kissed was when I was still in Chinese school."

"What was his name?"

"Bertram Wu."

"*Bertram?*" Len says this using more of his nasal cavity than is really necessary, and it cracks him up.

"Okay, *Leonard*," I say in the same tone.

"That kinda just makes it worse for you."

I shove him, but he keeps on laughing, and then I join in, too.

"Whatever happened to Bertram?" he asks, finally recovering.

"His family moved back to Singapore, and that was the end of that."

"Were you in love with Bertram?"

"Probably not. Also, you don't have to keep saying his name. Especially like that."

"Okay, okay." Len's amusement hasn't quite faded, but he's a little more subdued when he asks the next question. "Have you ever been in love?"

I don't answer right away. "I'm not sure," I say eventually. "What about you?"

"Maybe." Len reaches over and takes my hand, running a finger down the lines in my palm. This seems to calm him, but it has the opposite effect on me.

I slip my hand away. "Do you think it's possible for someone to go through an entire life—getting married and having kids and growing old—and never truly fall in love?"

"Maybe what's more likely is falling out of love."

"I don't know if my parents were ever in love. My mom married my dad so that she could come to America."

"She told you that?"

"Yeah, she says that all the time." I tell Len the story that Mom likes to share, about how Dad used to be a terrible letter writer. He was already living in LA, having been granted asylum straight from Vietnam, while she had ended up in China. So when her aunt said a friend in America had met this Chinese-Vietnamese boy in ESL class, an introduction was arranged. At first he wrote her a few stiff messages, which she responded to (with a photo), but then, quite confusingly, she stopped receiving correspondence of any kind. This sent everyone—A Gūng and A Pòh, plus various aunts and great-aunts—into a panic, because Mom was supposed to be the first link in their chain migration to the golden country. What could be the problem? She was the prettiest girl in the family! If he didn't like her, what could they do? Finally, a few months later, a reply arrived. "Sorry I haven't written in a while," he explained. "It's been basketball season on TV."

Len doubles over in laughter. "I should use that line."

"Anyway," I say. "That's how my parents got together."

"If it makes you feel any better, my parents got married because I was an accident."

"Wait, really?"

"Yeah. They were kind of young. My dad was two years into his PhD at Columbia, and my mom was just about to start law school. But my dad's family is pretty Catholic, so they wanted me. My mom says I need to make her capitulation to conservatism mean something by swearing I'll always support women's reproductive rights."

Now it's my turn to laugh. "She told you *that*?"

"Yeah, so not the most romantic origin story, either."

"Well, your parents are still together."

"Yeah."

"I guess mine are, too."

Len has taken my hand again, and this time, I wrap my fingers around his.

Then my phone buzzes.

"Shit," I say. "Speaking of, that's probably my mom."

When I pick up, she sounds frantic, even though she's probably only been sitting in the school parking lot for about two minutes. "Eliza! Where are you?"

"Sorry," I say, "I, uh, had a meeting after school, so can you pick me up at a classmate's house?"

"Why didn't you remind me?"

"Sorry, sorry, I forgot."

"Where?"

"The same place as the other time."

After I hang up, some of Mom's agitation has worked its way into me, and I scramble to gather my stuff. Then I remember I'm still wearing the Lady Justice dress.

"Can I change somewhere?" I ask Len.

"Here's fine." When I give him a look, he adds, laughing, "Or, bathroom's down the hall."

Once I close the door behind me, I step out of the dress in a hurry and roll it up into a ball so I can stuff it in my backpack. But then, seeing my reflection in the mirror, I realize there's work to be done on my face—namely, scrubbing off the lipstick that, lo and behold, has turned out to be certifiably make-out-proof. *Thank you, Serena,* I think, as I splash cold water on my face. I also realize that my hair is still in a braid crown, which in itself would be an innocent thing, except that I have not traditionally been the type of girl who gets her hair done by friends at school, and I don't need any extra reasons to be grilled today.

I extract the pins from my hair as I walk back to Len's room, where he's lying on the bed, reading *Well-Behaved Women Seldom Make History.*

"Don't you have your own book?"

"Yours seems more interesting."

But he's only pretending to read now. I sit on the edge of the bed and undo my braid, loosening the strands with my fingers—unceremoniously, even though I know he's watching.

"Your hair looks pretty like that," he says, when I'm done.

My face warms. I'm not used to hearing something like that so directly from a boy—especially from Len, of all people. And I admit that it sends me into a euphoria that I'm immediately afraid of losing, like a Lindt truffle that you can only savor while it melts. *This* is the male gaze, I realize. It's wonderful and horrible at the same time.

I jump to my feet, gathering my hair up in a bun. "Good call," I tell Len. "If you noticed something, then my mother definitely would."

Downstairs, at the door, I struggle to put on my sneakers without sitting, putting my books down, or taking my backpack off. This involves hopping on one foot while waving around the other, trying to fit a shoe over my heel.

Len takes the books from me, which then makes everything a lot easier. "So . . ." he begins, leaning against the foyer railing. "What happens now?"

I try not to look at him. "I don't know," I say, retrieving my books from him. "What do you think?"

Len studies the tile on the floor. "You're probably right," he says. "Even if I resign, maybe we should let this . . . cool off."

I swear, all sense must have deserted me, because even though he's saying exactly what I think he should be saying, it's not at all what I want to hear.

"Okay," I say, swallowing. "Thanks again for getting me out of detention. I guess I owe you one."

"Don't worry about it."

Now that both my shoes are on, I have no idea what to do with myself. "Well," I say, sticking out my hand. "The ceasefire was nice while it lasted."

Len grins a little bit. "Until the next battle, then," he says, swinging his arm around like he's about to offer me a hearty handshake. Then he pulls me in and kisses me.

When my phone buzzes again, announcing Mom's arrival, I don't have time to ask any questions. "See you," I manage, stepping away from him.

"See you," he says, before I run out the door.

27

THERE'S NOTHING QUITE LIKE A CAR RIDE WITH your mother to throw cold water on the kind of lingering feelings that, just a few minutes ago, while you were busy making out with a boy, seemed impossible to get rid of. It's not a solution I would necessarily recommend, but it's definitely effective.

"Who was that?" Mom asks when I get into the car. She's parked in the DiMartiles' driveway and, judging from her very focused interest, apparently got a good look at Len as he was closing the door.

"Len," I reply. "He's in my group for an English project." Fortunately, even though we have discussed him before, I'm pretty sure there's no way she remembers his name. But to further distract her, I add, "That Korean girl, Serena Hwangbo, is also in our group."

"The one who is always at Back to School Night?" Student-council members volunteer to help teachers at parent events, so Mom tends to be most familiar with them.

"Yeah."

"Where is she?"

Mom seems to know something is up. She claims she has a sixth sense about things that happen to Kim and me, and it tends to manifest when you least want it to. It never seems to work when, say, you insist that you did not intentionally leave the kitchen drawer open to piss her off, even though, yes, you *know* she has asked you to remember to close it a million times.

"Oh, she went home already," I say. "She lives around here, too."

"This is a rich person's neighborhood," says Mom, observing the houses as we drive down Holyoke Lane, back toward the main thoroughfare that leads to our part of town.

"I guess so," I agree. Then, because it's the sort of thing that would interest Mom, I add, "A lot of Koreans live here."

"Is that boy Korean?"

"No, he's half-Japanese and half-white."

"Oh, that's why. He's very tall." She pauses, as if mulling this over. "His eyes are small, though, for being half-white."

When I fail to respond, Mom looks over and does her best approximation of playing it cool. It is about as successful as a car wreck. "So, you like this boy?"

What the actual F. Do I have it written on my forehead? How does she know? Is everyone going to know?

"No," I lie.

"That's good," says Mom, even though I can tell she doesn't believe me. "Your dad and I wouldn't like it if you had a boyfriend right now. You should be focusing on your school-work and getting into a good college."

"Yeah, I know."

"Also, you should be careful when you are alone with a boy. Some boys will try to take advantage. The nice ones won't, but you never know. Do you understand what I'm saying?"

Oh my God. This reminds me of the time Mom asked whether I knew how babies were made, and I had to hurry up and tell her that yes, I already did.

"Yes, Mom."

"It's a problem when you're naturally pretty. A lot of boys will try to bother you, but you can just ignore them. You don't need to like the first boy who likes you. You can be discerning, even a little uppity. There will always be someone chasing you, but you need to maintain self-respect."

Somewhere in this, I think, is a pep talk, although as far as I'm concerned, it seems gratuitous. I have not, so far, ever been pretty enough to cause myself any problems whatsoever. I'm also galled by the way that, in Mom's universe, Len and I have become characters in a sordid morality drama: danger-ous boy, virtuous girl. There's no room in the story for how I actually feel. Wanting the boy makes him less dangerous, but it also makes the girl, to put it plainly, *not* virtuous. That kind of virtue doesn't exist on a spectrum, which means one wrong move and you're done.

I think of what Len and I were talking about and decide to ask a risky question. "Did you ever like any boys?"

"No!" Mom seems horrified. "When I was your age, I was in a detention camp in Hong Kong. I just wanted to go to America. Why would I like any boys?"

Before Mom resorted to her epistolary courtship with Dad, she and my grandpa had tried to get to America by way of Hong Kong, which served as a port of first refuge during and after the Vietnam War. This was, unfortunately, after they'd already been granted asylum in Nanning, so the authorities did not look kindly upon their attempt to pass themselves off as refugees requiring resettlement elsewhere. When they were discovered, Mom and A Gūng were detained for a whole year as illegal migrants, and at the end of it, they were deported back to China. A few years later, Mom agreed to marry Dad.

I know all of this because it gets referenced frequently in our household, sometimes in an offhand, shoot-the-breeze fashion, and sometimes in conversations like these, shutting down—inadvertently or not—my inquiries into whether Mom and I have anything in common at all. Mom hates it when I try to understand, because she sees it as comparing. "You cannot compare the life you and your sister have to mine," she always says. "It's too different. You are too lucky."

I try to imagine what it would be like if I had met Len in a refugee camp—knowing, like Mom did, that I didn't want anything (or anyone) holding me back if I could find a way to get to America. In truth, it's hard to even picture him in a place like that. There probably wouldn't have been any baseball at this camp. Would I have liked him? Would I have blown my

chance to leave the country on him? Would liking him necessarily have meant blowing it? She's kind of right, in a way.
Seems hard to know.

"A lot of men were not good in the camp," Mom says.
"There was one who even got a girl pregnant. He followed
me around, too, but I was too smart. One day, he wouldn't
leave me alone, no matter where I walked, so I ran into the
block where a family friend stayed, and I hid there until A
Gūng came to find me."

This is a story I have never heard before, and it shocks me
how casual the telling is, how the crux of it involves Mom
seeing herself as a trickster, rather than a potential underage
victim of sexual assault. How she simply accepts the fallacy
that a crime like that can be avoided, just by being clever
enough.

"That's horrible." I think of Mom in the sepia photos from
when she was younger, with a rounded, oval face and hair in
thick braids. She looked like Kim, but her wide-eyed expression was always the same: unsmiling, with a curled bottom lip,
like she didn't, and wouldn't, trust the camera.

"Yeah, you see? You have to be careful when you're a girl.
You can't let others hurt you." Mom eyes me pointedly and
pronounces, as if it is the grand moral of the lecture: "Don't
do anything stupid."

It is all the same to her, I realize. Or, she believes that thinking it is all the same is the only way to preserve oneself. It
reminds me of the way she insists on taking a full-strength
Tylenol Cold capsule whenever the mildest symptom appears.

"You have to battle the germs early," she says, no matter how many times Kim and I explain that Tylenol Cold doesn't work like an antibiotic, and anyway colds are caused by viruses, not bacteria.

It's easy to dismiss Mom's beliefs about germs, but when it comes to this sexuality stuff, it's another story. I hate to admit it, but her conviction rattles me. Part of this is due to the fact that my counterauthority, also known as American culture, seems itself divided. Was hooking up with Len stupid or empowering? Did I lose any self-respect in the process? Am I going to get hurt now?

Unnerved, I pick up my phone and scroll through the million notifications that accumulated while I was off playing fast and loose with my sense of worth.

First there are messages from Winona:

How's detention?

That was some move you pulled! Everyone is talking about it.

Wait, where are you?

And, of course, from Serena:

WTF?????

GIRL YOU ARE UNREAL.

But also . . . a genius?

Are you seeing what's been posted?

Where are you?

ELIZA WHERE THE F ARE YOU?? CALL OR TEXT ME.

Both Winona and Serena are right—the walkout is dominating the Willoughby social-media sphere. The comments are overwhelmingly positive, which I guess is what we want?

@jennyphan03: OMG @elizquan taking a hit for gender equality and free speech . . . what a queen. #goals

@fleur1618: Sooooo inspired by @elizquan right now!!!!

@sayitagainsam: When is @lendimartile gonna step down? #ElizaforEditor

A headache, which grows worse by the second, forces me to quit reading, and I have to shut my eyes to make everything stop spinning.

28

I LIE ON MY STOMACH SO THAT MY LEGS DANGLE off the edge of my bed, fingers poised over the keyboard on my phone. It's starting to get uncomfortable because I haven't moved from this position in at least half an hour, but time doesn't seem to exist anymore as I type and delete and retype, trying to figure out what I should say to Len.

What exactly happened today? It all seems so wild. I look at the last text he sent me, from days ago.

You were right.

It makes me feel the way I did when we were kissing, a kind of lurch that gets my heart pounding like it's desperate to break out, like it's shouting, *Let me at him!* I flip over onto my back, but the disquiet lingers in my body, like a deep itch I don't know how to scratch.

Suddenly, the ". . ." pops up, and I sit up, alert. Then, a message:

I thought you said we should let this cool off.

My grin is so wide, you'd think we'd just elected a female majority to Congress.

YOU said that.

His response comes pretty quickly.

No, that doesn't sound like me at all.

I exhale something between a snort and a smile.

You're right. It didn't really seem like you wanted to stop.

The ". . ." appears for a long time before he replies:

I don't.

Another lurch, a great big one that triggers a fresh bloom of that warm, unsettling strangeness. I realize then that it's not the feeling itself that is unfamiliar, but its insistence. Because it's not that I've never imagined kissing other boys—it's that I never imagined what would happen next.

But now, I don't know what's come over me. I can't *stop* imagining what might happen next.

"Eliza!" Mom calls from the kitchen. "Kim! Time to eat!"

I manage to tear myself away from my phone to sit down at the dining table, but all I'm thinking about is how fast I can get back to it. Kim, who was in and out of the bedroom earlier, gives me a funny look, although she doesn't say anything.

"You didn't hear back from any of the companies yet?" Mom asks Dad, just as he shovels a mouthful of rice into his mouth. When he sets the bowl back down, only about two-thirds of the rice is left. Mom says Dad eats so fast because he has six brothers, which meant that when he was a kid, not eating fast meant not eating anything at all.

Dad shakes his head.

"*Aiyah,*" Mom reproaches. "What you need is a referral. It's always easier if you have someone on the inside." She chews thoughtfully. "What about those friends you're always going to see at the Jūng Wàh High School reunions? Can't any of them help you find a job?"

Dad doesn't say anything, only puts a heap of sautéed ong choy into his bowl.

Mom sighs. "Maybe I should call Siu jē."

After dinner, as Kim and I are finishing up the dishes, I hear Mom on the phone in the bedroom. "Wái, néih hóu Siu jē," she chirps, making her voice more cheerful than it's been in weeks. "How are you?"

Back in my room, I have my calculus book open on my desk, but really I've been texting Len. I barely notice how dark it's gotten. Illuminated only by the private glow of my phone screen, I get lost in a conversation about nothing and everything.

On the vegetable tempura Len's dad tried to make for dinner:

Len: It was pretty soggy, to be honest.

Me: Haha did you eat it?

Len: Yeah, but my mom rejected it.

On our neighbor's new karaoke machine:

Me: We can hear him singing sad Vietnamese songs through the living room wall.

Len: Is he good?

Me: Not really. Kim is about to lose it because she's actually studying. Unlike me . . .

Len: Oh, is someone else already distracting you?

On Joan Didion, whose books (of course) just happened to be lying around his house, waiting for him to take an interest:

Len: I can see why you like her. She writes so precisely, it almost hurts. Like it's just you and these facts that you can't look away from.

Me: Yeah exactly! She's austere, but in a good way.

Len: I guess I might have a type.

On Len's favorite band:

Len: They're from this beach town maybe half an hour from here. I first heard about them from Luis.

Me: Wait, Luis has good taste in music?

Len: Don't hate on my man Luis! His boyfriend's in a real band, so he knows what's up.

Me: Fine, what kind of music are we talking about?

Len: Imagine drugged-out surfers moonlighting with a doo-wop group. But with lyrics that can really cut you open.

The newness of this—finding that the most eloquent expression in a conversation can come from someone other than me—is dizzying. Slipping my headphones in, I lie back and listen to all the links that Len sends me, searching for pieces of him between the notes of each song.

Me: All right, they are pretty good.

Len: Yeah, they're actually even better live. We could go, if you want.

Before I can wonder whether Len has just asked me out on a date and, if he did, how I should respond, Mom calls from the living room. "Eliza! Can you email Dad's résumé to my friend Siu?"

Her tone makes me decide I'd better pause the discussion with Len.

Brb, my mom wants me to help with some job stuff for my dad.

I grab my laptop and dash off the email, so quickly that I almost forget to include the attachment. Then Len's next message appears, with a ping that is now the exact sound of joy, as a notification at the top of my computer screen:

Oh yeah, how's all that going?

I hesitate before responding, my euphoric fog fading a little.

I don't know. Not that well, I guess. My mom is definitely on edge.

For the first time all night, I notice the hushed sounds of Mom and Dad's conversation down the hall. I sink back against my chair.

I guess I'm kind of worried, too.

Len's ". . ." is strangely comforting.

Can I do anything to help?

What a useless, unrealistic question—what could he possibly do? And yet his words enfold me anyway, like a hug I didn't know I needed. Because I'm getting the sense that if I *did* ask him to do something right now, he'd drop everything and do it.

While turning this all over in my head, I almost don't notice when Kim appears at the doorway of our room, and I only just manage to snap my laptop shut in time.

Kim gets into bed and sits back against her pillows, knees folded under her old comforter with the pink Hello Kitty print. Now she's pretending to read some article, highlighter in hand, but I know she's actually trying to guess who I've been texting.

Maybe I'd better call it a night. I pick up my phone again.

No, it's all right. But I should probably work on some calc homework now.

His response, which comes lightning fast, isn't one I'm prepared for.

Okay, me too. Want to compare answers?

I never thought that question could thrill me quite this much, but it's because no one has ever meant it the way he does now: *Wait, don't get off the phone. I still want to talk to you.*

I practically smile out loud as I write back, **Yeah sure.**

"You seem like you're in a good mood," Kim opines from behind her photocopied pages, and I ignore her, but it's true.

I'm in an even better mood an hour or so later, as we're working through the problem set, when I realize that there *is* something Len DiMartile isn't good at after all: calculating derivatives.

You're terrible at this, I tease, after he's gotten three wrong in a row. **Looks like I've finally discovered your weakness.**

When his reply arrives, I can't decide whether to be embarrassed or exhilarated.

I think you've found more than one.

One thing's for certain—it sure makes me wish Kim weren't in the room.

29

AT SCHOOL THE NEXT DAY, LEN AND I FOLLOW through on an unspoken agreement to appear as though we are still avoiding each other. It seems like the most reasonable thing to do for now, because I'm frankly still not sure what to make of it all. Or even what all of "it" is. So we don't make eye contact, we say very little to each other in the classes we have together, and we never stand close enough to touch.

What no one knows, though, is that we're texting all the time. Last night, we kept it up long after we'd finished the calc problem set, long after both of us should have gone to sleep, and I can see it in his face: a little more wan than usual, with faint dark circles forming under his eyes. But there's also something in his stealthy grin and the way it lights up at me when no one is looking. I feel it, too—a kind of jittery high that exists just this side of being found out.

During lunch, when I see Len in the *Bugle* newsroom, I give him some article to edit, and then he hangs around for a bit, talking to Tim.

"So, DiMartile," says Tim. "Are you gonna resign or what?"

I put on headphones and pretend to be super focused on my laptop screen, but I sense Tim flicking a glance over in my direction.

Len is sitting on a counter at the side of the room, his feet propped up on a chair. He tilts it forward, then backward, each time bringing it down onto the carpet with a cavalier thud. "I'm still thinking it over."

Mr. Powell is out today, because he's one of the chaperones for the annual senior field trip to the Getty Villa. James is out, too, for the same event, which means Len hasn't had a chance to tell either of them about his plan to resign. It made sense to both of us that Mr. Powell and James should be the first to know, so Len's been playing it cool whenever anyone else has asked.

"Man, would you really?" Tim's voice lowers. "You were elected, fair and square. Don't let them bully you out of it!"

Len laughs. "She *is* more qualified than me, though," he points out. "You know that."

"*I'm* more qualified than you, dude. That's not the point."

"Sounds like maybe you should've run, O'Callahan. You missed your chance."

Tim folds his arms across his chest and chuckles. "Guess I did!"

After a while, they switch to talking about how the Dodgers are doing this season, and that's when I tune out. Then my pocket buzzes.

Do you want to come over today?

I tuck my phone under the desk and try not to smile.

Me: To do what?

Len: Calculus, of course.

Len isn't looking at me, but he's smirking big-time down at his phone. I don't know exactly what this feeling is, but it's like wearing in an extremely annoying, scratchy sweater that also, somehow, warms you all the way inside.

I don't really get much out of doing calc homework with you. Just saying.

His phone gets a little smile that's meant for me, and he types out a reply before pocketing it.

Well, let's not do homework then.

Across the room, he slides off the counter. "I'm gonna go get some food."

"Yeah, me too." Tim slings his backpack over his shoulder, and then, as he passes where I'm sitting, says, "See you, Eliza." Len, following behind him, raises an open palm at me, like an afterthought to Tim's afterthought.

"Bye." As I watch them disappear through the door, the newsroom doesn't seem as alive as it did just a few seconds ago.

God, what is *wrong* with me?

My phone vibrates again, and I grab it like I haven't heard from Len in days.

Let's do whatever you want.

Just then, Cassie bounds into the newsroom, the camera around her neck as usual. She was out on assignment during zero period, so I haven't seen her since yesterday afternoon. I notice that she's still wearing her *I AM A FEMINIST* button.

"Hi, Eliza!" Her grin is enormous. "Boy, am I glad I ran into you. I wanted to show you the photos from the walkout."

She plops down in front of the computer with her jacket askew, books spilling out of her arms and her lunch bag toppling onto the floor. The camera, though, she unloops from her neck and sets down gently, like a baby. "I have to upload some new photos from this morning," she explains, connecting the camera to the computer. "But the walkout ones are already here."

I pull up a chair next to her as she opens the folder.

"Wow," I say, as the images flash across the screen. "These are really good, Cassie."

And it's true. There are bright, sunny shots of us all flocking together in the quad, of everyone smiling and shouting and holding up signs, of teachers peering curiously through open doors. There are also shots of me, of course, walking blindfolded between Winona and Serena, climbing up on the lunch table, raising my sword in the air.

I don't think I've ever looked so badass in my life.

"It was *so* cool, Eliza," says Cassie. "I felt proud to be there. It's probably the most exciting thing I've ever photographed for the *Bugle*."

"Yeah, well, you did a great job!"

Cassie seems flattered by my genuine compliment, but she

shakes her head. "Nah, I was just taking pictures. You're the one who did something."

Some of my lunch starts to sour in my stomach. "I didn't do *that* much."

"Are you kidding?" Cassie makes an incredulous gesture at the computer screen, which is currently displaying a close-up photo of me, my braid crown glinting in the light. "You took a big stand for what you believed in," she says. "Not many people are brave enough to do that."

I shift in my seat, feeling increasingly unwell. "I don't know. I did basically give in at the end."

"No, you stood up to Dr. Guinn!" Cassie cries. "You didn't let him punish everyone just for making their voices heard. You were *totally* fighting the patriarchy!"

I manage not to throw up all over the computer, but only just.

Somehow, I get myself to stand up and mumble something about needing to stop at my locker before class. Then I gather up my stuff in a hurry and wave at Cassie before scurrying out the door.

As I hasten across the quad, I feel rudely reacquainted with the detailed solidity of the world—the uneven asphalt beneath my shoes, the unforgiving sunlight on my forehead, the boisterous noise of the lunchtime crowd. The questions I've been evading are now closing in. What will it mean if Len resigns, and then everyone finds out we've been hooking up? What if he doesn't resign? Will we still keep hooking up?

And is that all we're doing, hooking up? It doesn't really feel that way, but I have no idea. The last time anything like this happened to me, I barely got anywhere with Bertram. I've never been anyone's girlfriend before. Do I want to be Len's?

This last thought makes my insides contract in at least three different ways.

I dig up my phone and reread Len's last text: **Let's do whatever you want.** My heart, of course, flutters to see it. But it's so easy for him to say that, to be gallant and accommodating. Because if the truth comes out, it's not *his* identity that will get boiled down into a single hookup. No, *I'm* the one who doesn't want anyone to know. Because I'm the one who everyone will say is doing something wrong.

I type out a message to Len and hit send before I can change my mind.

Thanks, but I think I have to pass.

His response is almost instantaneous.

Oh yeah? How come?

Goddamn it, Len.

Because things get complicated when I go over to your house.

And I definitely don't need any more of that.

30

UNFORTUNATELY, I FORGET THAT OUR *MACBETH* group is supposed to have another meeting this afternoon, given that the performance is on Monday. Len apparently didn't remember either. Ryan, of all people, reminds me during English class.

"Going to Len's today?" he asks, pausing at my desk.

I jump maybe five inches off my seat. Then I remember what he's talking about.

"Oh." My face flushes. "Do we have to? We all know our lines, right?"

"You're the one who said we needed to rehearse more," says Ryan. "I think your exact words were 'Especially for your benefit, Ryan.'"

"Okay, I'm sorry. I shouldn't have said that. You're doing fine."

Ryan has trouble wrapping his head around this. "Eliza thinks we don't have to rehearse anymore," he says to Len, who is walking by.

"How uncharacteristic of her," Len remarks.

"That's what I'm saying!"

When Serena is consulted, however, she brings up a more crucial issue. "We still have to decide on our costumes, don't we? For the extra credit?"

Shoot. "Well, let's just meet in the quad," I say. "We don't have to go anywhere."

"Especially not my house," Len puts in.

"I meant anyone's." I give him a warning look that he pretends not to see.

Luckily, Serena's attention is already back on her phone. "Sure," she says genially, "whatever."

After school, the four of us congregate at the lunch table under the big oak tree. Len is wearing, unusually, a Willoughby baseball cap. I do a double take, because I don't think I've seen him in one since before he joined the *Bugle*. It seems like his hair is getting a little long again.

Len sits down right next to me, acting totally natural, and it sends my heart rate way up. What does he think he's doing, getting so close? He never replied to my last text, so I wonder if this is his idea of an amusing way to respond.

I scoot away and flick the bill of his cap. "What's with the hat?"

"Len and I have a costume idea." Ryan takes his own baseball cap from his backpack and twists it backward onto his head. Then he crosses his arms and puffs his chest out, elbowing Len. "Come on, show them."

Obediently, Len swivels his hat around and assumes a similar stance, looking only slightly abashed. His grin makes his eyes crinkle up like they normally do.

He looks absurd, and also really cute.

Serena bursts out laughing.

"I don't get it." I frown hard, attempting to maintain some pretense of composure. "Are you . . . bros?"

"Yeah!" Ryan is ebullient. "Genius, right? It's, like, zero effort!"

"Okay, no." I start to get up from the table.

"Aw, wait." Len grabs my elbow. "Hear him out."

I shake him off, but I do sit down again, landing almost near enough to brush against his hip. I refuse to let on that I've noticed. "Fine. I'm listening."

"So I was looking for some summaries of *Macbeth* on YouTube—"

"Ryan, have you not read the play?"

"Sure, I've read parts of it."

"Which parts?"

". . . My part."

I practically knock Len over when I lunge at Ryan. "Are you serious?"

"Hey, as long as he's got his lines memorized, why do you care?" Len pulls me back down next to him. "Let the man speak."

"Thanks, dude." Ryan gives Len an appreciative nod, and I roll my eyes. "As I was *saying*, I was watching these videos, and in one of them, Macbeth was a bro who wanted to be president of his frat—"

"Are you telling me this utterly asinine suggestion wasn't even an original idea?"

Ryan looks miffed. "Why you gotta be such a hater, Eliza?"

"It's not a costume if you're dressing up as yourself!"

Len leans in, and for a few brief seconds, our shoulders touch—long enough for me to lose track of whether it's Ryan's inanity that's got me feeling worked up, or something else. "Well, technically, it would be a costume for you," Len says, almost in my ear. Then he straightens up, grinning again. "And you, too, Serena."

Unlike me, Serena has been fairly sanguine about this whole situation. She reaches over and steals Len's hat, placing it on my head, her expression sly. "Let's see," she says, adjusting the brim. "Eliza, give us your best bro face!"

"This is stupid," I complain. But on impulse, I jut my chin out anyway and approximate a *sup* nod.

Serena collapses in a fit of giggles, and I can't help breaking into a goofy smile. "You're a natural!" she jokes.

Len's laughing, too, but oddly, he makes no comment, and his look lingers in a small, quiet way that feels like it should be private even from me.

Abruptly, I yank off his baseball cap and drop it on the table.

"Does this mean we're all cool with the idea?" asks Ryan, hopeful.

I get up and take a few strides across the grass, trying to collect myself. "We'll go with it for now, until I can think of something better," I announce briskly. "But let's just start rehearsing, shall we?"

After we've run through our scenes a few times, the boys decide to get a snack, and I feel almost relieved to watch the two of them traipse toward the vending machines. I'm letting out an exhale when Serena says, "So, what's up with you and Len?"

I choke. In the distance, Ryan is putting some coins into the machine while Len waits behind him.

"What?" I stare at them because I can't look at Serena.

"Something seems up," she teases. "You're not falling for him, are you?"

"No," I say, much too defensively. "No way."

Serena is thoroughly enjoying this until she peers into my face. "Oh . . . ," she says, like she's realizing something.

I panic. "What is it?"

Serena leans over seriously, like she's my lawyer and she needs to know the truth. She pauses for a very long time, head tilted, eyes squinting at me. "Are you . . . hooking up with him?"

The last syllables climb up to the heights of incredulity, and I want to die. I try to make my mind go completely blank, but like a traitor, it jumps to yesterday afternoon and Len's room.

"Holy shit." Serena covers her mouth. "You are." She's almost laughing, but I can't tell if it's because she's amused or appalled.

"We're not hooking up," I say.

Serena sizes me up in a way that suggests she is extremely skeptical about this claim.

"It only happened once," I falter, bracing myself for the imminent blowup.

But all Serena manages to say is "Wow." She fans herself, like she's imagining the special place in hell for feminists who hook up with the enemy.

"I'm sorry. I really am. It was a horrible decision."

"You can say that again." Serena shakes her head. "Of all the guys, Eliza!"

I let my forehead drop to the table. "I know, I'm sorry." I wonder if things will get better for me if I keep my face planted there.

But then Serena surprises me.

"It's fine," she says, in the tone of someone about to clean up a large mess.

I blink up at her, strands of my hair falling in front of my eyes. "What?"

"I get it." She shrugs. "He's hot, and a jock. It's like, do you have a pulse?"

We both look over at Len, who is stretching his arms over his head so that his hoodie rides half up his back, taking his shirt along with it.

"He's not really a jock anymore," I try to explain.

Serena tosses Len's baseball cap in front of me. "Isn't he?"

I wince.

"You know, I always thought your type would be more like a James Jin. But I guess . . ." She sounds almost wistful. "It's hard to resist a baseball player, huh?"

I open my mouth to dispute the implication that Len is *just* a baseball player, but then I close it, because I'm not sure I'm ready to say it out loud.

Serena rotates the bangle around her wrist in a meditative motion. "I assume you haven't told anyone else?"

The question reminds me that Winona is now part of the "else," which makes me feel even shittier. "Not yet."

"Well, keep it that way." She sighs, a long and jaded exhale. "If it had been literally any other boy . . ."

"I know," I say, rubbing my temples.

Serena appraises me sharply. "This divide at school is bigger than you and Len now. So whatever is happening between you . . . shut it down."

Her words have an ominous certitude to them, and I'm chilled both by her conviction and my inability to match it.

"You're a girl," Serena warns, when I don't respond. "Len will get a pat on the back, but you're gonna get torn apart by the judgment. You won't survive it if this gets out."

The boys are making their way back to our table now. "What'd you get?" I ask as they approach, because I have no idea what else to say.

"Raisins," says Ryan, his mouth full of them. Len shows me his bag of trail mix, and then holds it out. I start to reach for some, but Serena intercepts me.

"So, Eliza," she coos, arm coiling around my shoulder. "You're coming to this party with me tomorrow night, right?"

I look at her, confused. "Wh—"

"We should both get out there," Serena interrupts. "It'll be a chance to meet some boys."

"What's wrong with the boys you already know?" says Ryan, forehead furrowed.

Serena gives him a gentle smile.

"What party?" Len's question is casual, tossed up with a handful of his trail mix.

Serena leaves him hanging with a coquettish dip of her shoulders, but then Ryan supplies the answer. "Nate Gordon's the only one having a party tomorrow."

"Ah," says Len, like this is all very enlightening.

Serena knows, I text Len later, as I'm waiting for Mom in the school parking lot. **She figured it out.**

Len: Really? How?

Me: What do you mean, how. She read you like an open book!

Len: Me? I was taking Ryan's side against you the whole time!

Me: Well, she knows. And she's not thrilled.

Len takes a couple of seconds to react to this, and when he does, his tone has lost some of its lightness.

Man, I'm sorry, Eliza. Are you gonna be okay?

I try to wall up the part of me that wants Len to drive back here and hold me, letting my face burrow into his chest until everything does feel okay. It would be so simple to ask him, and he'd come running—except that's exactly what *can't* happen.

Serena said she'll keep the secret. But . . . I also kind of told

her it was a one-time thing.

There's a pause before he replies again:

That's technically true. It has only been a one-time thing. Mostly.

I lean against one of the concrete parking-lot posts and bite my lip. Then I type what I really don't want to say.

It should probably stay that way, like we originally discussed. And we should stop doing this, too.

The ". . ." flashes on and off for a while before his reply comes through.

Stop what?

Suddenly, the afternoon sun feels unbearable.

I dunno, whatever this is. All the . . . texting.

Len doesn't reply for a few solid minutes, and my skin starts to feel prickly all over, like the start of a sunburn. I wonder if Len has just decided not to respond at all. But he does, finally.

Okay. I guess I'll see you then.

My heart stops. That's it, then? I swallow hard.

I've never, ever cried over a boy, but I feel like maybe, now, I can understand why someone might.

Len, though, isn't done typing, and his next message makes me laugh out loud, though whether out of exasperation or relief, I'm not sure.

At Nate Gordon's.

31

ABOUT TWENTY MINUTES AFTER I TELL SERENA
that I'll go to the party with her, Winona texts me.

**Serena is trying to get me to go to some party tomorrow
night. She says you're going.**

Yikes. I guess it makes sense that Serena would also want
Winona to come, but she must not know the battle she's in for.

Me: Yeah, I guess I am.

Winona: Why???

I definitely don't have a good answer, so I try to stick to the
facts.

**Me: She kept badgering me about it, and it's hard to say no to
her. You know how she is.**

Winona: Uh yeah, I do. That's exactly my point.

Serena has, in fact, been very persistent with her texts, and
another one arrives now:

It'll be so fun!!!!! You'll forget all about Len.

Right . . . about Len. The last I heard from him was earlier this afternoon, when I asked him whether he was really going to Nate Gordon's party and he responded with a single emoji: 💀

This is good, right? We're cooling off, just like Serena said we should. Just like I wanted. It's almost okay, maybe, that I still haven't told Winona anything about the situation.

Except it isn't. Not really. And the longer I wait, it seems, the worse it gets.

I type something out now.

Hey, FYI, I hooked up with Len. Yes, the Len that we made into the poster child for the patriarchy. It's not a big deal, though. Really.

I hit backspace over and over, like I'm afraid my phone will somehow transmit the message if I don't delete it fast enough. I've known from the beginning that the confession wouldn't be easy, but now it's definitely too late. Her reaction is going to make Serena's seem almost congratulatory.

Me: Serena's not as bad as she seems.

Winona: You've just drunk the Hwangbo Kool-Aid.

Five minutes later, though, more texts come through:

Damn it, Eliza. She's blowing up my phone. I had to give in for my sanity.

To distract her, I volunteer to spend all Sunday filming *Driveways*—which, I realize with a start, is now due in less than a week. In all the chaos of the last few days, I haven't thought about the film once, and acknowledging this adds a new layer to the guilt that's already congealed in my chest.

I'll at least fix that, I vow to myself. After tomorrow night, once this Len absurdity has had a chance to settle, I'll switch back to full producer mode so we can finish this thing and tie it up with an award-winning bow. The National Young Film-makers Festival is in for a major Winona Wilson hit. I'll make sure of it.

On Saturday, Mom and Dad get into a pretty big fight. Well, it's really more Mom yelling and Dad sitting at the dining table, testy and silent. Their arguments tend to be mostly in Vietnamese, with only some Cantonese interjections, and this one's no exception.

"Why do I have to do everything in this family, *há*?" Mom laments.

From the couch, I flash apprehension at Kim, who is sitting at her desk in the living room, studying. The fluorescent lamp overhead is too harsh for the afternoon.

"This is for *your* job," says Mom. "You should be looking for yourself, asking around. Why do I have to make all the phone calls for you? Do you think I like to ask people for help? Do you think I am not embarrassed?"

Still Dad doesn't say anything. Kim and I both start to gather our things and try to creep into our room unnoticed, but we get caught in the maelstrom.

"Of course I don't like to do any of those things. But I do it for them." Mom points at us over the stove. "For your daughters," she emphasizes, as if he's forgotten that he has any.

"If I go back to working in a restaurant, I could get a job tomorrow," says Dad. He sounds irritable.

"And what? Go back to never being at home? Eliza is almost done with high school, and Kim is in college. When are you going to spend time with them?"

"Some things can't be helped," says Dad. "It's fate."

Mom makes a dismissive sound, the contempt sharp enough to slice right through my stomach. "That's right. I don't know what I did to you in a past life to be cursed with this suffering."

Mom says stuff like this all the time when she's mad, even to Kim and me. Sometimes she works herself into such a state, flinging every emotional grenade she can get her hands on, that I can't do much more than watch in detached horror, as if she's pantomiming behind glass.

"If you were a different type of man," Mom continues, "I wouldn't have to worry about anything. Not about money or finding you a job. I should have married a man who could take care of me!"

I follow Kim into the hallway. She signals at me to stay quiet, then opens the door to our room. We tiptoe in, slowly shutting ourselves against the noise. It reminds me of when we were younger, how we'd crawl into the closet together and wait, among long skirts and pants legs, for the crisis to pass. It's been a while since we did that.

"Ugh." I roll onto my bed. "I can't believe she went there."

"She didn't mean it," says Kim automatically, sitting down on the edge of her own mattress.

"I don't know . . ."

"She's not going to leave Dad, if that's what you're thinking. She wouldn't go through with it."

"I know. But that's not even what I'm talking about. I meant the part about marrying a man who could take care of her. I wouldn't want a man to take care of *me*."

"You've always had someone to take care of you," says Kim. "So it's easy for you to say that."

"Well, I meant when I'm grown-up."

"You might find it harder than you think."

Kim can be so annoying sometimes. Always acting like she's so much more mature than me, just because she's a little bit older. But it's not like she's had that much more life experience. She still lives at home, after all. I want to tell her that I'm not like her, that I'm not afraid of how hard it will be. But she's already putting in her headphones, so I turn back to reading *Life: A User's Manual*.

After dinner, I tell Mom that I'm going to Winona's house. She's still so caught up in the argument with Dad that she doesn't ask me any questions, which gives me the courage to request an extended curfew.

"Can I stay until midnight tonight?" I say. "Winona and I have a lot of work to do on her movie."

"Okay, fine."

"Did you hear that," I say to Kim, because I'll need her to be my backup if Mom forgets that she agreed to this. "Midnight."

Kim rolls her eyes. "Yeah, sure."

Later, though, as I'm standing in front of the bathroom mirror, Kim walks over and leans against the door frame. She meets my gaze in the mirror as I'm braiding my damp hair into two plaits.

"Eliza, do you have a boyfriend?"

I pause mid-braid, wondering if maybe Mom wasn't so distracted after all.

"Did Mom tell you to ask me?"

"No."

"Then keep your voice down, would you?" I finish the braid and secure the end with a rubber band.

"So you *do* have one?" Kim brightens like someone has just set a big ice cream sundae in front of her.

"No," I say again.

"But there obviously is a boy."

"What's that supposed to mean?"

"The other night, you were chatting with someone until way late. Don't think I didn't notice."

Apparently she hasn't noticed the current text hiatus. "I went to bed at eleven last night."

"Okay, but now you're bothering with all this." Kim gestures at my hair.

I hate that she's right. Other girls, including Kim, fuss over their hair all the time. But I don't, and now I feel self-conscious about trying. When you look a certain way every day, and people are used to seeing you that way, it feels like drawing too much attention to yourself to change it. The wrong kind of attention. Because a serious, self-respecting girl should want to be noticed for her mind, not her appearance. Right?

Kim presses her lips together into one of her knowing smiles. Then she pulls open a drawer. "Spray this over your hair." She hands me a metallic teal can. "Otherwise your waves won't hold."

"I'm not going for waves," I say, even though I was. I change the subject. "Can I borrow your car tonight?"

"Only if you admit that there's a boy."

"I'm going to a party." Sometimes, the only way to avoid telling one truth is to tell another truth.

"Really!" Kim exclaims.

"Yes. So, about the car?"

"Okay, fine." Kim crosses her arms and grins. "Is the boy going to be at the party?"

"Kim!"

She simpers fondly at me before turning to go. "I'm just glad you finally get that it's okay to care about how you look."

I check myself out in the mirror again and decide to leave my hair in braids. No need to go through the trouble of waves, just for a boy. I also decide not to wear anything special, either— just the same old jeans and my sweater-substitute-of-the-day, a white pullover that's only a little bit too short.

At the last minute, though, before leaving, I rummage through Kim's drawer and pocket a tube of red lipstick.

Nate's house is just outside Palermo, less than half a mile from Winona's, so we decide to walk.

"I'd rather be watching a movie," grumbles Winona as we

shuffle down the empty sidewalk. The evening still has a bit of blue to it, but the streetlights are already on.

"We'll watch a movie after," I say. "We're just gonna say hi to Serena and then leave."

I've obviously never been to Nate's house, but as soon as we turn onto his block, it becomes clear which one is his. There's the music, of course, pummeling the evening air with its obnoxious bass, but also the layers of voices floating out on top of one another, punctuated by shouts and squeals. The front shades are drawn, but the back window is illuminated, and through the semi-sheer curtains, you can see people crowded around a table, erupting every so often in a histrionic roar.

When we ring the doorbell, the man himself answers. To his credit, Nate does not behave as if it is at all weird that we have shown up on his doorstep, despite the fact that neither of us has spoken a word to him in the last three years we've been at school together.

"Eliza Quan!" he says, stepping aside to let us in. "The feminist!" He is being facetious, but in that way that is past ridicule. He either has had enough to drink or is more good-natured than I realized.

Serena comes running and immediately envelops Winona and me in a tight hug. "Heyyyyyyy!" She smells like cool-girl shampoo. "I'm so glad you came," she says. Then she leans in closer to me. "Oh my God, Eliza, have I converted you to lipstick?"

I turn about fifty percent as red as my lips, but Serena loops her arm through mine, then Winona's. "I love it," she says, and

I feel like maybe getting noticed for your appearance isn't so bad after all.

We run into Esther and Heppy on our way to the kitchen, which earns us another round of high-pitched greetings and hugs. Winona seems drained already.

"Drinks?" Serena waves her arm in a flourish over the island counter, which is covered with an assortment of alcohol.

I shake my head, but to my surprise, Winona says, "Sure." When I look at her, she shrugs. "Why not?"

Serena pours about a half inch of vodka from a near-empty plastic bottle, filling the rest of the cup up to the brim with orange juice. She hands this to Winona before freeing another red tumbler from the plastic, which she holds out to me. "We need to do a toast," she orders.

I comply by serving myself some orange juice, and then we raise our cups in the air, bolstered by Serena's salute: "To feminism!"

My juice is room temperature and leaves a sourness in my mouth. "Is it any better with the vodka?" I ask Winona. She tilts her cup toward me, and I take a sip. Now the aftertaste is bitter, with a burn that feels like blushing. Unimpressed, I return the drink to Winona.

"Hey, Hwangbo!" Dylan Park is over at the dining table. "You gonna join my team or what?"

Serena smiles coyly, a move so practiced it's effortless. "Sure," she says, like a magnanimous grand dame. "I'm bringing Eliza and Winona, too."

I try to explain that I should abstain because I'm not any

good at drinking games, and also I was kind of serious about the whole not-drinking thing.

"That doesn't matter." Serena sets my orange juice on the table. "Just use that." And because Serena says it's fine, it is.

"Okay," says Dylan, as we move into place next to him. "Do you know the rules of flip cup?"

Neither Winona nor I have played before, so Dylan explains. There are two teams, each forming a line on either side of the table. Once the game begins, the first person in each line has to down their drink, place the cup on the edge of the table, and then flip it so that it rests upside down. Then—and only then—the next person down the line does the same thing, and so on, and so on. The team that gets through everyone first wins.

The referee is a white kid I don't know, maybe from Hargis. "On your marks," he says, "get set . . . go!"

Dylan is up first, and he's a real pro. He drains the beer like it's water, and then, in one expert swoop, he's flipped the cup.

Serena's next, and she is elegantly abysmal. Next to her, Dylan bobs up and down, howling, "You're killing me, Hwangbo!"

She finally gets it after about seven tries, and she shrieks as the cup wobbles into place. Dylan holds up both hands for a double high five, and she bounces up to slap them.

Meanwhile, it's Winona's turn, and she seems her normal composed self. Our team is a little behind because of Serena, but Winona is unfazed. She gets it after only three tries. "Woooo, Winona!" Serena squeaks, clapping her hands.

Now it's my turn, and I'm slightly nervous. I swallow the disgusting orange juice in two big gulps, and then set the cup down. Okay, I tell myself, focus. Envision the cup standing up after a tight somersault. I flick the rim of the cup with my finger, and, miraculously, it lands on the first try.

"You go, girl!" Dylan is beside himself. Thanks to me, we've caught up to the other team. Tony Mercado takes his turn next, makes it in two flips, and then we've won.

We're all screaming now, even Winona, and Dylan gives us high fives. "Who knew feminists were so good at flip cup?" he says, grinning.

In all the commotion, no one noticed until now that the Willoughby baseball contingent has joined our ring of spectators. Notable among them: one especially sullen Jason Lee. And also . . . a particularly tall ex-pitcher.

Len leans casually against the refrigerator, one hand in his pocket and the other holding a drink. He's wearing his green flannel, the one that's the color of pine needles, which goes terrifically well with the dark brown of his hair. I want to run over and thread myself under his arm, snuggling up against him the way Winona's dog Smokey does when you stoop down to greet her. But I don't, because I am not a dog and also, seriously, what is *up* with me?

Luckily, everyone is too riveted by Serena and Jason to notice. Well, everyone except Len, who raises his cup at me with a small tilt of his hand. A nearly imperceptible *cheers*. It's nothing, but it warms up my chest, not totally unlike the way that sip of Winona's vodka orange juice did.

The music's still going strong, and people around us are laughing and arguing and noisily tumbling in every direction, but in this little flip-cup corner, the silence is funereal as we all wait to see what will happen.

"Hey, guys," says Dylan, bravely, even though you can tell he's feeling uncertain.

But Serena doesn't need his heroics. "I think we're done here," she says, linking her arms once again with me and Winona, and we parade outside to the backyard.

An hour and a bit more alcohol later, Winona and Serena are the best of friends.

"Winona, you are, like, so brilliant," Serena is saying. The three of us are sitting together on Nate's wicker sofa, and I'm in the middle, hugging a pillow to my chest. Serena rests a doting arm on mine. "And you are, too, Eliza. Obviously. Aren't you glad all this has brought us together?"

Winona leans over me from the other side. "Not gonna lie, Serena. For a while, I thought you were way too obsessed with boys and appearances and all that stuff to be a serious feminist. But you really came through for the walkout, so I'll give you *some* credit."

"Listen to her!" cackles Serena, and then they're both laughing, a concerted fit that ends with the two of them almost in tears. Things must be funnier somehow when you're drunk.

"Ugh, why have we never hung out before this?" Serena is almost maudlin now. "I fucking love you both. I fucking *love* feminism."

Esther rushes over to us then, a bit red in the face. She crouches down in front of Serena and whispers, "She's here."

"Who?" Serena sits up. We all fix our eyes in the direction that Esther's head is cocked, and then I realize exactly who she means.

It's the girl from the baseball game. Jason's . . . whatever she is.

"The *slut*?" Serena grips my arm, and the word digs a little into my skin, like her nails. "Oh my God."

Her name, Esther tells us, is Vicki Wang, and she's a junior at Hargis. We get a good view of her as she stands with a group of boys, floodlit by the patio door. She's moon-faced and petite, with stocky shoulders like a swimmer's. Her ears stick out through her hair, a strand of which she twists around her fingers, held up like she's dangling a cigarette.

"She looks so trashy," says Esther. It's hard not to compare her to Serena, who's practically channeling Grace Kelly in an all-white jumpsuit that bares only her shoulders. Especially now, as she sits perfectly still, chin up, casting icy judgment. It is a little depressing that Jason would throw her over for . . . well, this girl.

"She *is* trashy," Serena declares. "Who hooks up with someone else's boyfriend?"

"My cousin says she'll hook up with anyone," Esther confides.

We watch as Vicki leans in to a boy who isn't even Jason, laughing so hard that her inauthentic trill grates all the way over here. She's wearing a velvet cami that, despite the line of buttons down the front, isn't quite containing her chest.

"She's embarrassing herself." Serena's nose rises high in the air. "She ought to have a little more self-respect."

Something about all of this, the way it cuts, reminds me of my conversation with Mom.

"Maybe we should lay off her," I say suddenly.

The three of them fasten their attention on me. "That's unlike you," says Winona, her glasses slipping down to the tip of her nose.

"Well . . . I just don't think we should slut-shame her." I droop a bit into the sofa cushion.

"We're only slut-shaming her because she did something *wrong*, Eliza," says Serena. "Like, I don't think you're a slut just because you—"

She stops herself, teetering on the edge of the revelation, and I freeze. But then she makes her gaze go purposely fuzzy. "I mean, *if* you hooked up with some guy, I wouldn't think you were a slut."

"Yeah, you're like the complete opposite of slutty," Esther chimes in.

I start breathing normally again, but I glance back over at Vicki, unsettled. Even though Jason is really the one who deserves the blame, there *is* something kind of off-putting about her. The way she keeps letting her bra strap fall down over her shoulder. The way she is performing some mono-logue for those boys in a singsong voice full of false notes, so animatedly that her hair is starting to stick to her shiny forehead. She wants their want, and so nakedly. We all see it, maybe even the boys. And I think we all see something else, too: we're over here, on this side of an invisible line, because we're different. We're not like her.

And yet. I also hooked up with a boy I wasn't supposed to. It's not the same, of course, because he wasn't anybody else's boyfriend, but still . . . which side of the line was that?

We're always making these distinctions, I realize, because we hope they will somehow protect us—just as I once insisted on separating myself from Serena, we're now desperate to distance ourselves from Vicki. But the harshness we fear, in reality, seeps through to all of us, no matter how many lines we draw.

"I think I'll go get some water," I say, standing up abruptly.

On my way back inside, I pass by Vicki and her crowd of boys. If she sees me watching her, I'll smile at her, I decide.

But she doesn't notice me at all.

32

AS I APPROACH THE KITCHEN, I NOTICE A FAMIL-iar figure checking out the bottles on the island. He's taller than I expected, but not quite as tall as Len. I recognize him from the red hair under his baseball cap. It's McIntyre, the pitcher from the Hargis game.

He steps aside as I walk over to the refrigerator and pop my cup under the water dispenser.

"Actually, that might be a better idea," he says, and comes around to wait his turn, leaning against the island with his legs outstretched.

Up close, I see that he's got brown eyes the same shade as his freckles. I don't reveal that I know who he is—when my cup is filled, I just smile, the way you do at strangers, and then gesture at the fridge. "All yours," I say, leaving him to it.

"So, do you go to Willoughby?"

I pause in mid-step. "Yeah," I reply. Then, because he seems to be waiting for more, I add, "I'm Eliza."

He holds out a hand. "I'm—"

"McIntyre!" Len, who has come up behind him, claps him on the back. "How you been, man?"

"Hey, it's Len DiMartile!" McIntyre laughs. "You know this guy?" he says, turning to me. "A legend."

I give Len a dry look. "I hadn't heard."

"I'm old news," says Len. "She didn't start going to baseball games until after I quit."

"Oh yeah?" McIntyre seems to sense, correctly, that I do in fact know this guy.

"I was at the last one," I explain. "That was my first."

"You pitched a pretty good game that day," Len says to McIntyre. "Especially in that weather."

"Aw, man, the wind was unbelievable."

They talk a little while longer about the game, and then McIntyre asks about Len's recovery.

"Oh, you know." Len brushes off the concern. "It's going."

"Must be tough," says McIntyre, and you can tell he's wondering what it would be like if the same thing happened to him. And there's something else in his face, too. Pity? Guilt? Whatever it is, I don't think he means it in a bad way, but Len doesn't like it very much.

"Well, listen, it's good to see you," says Len. "Good luck with the rest of the season."

"Yeah, thanks," says McIntyre. "Hope you're back at it soon." To me, he adds, "Nice to meet you, Eliza. Maybe I'll see you next time we play Willoughby."

We watch him walk away. "He seems nice," I say.

Len takes a sip from his drink. "I didn't know you had a thing for pitchers."

"I didn't know pitchers had a thing for *me*."

I wait for Len to follow this up with a wisecrack, but he doesn't. He just chuckles. And I realize I've never noticed before what his laugh is like: deep and generous in a boyish way, with a goofy current skimming over the top.

Suddenly, I feel kind of shy.

I get up on my toes, like I'm trying to get a peek into his drink. "What're you having?" I ask. He hands the cup to me and it feels strangely intimate, like we share drinks all the time. Like we've been friends for a while. Or more than friends.

I take a big gulp so he doesn't notice my face.

"Wait . . . is this ginger ale?"

Len snickers. "What'd you expect?"

"I don't know. Something bro-ish. Beer?"

"I drove here, and I didn't know how long I'd be staying." He kind of glances at me when he says this.

"You're very responsible."

"Sometimes." He musses the back of his hair, glancing down at his shoes. Then his gaze curves up slowly, a hesitant adagio of a look. "Do you want to go outside for a bit?"

Yes, I think, my heart already skipping out the door. *I'll go outside with you. I'll go anywhere when you ask me that way.* But I don't say any of this aloud. Instead, I just slip my hands into my front pockets. "What if someone sees us?"

"Well." He sets the cup down on the counter and grins. "Guess you shouldn't do anything you don't want them to see."

The front yard is empty, so Len and I sit down on the front steps. Neither of us says anything for a while. By now the blackness of evening has fully descended, and the light from the streetlamps is soft enough that I can still pick out stars in the sky. I like the chill, too, surprisingly sharp in the way of the desert night, washing over the concrete and stucco as if the sun never existed. Behind us, the muffled sounds of a party beat on. But here, on this unremarkable step, at the edge of this expanse of lawn, I discover a pocket of solace. Or, I suppose, Len and I discover it together.

He's leaning against the side of the house now; I'm not. We're close enough to touch, but we don't.

"I wanted to tell you." I stretch out my legs so that my shoes are next to his hip. "I listened to more of that band that you and Luis like."

"Yeah? Any new thoughts?"

"I'm torn, actually."

Len seems amused. "How so?"

"Well, I like them a lot. The lead singer's voice, especially, strikes a nerve, but in a good way. It's grating but soothing at the same time."

"Yeah. Like it's been soaked in the alcohol from a honey-lemon cough drop."

The specificity of the image, thrown so casually into the conversation, startles me, like he's just grabbed hold of my hand. I even pull back, as if he's really touched me, and retreat my fingers into the sleeves of my sweater. "You do have a way with words," I admit slowly, with a joking admiration. But I mean it.

He shrugs. "I've always liked his voice, too. I guess I've spent a lot of time thinking about how I'd describe it."

Something about the way he reveals this, as he plucks a jagged leaf from the rosebush by his shoulder, makes me want him to kiss me. I want to feel it dissolve everything, like all the other times, and then I want to hear him describe it, so that I can have his words, too, the memory spun into poetry that I can tuck away into a little corner of my heart.

"Anyway," I say, shaking off these thoughts, "I guess my issue is that some of their best songs are . . . well, kind of misogynistic."

"Tell me more." His eyes roam over the houses across the street, their sameness shrouded by the dark.

"Like that one song about the woman who's so awful that she makes the guy want to off himself by jumping into a lake. I think there's a line about how her beauty is the only thing she's got going for her, and she's wasting it."

Len laughs. "Okay, I see what you mean," he agrees, tossing the leaf at me. "I will say, though, the perspective does vary from track to track. Each one is like a different story. So the persona in one doesn't necessarily correlate with the views of the band in general. I hope."

"Yeah, but I guess it's not totally clear sometimes how the band feels about a particular persona. Or how they want us to feel about it." Impulsively, I reach over and tug on the frayed end of his shoelace, though not hard enough to undo it. "So I just wonder if that's a problem, you know? But I find myself drawn to the music anyway." I look at him out of the corner of my eye. "I can't stop listening to them."

Len leans forward, arms dangling over his knees. If I wanted, I could brush a lock of hair off his forehead. If he wanted, he could reach over and pull me to him. And for a second, it does seem like one of us might do something. But then he picks up a pebble and flicks it onto the lawn. "I think it's okay to like problematic art," he says. "As long as you see it for what it is." He offers a mischievous smile. "You're good at that."

Sometimes, I don't understand how I haven't completely melted into the atmosphere by now.

Then, unexpectedly, Len takes his phone out. "Here," he says, unlocking it. "I made you listen to some misogynistic songs. Let's listen to something you like."

He passes me the phone, and I cup it in both hands. "Now?" I check around us. "Out here?"

"Why not?"

The night surrounds us with its stillness, and I almost don't hear the party anymore.

"Okay." I think for a moment, and then I know exactly what to type into the search. "Here's my favorite band."

That's how Len and I end up with our heads close, foreheads bent over his phone screen, piercing the suburban calm with a girl-group punk-rock anthem blaring from a tiny mobile speaker.

"This is awesome," says Len, grinning at me.

The song I picked involves the lead singer telling off everyone who talks down to her because she's a girl. At different points in the music video, she is dressed up as the president, a witch being burned at the stake, and a suffragette. She gets to be really angry, riot grrrl–style, but she's also having a lot of fun. I'm always super pumped up after listening to it, and that's how I feel now, giddy not just from the music itself, but from the headiness of sharing it with Len.

"I like how the guitarist, bassist, *and* front woman are all girls," I explain. "They're our age, and they're all ridiculously cool. Especially the front woman. She's so hot."

"She is."

"I wish I could be as badass as her."

"She kind of reminds me of you."

I turn toward him, surprised, and that's when he catches me with the kiss. Even though I've been waiting for it all night, I'm still not prepared for how good it feels—how completely lost I can get, how much I want to be lost.

But then he pulls back abruptly.

"It's okay." I think that maybe he's stopped because of what I said earlier, but in this moment, my fingers caught in his flannel, it's hard to remember why I cared. "No one's out here."

"No."

The grim syllable makes me go still. His expression is stricken with uncertainty, and I see a flash of what he might have looked like when he was a little kid, long before he learned how not to let his face betray him like this.

"What's wrong, Len?"

He looks away. "I posted the manifesto."

This comes at me from nowhere, like a slap in the face, and my brain, normally so reliable, refuses to connect the synapses. "But I thought Natalie did," I try. "You told her to?"

"No, I posted it originally. On the *Bugle* home page." Another slap, on the other cheek.

I sit back, disbelief squeezing my throat tight. One second ago, the manifesto posting seemed so far away, and now I'm back in the *Bugle* newsroom, awash in a dread that makes me feel like throwing up all over again. This time, though, it's even worse than before, because I know it was *Len* who first ripped open my private thoughts and scattered them around for everyone to read. It was Len who violated a place I thought was safe, setting off a whole heap of humiliation and vitriol that I had to fight off without any help from him. And, worst of all, he never said a word about it. He's been as good as lying to me this entire time. Len, the boy who twirled me into falling in love, trampled on my trust before I even consented to dance.

In one instant, everything—the noise from the party, this sitting on the steps, the kissing—turns sordid.

"Why didn't you tell me?"

"I'm sorry." Len closes his eyes. "I'm sorry, Eliza. I didn't mean for any of this to happen."

For some reason, that makes me feel even more like shit.

"You could have just told me." I sound calm, but inside I'm filling up with something hot and angry.

"I meant to, especially before . . ." He sighs, and I know he means before we hooked up. Involuntarily, I think of us that afternoon, his hand bunching up my skirt, my hand traveling down his shirt, and for the first time, I feel the way I thought I'd never let any boy make me feel—cheap.

"Why'd you do it?" I force my voice not to quaver. "I tore into you in that manifesto. Why would you even want to post something like that?"

He doesn't answer right away, just tips his head back and studies the eaves. Finally, from the back of his throat, comes the response. "I guess I thought you were right. It's like what I was saying. You see things the way they are."

I don't move, waiting for him to go on. He takes a deep, long breath.

"The stuff you said in the manifesto, it was all true. I felt like you were the only one who saw through my bullshit. I felt like you really saw . . . me."

His eyes meet mine, and I feel a shiver in spite of myself. There isn't a trace of his normal glib humor, no layer of sardonic bubble wrap around his words. He seems exposed and soft in a way that I've never seen before—in a way that I think few people have. And strangely, because of that, I feel responsible for protecting him. Honored, even. I want to take his head in my arms and stroke his beautiful hair, saying, *You're right, I am the only one who sees you.*

But that's when I realize something: I'm not special. I'm just like everyone else, getting swept up in his bullshit. I'm letting him off easy.

"No." I'm plenty assertive now. "I didn't see you at all. I thought you were just some stupid jock coasting through life. But I was wrong." I get to my feet. "You're not stupid at all. You're something worse."

He stands up, too, and suddenly, I have to look up to spit out the words.

"I knew you were a coward, but I didn't know you'd let it hurt someone else."

He flinches. "That's not fair."

"Which part?"

That makes him hesitate. "I wasn't trying to hurt you."

"I don't care about what you were *trying* to do. I care about what you've *done*. And the way I see it, you couldn't do the right thing, even though it was so simple." I shake my head. "You're nothing if you can't do the right thing."

"Come on, Eliza." Len fans his fingers through his hair, pulling on the strands tightly, like he wants to rip it all out. "You know it's not always that easy. Especially with you. How would you have reacted if I'd told you?"

"I would've never talked to you again."

"Is that what you want? For us to have never been friends?"

"Yes."

"You really mean that?" His voice cracks on the last syllable, and my chest pinches. But I don't back down.

"I mean everything I say. Not like you."

Len is silent for a long time. When he does speak, something in his tone has shifted. "That's right, you've got a code."

His face is closed up, and I start to regret my lie.

"Okay, Eliza. Why don't you tell me about it?" He crosses his arms. "I'm a coward and a liar. I'm not your idea of how a person should be, and I think you knew that before tonight. So why did you come out here with me?"

I can't seem to utter a sound.

"Do your feminist friends, the ones who helped you plan the walkout, know what you're doing here?"

I turn toward the door, but Len steps in front of it.

"You're so goddamn self-righteous, Eliza. You have so many principles. But when are you gonna admit that even you can't live up to all of them? When are you gonna admit that sometimes, you don't even want to?"

I push past him, because I'm sick of everything and I need to find Winona so that we can leave this god-awful party. I try to swing open the screen door in defiance, but it gets caught in the jamb, and I end up having to fumble with the handle until it finally breaks free.

"Eliza, wait." Len's voice sounds different than it did a second ago—smaller, like I could break it into a million pieces if I wanted. But what's it matter to me? I abandon him on the porch.

33

INSIDE, THE PARTY IS GOING ON EXACTLY AS I left it. Except now the smell of sweat and spilled beer sickens me. I'm about to make a beeline for the backyard when a couple, sloppy and entangled, veer across my path. I manage to avoid colliding into them, but just barely.

"Hey, watch it!" Then I realize who the girl is. "Natalie?"

Hearing her name, Natalie turns. "Elizaaaaa!" she squeals, like she is thrilled to see me.

This is the first sign that something isn't right.

"Are you okay?" I ask. The guy she's with is someone I don't know, pale with stringy hair, and he doesn't seem to register that Natalie has become engaged in a conversation. If you could call it that.

"Yeah," Natalie answers. "Totally. For sure." She giggles as the guy leads her toward the stairs, all the while kissing her neck. "Stop it, Austin!" Then she hiccups and stumbles, landing on her knees.

There's a vibe in this situation that unsettles me, but I'm not quite sure what to do. Natalie is noticeably drunk, but is she too messed up to decide whether she wants to go upstairs with Austin? Would she be pissed off if I cockblocked this liaison? I have no idea. We're not, after all, even friends.

"So, uh, how do you know Austin?" I try to buy some extra time and information.

Natalie's face knits into a frown. "What?" she says, but her eyes are on the floor.

I bend over to read her expression. "Natalie . . . ?" I say, growing alarmed.

A plastic trash bin, smooth and rounded like an eggshell, appears between us, just in time for her to puke into it.

I turn around to see who's holding the container, and it's Len. "I've been to enough baseball parties to recognize that look," he says soberly.

Austin, who is pretty drunk himself, is still hovering. "I think she's done for the night, buddy," I snap at him, kneeling down next to her, and he finally scuttles away.

Natalie coughs, apparently nearing the end of her supply of vomit.

"She looks like shit," I observe, pushing the bin a bit closer.

"She'll feel better after," says Len.

I cringe a little as Natalie wipes her mouth with her sleeve. She keels over the trash can, her white high-tops splayed in opposite directions, and as she continues to empty whatever's left of her sorry dinner—if that was her dinner—into the bin, she seems very small. I search around for her friends. She must have come here with other people, right? Where the hell are they? I don't know how to take care of a drunk person. Especially when I can't stand them.

"Someone should probably take her home." I gingerly brush back the strands of hair that have fallen past her chin. But I don't have Kim's car here, and everyone else in the room seems too wasted to entrust with the task.

Well, except one person.

"I'll drive her," says Len. "But you have to come with me, because I'm not showing up at her house alone. Not when she's like that."

He holds my gaze when I glance up at him, and it's a plea and a challenge at the same time. I want to refuse, just get up and walk away, leaving him to deal with Natalie on his own. After all, they seem to know each other well enough.

But then I reconsider Natalie, green over her bin of sick.

"Where do you live?" I ask her.

Despite her compromised state, she manages to recite her address, which I type into my phone.

"It's only a five-minute drive," I tell Len.

"I can drop you off after," he says.

I try to find Winona, but I don't see her anywhere, and Natalie is about to fold herself into a wobbly sleep over Len's arms.

"No, it's okay," I say, because I don't want to leave without Winona. "Just bring me back here, I guess."

I send a quick text to Winona.

Taking Natalie home. Long story. Brb.

In the back seat, Natalie has the window rolled down, so the night air invites itself in. She dangles her arm outside and sighs.

"Where are we going?" she asks.

"We're taking you home," I say from the front passenger seat.

"Is Len driving?"

"Yes."

Natalie's voice trails into a whisper. "He's so nice."

I don't look at Len. "Mm-hmm."

"I totally had a crush on him."

"Mm-hmm."

"He doesn't like me, though. I mean, not like that."

In spite of myself, this revelation intrigues me. "How do you know?"

"He told me," says Natalie, and once again, she sighs.

I glance over at Len, who stares straight ahead.

Much to my relief, the lights are still on at Natalie's house, which turns out to be yet another masterpiece of Palermo architecture. Len and I walk along familiar stone steps to the front door with Natalie propped up between us. "Do you have your keys?" I ask.

Natalie starts fumbling in her little zippered pouch of a purse, but then the door opens. Her moms appear, one straightening her glasses and the other wrapping a bathrobe around her waist. Both look highly concerned.

"Don't worry," Natalie announces, blinking through her daze. "I'm okay."

The whole ride back, Len and I don't talk. But when he pulls up to the curb in front of Nate's house, he turns off the ignition. "Eliza—"

Immediately, I reach for the door, but it's locked.

"I have to go," I say, yanking on the handle.

"Can we talk?"

"No."

Sighing, Len unlocks the car, and I stumble out. To my surprise, I see Winona standing on the front steps. Thank goodness. I start to run over to her, but I slow down as it becomes obvious that she's not so happy to see me.

"What the hell, Eliza?" Face puckering, she fixates on something over my shoulder.

I turn around to see Len getting out of his car.

"What's the matter?" I say. "I had to help Natalie get home, I texted you—"

"My phone was dead. But Esther showed me."

I'm really confused now. "Esther?"

Winona holds up a phone in a giant koala bear–shaped case.

"Oh my God," I say, grabbing it from her.

Someone has posted a photo of Len and me, taken barely an hour ago. We're sitting on these very steps, clearly making out.

Below, the comments are already starting to pile up:

@fiverjlg: Omg . . . is that @elizquan and @lendimartile?

@cooliobeans23: Guess she'll do anything to be editor in chief 😏

@xlive328: All hail @lendimartile, getting some for the patriarchy tonight!!

"Oh my God," I say again. I can't form any other words.

Len comes up behind me. "What's wrong?" He takes the phone from me before I drop it, and then he too sees the incriminating image. "Holy shit," he says. "How—"

Just then, Serena bursts unevenly through the door, with Dylan right behind her.

"Eliza, we talked about this," she scolds. "You really couldn't keep it in your pants?"

Winona looks from Serena to me, a realization dawning on her. "*She* knew?" she says, the disbelief stoking her voice up an octave. "You told *her*?"

"No—" I try to explain, but everything is muddled in my mind, as if I'm the one who's been drinking all night, not everyone else. "No, I'm sorry—"

Winona turns around and storms back into the house, pushing past Serena and Dylan.

"Winona!" I call out, but she doesn't stop.

"See?" Serena says to me. She sounds almost sorry for me. "This is only the beginning."

I feel Len about to put his hand on my shoulder, but I jerk away.

"Don't touch me," I say, and I run off down the street.

34

I JOG ALL THE WAY TO WINONA'S HOUSE AND GET in Kim's car. I'm sweating, but the night air is chilly, so my body has no idea how to react. Neither does my mind. Closing the door, I bury my face in my hands.

What is happening to me?

Even though I'm afraid to, I check my phone. The comments on the post are still popping off, and I have to force myself to stop scrolling. I've also got texts from Len, which I ignore, and a text from Kim, warning me that I'd better be on my way home because she can't guarantee that she can keep covering for me much longer.

I start the car and begin driving, because it seems like a logical immediate first step. I make it home in one piece, and, much to my relief, the apartment is quiet when I unlock the door.

Kim swivels around at her desk. "Mom and Dad went to bed," she says in a low voice. Then she stares at me. "What happened to you?"

I step out of my shoes like a zombie.

"I don't want to talk about it." I blow past her before she can say anything else.

After brushing my teeth, I scrub my face extra hard with a washcloth until my skin is raw. When I undo my braids, my hair is super wavy, and I turn away from the mirror in disgust.

In our room, I climb into bed in the dark, but then my hip hits something heavy. I reach down to feel for it, and then I remember it's *Life: A User's Manual*. What a ridiculously misleading title. As fucking misleading as Len himself. The book is certainly the most useless manual I've ever read. All those hours I spent parsing its dense descriptions and meandering anecdotes—I thought all of it would somehow illuminate something profound about Len. Or, at the very least, about life. Instead, over 350 pages in, I'm as confused and frustrated as ever. The whole thing has felt like an exercise in futility matched only by the central character's quest itself, and I can't believe I once thought it was so goddamn interesting.

I throw the book over the side of my bed and roll toward the wall, curling up under the covers. I feel like shit. Being a feminist was supposed to mean being part of a sisterhood. But I've ruined all of that, including the one friendship that's been there for me since before I even knew what feminism was.

And for what?

A boy.

Every time I think about him, I get angry. I'm still not over the fact that he was the one who posted the manifesto. It was him the whole time. The whole time! Remembering how oblivious I was makes me feel sick. I can't believe I kissed that jackass. I can't believe I *liked* him.

I feel my eyes sting, and that's when I realize the biggest betrayal of all: I still like him. Goddamn. And in typical jackass fashion, he threw it in my face, too: *So why did you come out here with me?*

I try to shut out his words and go to sleep, but instead I crush my face into my pillow and let the tears finally well up.

35

WHEN I WALK INTO ZERO PERIOD ON MONDAY,
Tim O'Callahan stands up to do a slow clap. "Way to go,
Eliza," he says. "Way to show us what feminism is all about!"

Turning bright red, I open my mouth to snap at him, but
James beats me to it. "Lay off, O'Callahan," he says. Len
sits upright in his corner, posture tightening, but Tim just
smirks.

I avoid all other eye contact as I make my way to my seat,
willing the minutes to evaporate so that I can make a run for
it. As soon as I lay my backpack down, however, Aarav has a
question.

"So," he says. "Is it true you guys did it in his car?"

Everyone around us goes silent, and Natalie and Olivia
swap stricken glances. Len, now looking really pissed, slides
off the desk like he's coming over to punch Aarav in the face.

But I save him the trouble.

"When's the last time *you* did it, Aarav?" I say.

Aarav is taken aback. "Wh—"

"Oh, you don't want to talk about it? That's weird. It's almost as if it isn't any of my business." I give the rest of the room a hard stare, and no one makes another peep. "Can I have everybody's drafts, please?"

The day gets progressively worse. In PE, I jog up to Winona during the Monday mile, but then she starts sprinting down the track and I can't keep up. Yesterday, when I went over to her house, hoping that she'd give me a chance to apologize, Doug answered the door.

"Sorry, Eliza," he said. "Winona told me to say that she doesn't need your help anymore." When he saw my face, he offered, "Do you want to stay to play Xbox with Sai and me?"

"*No*, Doug, we're still doing the scene!" I heard Winona shout from inside.

"Sorry," Doug said again, shrugging.

"Can you tell her I'm sorry, too?" I said, and Doug nodded. Then I went home, and Winona hasn't replied to a single text or call since.

Now, as I plod across the quad, I feel people's eyes on me, everyone tittering derisively among themselves, no doubt rehashing all the awful things they've already said online:

There goes that girl, the hypocrite. The one who made a big fuss over the fact that a boy was elected to be editor in chief, and then went and hooked up with him. Bet it was about him this whole time—bet she never cared about feminism at all. Didn't we call it? How could she have lied to her friends like

*that? After all the trouble they went through for her. Girls like
her give feminists a bad name. What an attention whore. She's
totally the type to sleep her way to the top.*

Everyone hates me. Those who dismissed my feminism are
elated, those who feel I've betrayed the movement are indignant, but all are finally in agreement on this one point: I am
the worst.

Underneath it all is a hidden current of something ugly,
which I discover is not so hidden when I see it scrawled across
my locker, below a scratched-out *FEMINAZI*:

SLUT!!!!!

I'm thinking about how bad it would be if I just left it there
for the rest of the year when Natalie comes up to me.

"Hey, Eliza," she says.

"What." I don't look at her.

"I just wanted to say thanks for helping me the other night."

"Oh."

"Len said it was mostly you. He said you asked him to drive
me home."

Len—telling the truth, but not quite, as usual.

"It wasn't a big deal."

Natalie eyes the new vandalism on my locker door. "Sorry
this is all happening to you. And for everything else, too."

"It's okay."

"For the record, I don't think you're a slut."

She smiles at me, and I smile back.

"Thanks," I say.

It's strange. This whole time, I assumed Natalie was the one who'd originally posted the manifesto, and I was convinced she was a bitch, through and through. Now, though, I'm not sure she deserved that, exactly. Maybe none of us ever really do.

Then it's fifth period, which I've been dreading.

As class starts, Winona's attention is absorbed by a conversation with Eddie Miller, who sits in front of her. She can't stand him, so if she'd rather talk to him instead of me, then things are *really* bad.

Serena, too, can't bear to acknowledge me. Tasked with passing out graded papers, she comes swishing down the aisle, handing them out as she goes. When she gets to mine, she sets it down on my desk primly. She doesn't need to say anything— the whole school already knows that she's no longer associating with me. And I don't blame her. If you're hoping to be the next female school president, I'm now a political liability.

As for Len, he's given up talking to me. He tried to catch me this morning, on my way out of the *Bugle*, but I brushed right past him, like he was a speck of dust in my universe.

Ryan and I, though, are apparently still on speaking terms: "So, Eliza, does this mean you're not a feminist anymore?"

"Fuck off, Ryan."

At this point, I'd really like to simply fade into the background and never have anyone notice anything I ever do again. Would it be so bad to be insignificant? Would it be so egregious to stand for nothing? I don't think so. Not anymore.

Unfortunately, today is when our *Macbeth* group is supposed to perform our scenes, and thanks to our train wreck of a cast, the class seems much more interested than usual. When Ms. Boskovic calls us up to the front of the room, everyone sits up a bit straighter, straining to avoid missing the debacle. They're disappointed when Len and I don't share a scene—Banquo and Lady Macbeth don't cross paths until later in the play—but they do get their taste of blood when Serena and I perform the grisly exchange between Macbeth and his wife after Duncan is killed.

Serena staggers across the room as she recites her lines, wearing a baseball cap backward because I failed, in the fiasco of this weekend, to come up with an alternative costume idea. Her Bro Macbeth is full of remorse, hands curled in guilty claws that she holds away from her body like they're someone else's—like she can't understand how they came to be hers. Watching her, you'd think Macbeth was a real stand-up guy who just happened to make the bad decision of listening to his wife.

Certainly, being played by me (nonsensically outfitted in my own baseball cap) doesn't score Lady Macbeth any points with this audience. It also doesn't help that, over the course of the scene, she (1) plants weapons at the scene of the crime because Macbeth can't bring himself to do it, (2) tells Macbeth that he's a sissy for having second thoughts, and (3) acts like washing their hands will make all their guilt disappear. "A little water clears us of this deed," she tells him, like a true psychopath. "How easy it is, then!"

In contrast, Macbeth ends the scene by wishing he hadn't killed Duncan. "I'll go no more. I am afraid to think what I have done. Look on't again I dare not."

As we take our bows, Ms. Boskovic claps vigorously and gushes, "The significance of your headgear was, I confess, slightly lost on me, but an inspired interpretation nonetheless!" Then she opens up the floor for a class discussion.

Sarah Pak raises her hand. "I think this scene contributes to the idea that Lady Macbeth is the true villain in the play," she says. "She seems really cold-blooded even while Macbeth is starting to feel bad."

The class murmurs, and a lot of heads nod.

"Interesting argument, Sarah," says Ms. Boskovic. "Other thoughts?"

But there aren't any. Instead, everyone decides to keep piling on Lady Macbeth.

"All she cares about is power," says Greg Landau. "She wants Macbeth to become king so badly that she pushes him to murder."

"Yeah, at least he questions whether it's worth it," says Veronica Patel. "He might have redeemed himself, but Lady Macbeth keeps egging him on."

More nods. Yes, everyone agrees, Lady Macbeth is a real pill.

Then Serena raises her hand. "Yes, Serena?" says Ms. Boskovic.

"I think *Macbeth* is an extremely misogynistic play," she declares. A buzz ripples across the room at this unexpected assertion. It's a big claim.

"How so?" says Ms. Boskovic.

"All the reasons everyone's been saying," says Serena. "Lady Macbeth is the main female character, but she's super evil. Which isn't cool because she also bucks gender norms by being strong and ambitious. She's totally being punished for behaving in masculine ways."

The class seems to consider this. Abby Chan raises her hand. "Should we really be reading something that portrays women so negatively?"

Now everyone is truly intrigued—was Shakespeare, that guy we've had to read in English class every year, actually a misogynist?

A few desks over, I see Winona roll her eyes to herself. For some reason, that emboldens me.

"I don't know if I agree." I speak out loud without raising my hand, and everyone turns to look at me. "I think it's too simplistic to say the play is misogynistic just because Lady Macbeth is evil."

"Please, elaborate," says Ms. Boskovic.

"Ambition is dangerous in Macbeth, too," I say. "We shouldn't be giving him a free pass. He's the one who actually commits the murders." My thoughts come together with increasing clarity as I forge ahead. "You could also argue that Lady Macbeth's ambition isn't really about her. It's about *him*. She wants him to be king, because that's what she should want, as a supportive wife. Plus, she does seem to feel guilty later, when she goes mad—"

"Spoilers!" Ryan exclaims.

"My point is," I continue, ignoring him, "I don't know if the play is necessarily claiming that Lady Macbeth is worse than Macbeth." I assess each corner of the room. "Maybe the fact that we see it that way says something about *us*."

The bell rings then, and Ms. Boskovic ends the discussion. "Let's continue this tomorrow, my dears!"

Across the room, Serena looks thoughtful.

36

SPARRING OVER *MACBETH* WITH SERENA Hwangbo wasn't the smartest thing I could have done for myself socially, given the circumstances—but then, what difference does it really make? Things are already pretty low. With each passing hour, the story of what Len and I supposedly did at Nate Gordon's party has gotten increasingly embellished, to the point where you might think I actually had a good time that night.

I used to believe that people didn't like me, and that it was because they thought I was a bitch. And, sometimes, maybe I was even proud of it. That's why I never really thought twice about labeling someone else that way either. Because if being a "bitch" meant I could do as I wanted without caring what I got called, well, I saw a power in that. But lately, I've wondered what kind of power that really was, if the word can still carry so much hate—the same kind, it seems, that gives *slut* its heavy stain, no matter who's saying it.

I know about that hate very well now, of course. Every-body's made sure of it.

After school, I trudge over to the *Bugle* newsroom and check if anyone's there. Luckily, I see only James, so I decide it's safe to stay awhile.

"How are you holding up?" James pauses at the whiteboard as I drag my feet past him.

"Not great."

"How are things with Winona?"

"Bad."

"She still won't let you apologize?"

I sit down, half sprawled, so that my chin rests on the desk. "No."

James goes back to erasing. "What about Len?"

I let my head loll to the side and don't answer.

"You won't let him apologize either?"

I spring up suddenly. "Did he talk to you about it?"

James turns around. "Len? No. But it's pretty obvious from the way he looks at you."

Oh my God. I press my nose and forehead into the top of the desk so that James can't see how red I've gone. I miss how much simpler things used to be, when James and I didn't dis-cuss my love life. When Len was just some jock I didn't care to know. When I didn't expect anything from him, and he didn't want anything from me.

But it's confusing, because even though the current state of affairs is about as pathetic as it can get, I'm not entirely sure I'd go back. I think of what Len asked me at the party.

Is that what you want? For us to have never been friends?

"It was a piece-of-shit thing he did, posting the manifesto," I say into the lacquered wood.

"It was."

"He told me he was going to resign."

James gives me a sympathetic shrug. "He hasn't said anything to me yet."

Figures. He probably lied about that, too.

I reach into my bag and pull out a draft from Olivia. It's a story on how few of the school library collection's "classics" are by female authors (and, especially, female authors of color). She actually pitched it herself, last week. It was the kind of data-driven story I would've liked to have written myself, if everything weren't such a disaster.

"I was inspired, you know, by all the feminist stuff you've been doing," Olivia said. "It made the topic seem, like, timely."

I could have hugged her, if I were the type of person who hugged.

I'm halfway through writing a long comment in the margin when I hear the door open.

"Uh, Eliza," James says, "someone's here to see you." My stomach drops because I think it's Len, but it's actually an even more unlikely visitor: Serena. She's got my old gray sweater folded over her arm.

"Hey," she says.

I'm too surprised to reply with anything except "Hey."

"I saw this in the girls' locker room lost and found," says Serena, walking over. "When I was looking for one of my earrings." She holds the sweater out to me. "I thought you might want it back."

As I reach out to take it, she adds, as if she can't help herself: "Even though it's really not a good look for you. No offense. I just thought I should let you know, as a friend."

"Okay, Serena." I laugh in spite of myself, because she is totally being serious.

"I mean," she says, "if we are friends?"

I finger my sweater, which smells musty from sitting among lonely socks and misplaced textbooks and who knows what else. It feels like a long time ago that I wore this every day.

"Depends," I say. "Are you here to say 'I told you so'?"

Serena gives me a dimmed version of her megawatt smile. "No, of course not." Then her expression fades altogether. "You know, all the stuff people are saying, it'll pass."

"Maybe." I shrug, like it's no big deal. "I'll be fine."

Serena nods. "I know, but I'm sorry I haven't been a better friend."

This catches me off guard. The last thing I expected from all this was an apology from Serena Hwangbo.

"It's okay." I fold and unfold the arms of my sweater. "I'm sorry I hooked up with the face of the patriarchy."

Now Serena laughs. "Is he going to resign, at least?"

"I don't know," I say. "He said he would, but he hasn't. I don't know how many more hand jobs it's gonna take."

Serena seems shocked for a second before a grin splits her face. "Oh my God, Eliza," she says, cracking up. "You *are* the worst."

And even though things still suck, it feels nice to know that Serena, at least, doesn't.

37

DAD GETS A JOB AT A QUICK-SERVICE CHINESE restaurant called Golden Chopsticks. It's different from his old work. Now he'll make orange chicken and lo mein instead of steamed lobster and fish-belly soup. The customers are younger, more white and Hispanic than Chinese and Vietnamese, and they place a lot of orders online for delivery and takeout. Dad says it seems like the hardest part will be keeping track of everything that comes in through the computer, because it's all in English.

I've never been to Golden Chopsticks, so I look it up. The Yelp reviews are mediocre, and I wonder whether they'll change once Dad has been working there for a while. I hope so. I use Yelp all the time, but it feels kind of funny to think about Dad getting reviewed on there.

On Tuesday night, when Mom is in the kitchen, mincing garlic with the big butcher's cleaver, I walk up and sit on one of the bar stools. She hasn't switched on the range hood yet, so the only sound is the rice cooker lid rattling from the bubbling steam. Since Dad started at Golden Chopsticks yesterday, Mom has begun cooking alone again. It dawns on me that when Mom complains that Dad isn't home enough to spend time with Kim and me, it's about her, too.

"Hey, Mom," I say. "Do you need help?"

Mom looks over at me, and then resumes mincing. "You're done with your homework?"

"No," I say.

"Go work on it. I'm okay."

"I'm just taking a break."

"School is hard now, but you'll reap the benefits later. *Sīn fú hauh tìhm.*" That's one of Mom's favorite sayings. First bitter, then sweet.

"Yeah, I know."

"You study hard, you won't have to be a laborer like your Mom and Dad. You can be the *lóuh báan.*" The boss.

"You think I should own a business when I grow up?" I'm semi-joking, because I already know what she's going to say.

"Are you the kind of person who knows how to do business? If so, then yes, you can make a lot of money that way." She evaluates me for a moment. "But I don't think you can. You're too honest. You're just like your dad."

Well, maybe if I'd been a little *more* honest, I wouldn't be in so much trouble.

"What about you?"

"It requires too much courage. I don't have it in me."

Mom moves on to washing the spinach, expertly agitating the submerged leaves before transferring them to a pink plastic colander. Whenever I've tried to help with this before, Mom has always critiqued my limp technique.

"Do you think Dad likes his new job?"

"What is there to like? Work is work." Mom shakes her head. "And your dad, for whatever reason, is stuck in this profession. They say a man's worst fear is picking the wrong career; a woman's worst fear is picking the wrong man."

I wrinkle my nose at this. "That's not true anymore."

"Still true. You marry the wrong person, it's a lifetime of suffering."

"But women can have careers now, too. They don't have to be dependent on men."

"Of course a woman should work, even if it's just part-time. What am I always telling you? If you make your own money, then you get to have a say in the family. You rely only on your husband's money, one day he'll throw it in your face."

I decide not to mention that a woman might not get married at all, because that could earn me a spin-off lecture.

"I just mean, now it's possible for a woman to be the one who makes more money."

"It's unlikely."

"I'm saying it's possible."

"Such a woman must be very fearless and cunning. It's not easy to do."

"Maybe I'll try."

"No."

I'm taken aback by her reaction. "Why not? You're always saying I'm so smart."

"It's not about how smart you are." Mom pours some vegetable oil into the wok. "As a woman, you should pick a career that is not too demanding. You'll see, having children and taking care of the family is hard work. It's too much to do both."

"Maybe if I'm the breadwinner, my husband will take care of the family."

"No, a woman is naturally more caring. You see your dad? He's a man, so his job is to make money to support you. He loves you, but I'm the one who takes care of you."

I remember her words from the argument that night. *Why do I have to do everything in this family?*

"I don't think things have to be like that," I say.

"But they are. You said yourself women get paid less than men do for the same work, right? Seems logical to have the husband be the one who makes more money."

I'm surprised she's listened to anything I've told her. "Yeah, but I also said I want to change that."

"It might be a long time, Eliza." Mom sounds tired. "To be human is hard enough. Don't make it harder for yourself." She reaches up to turn on the range hood, then slides the garlic into the wok, and the conversation evaporates into the sizzle.

In the living room, where Kim is working at her desk, I

climb onto the couch and lean an elbow on the armrest. "Do you think Mom is a feminist?"

Kim's pencil hovers over her problem set. "Um, no."

"It's weird, because sometimes it seems like she is, and sometimes it seems like she isn't."

"Isn't that how it is with most people?"

I guess Kim knew better than me all along.

"What do you think she would have done with her life if she hadn't had us?"

"And if there hadn't been the whole refugee situation?"

"Yeah."

"I don't know. She said once that she wanted to be an electrical engineer."

I had no idea about this. From what I've heard, it's always seemed like Mom didn't have any interests as a kid besides getting good grades, "because that's the only thing that matters."

"I wonder if she regrets it." I rest my chin in my hands. "Not getting to do that."

"Probably." Kim rubs her eye under her glasses, knocking them askew on her nose. She only wears glasses at night, even though she would look cool with them on normally, too.

I glance over at Mom stir-frying the spinach, tossing the wok every so often to give its contents a good shake.

"Sometimes I think that maybe I should major in engineering," Kim says. "You know, because she didn't get a chance to."

"You still could, couldn't you?"

Kim turns back to the spread of notes in front of her. "No, I'm not smart enough."

She states this without emotion, as if it were simply a fact of life, and I stare at her. What must it be like to write yourself off like that? Where did she even get that idea?

But I know. I've heard it said before a million times—by herself, by Mom, by everyone we know. Including me. Kim is the pretty one. I am the smart one.

It occurs to me that, lately, Kim has been studying a lot more than usual. Stacked on her desk is a pile of textbooks, including one for chemistry and another for calculus. How much harder would it really be, if she actually tried to become an engineer? If she just put in the effort?

"Of course you're smart enough."

Kim angles her head sideways. "Are things going well again with the boy or something?" she teases.

I blush. She doesn't know how wrong she is. "I mean it, Kim."

She picks out a section of her hair and smooths out the ends. "I don't really care that much, Eliza," she says. "I'm fine with biology. I'm just trying to get into pharmacy school."

"But electrical engineering could be so much cooler, especially because it's one of the fields where women are most underrepresented. If you were interested—"

"I'm not." Kim cuts me off, but not unkindly.

"Time to eat!" Mom calls out, scraping the spinach into a metal platter.

"I'm not like you, Eliza," says Kim, as I follow her to the kitchen. "I don't need everything in my life to mean something big." She opens the drawer to pull out three sets of chopsticks.

But what if it could, I think.

38

AT LUNCH THE NEXT DAY, SERENA SENDS ME A text welcoming me back to her table, but I beg off. As much as I appreciate a Hwangbo endorsement, I think it would probably be wise for me to continue lying low for a bit. So I retreat instead to a spot behind the art studio. It's quiet back here, and best of all, no one can watch me as I sit alone on the asphalt and unwrap my sandwich.

I peer into it and sigh. Too much turkey, as usual.

The door opens, and I instinctively crouch down, despite the fact that I'm pretty well hidden on the other side of the building.

"I heard she totally blew him at Nate Gordon's party," says a boy's voice. "On the front *steps*."

They're talking about me. I should just crawl under the building and lie among the spiders like a corpse.

"Gross, Jared!" squeals a girl.

"What, that's what everyone's saying!" Of course they are.

"I really didn't think Eliza was that kind of girl," says another voice, a boy's. "She seems way too uptight."

Jared cracks up. "Well, you know what they say . . ."

I give them both the finger even though they can't see me.

"I don't care what she does with him." Another girl has spoken up. "It's whatever. My thing is, like, why drag the rest of us into the drama? I wanted to have a real conversation about sexism on campus." I hear more footsteps coming down the ramp, and then the girl adds, "What do you think, Winona?"

I almost drop my sandwich.

"You mean about Eliza?" Winona's response is careful, the words stretched out slightly, the way they get when she's still formulating the best way to really lay into someone.

"Didn't you and Serena help her plan the whole thing? That must have sucked when she threw you all over for Len."

Another pause, but then, with a readiness that cuffs me hard in the collarbone: "Yeah, I thought she was better than that."

A shower of self-reproach descends over me, the shame pelting me in little savage shards. I've heard a lot of things said about me since that night of the party, but this one, by far, hurts the most.

"Eliza was supposed to take a stand against sexism, and she clearly failed," Winona continues, and I hang my head, wondering if I'll ever stop feeling like a complete shithead about this.

But then, with no warning, she adds, "Because none of you have noticed how everyone's reaction to this entire situation has still been one hundred percent sexist."

Winona's boots squeak down the ramp as she brushes past the others, leaving us all in silence with our thoughts.

That afternoon, after much deliberation, I decide to make one more attempt to apologize to Winona, even though I'm pretty sure she still won't want to talk to me. But I have to try, I tell myself as I clump along the sidewalk on Palermo Avenue. It's the least I can do.

"You said this was the last time!" Up ahead, Doug is standing in the middle of the street, arms crossed.

"I said it's the last time *if* we get it right!" Winona shouts from the curb. "That was the worst acting I've ever seen in my life. What emotion was that even supposed to be?"

Sai, half lying in the grass, sees me first. "Hey, look, it's Eliza."

They all notice me then, and Doug waves ecstatically. "Eliza! Come here and tell my sister she's gone nuts."

Winona grabs Doug's arm with one hand and her camera with the other, stalking away in the opposite direction. "Good luck getting Eliza to tell me anything. She's been getting *awfully* busy with other interests."

"Winona, wait." I jog closer, but she keeps walking, pulling a squirming Doug along. I pick up the boom mic from the grass and fall into step behind them, alongside Sai. "Winona, I'm sorry."

She doesn't turn around. "If you're not part of this

production, please leave."

I speed up so that I can cut directly into her path. "I *am* part of this production." I walk backward, thinking fast. "I'm the producer."

Winona shoots me a sour glare. "No, you're fired."

"Well, technically, firing people is my job."

"Fire yourself, then."

"Okay, if that's what you really want, I will. But it's also my job to make sure this film stays on schedule, and I seem to remember that the National Young Filmmakers Festival deadline is tonight?"

We're in front of the Wilsons' house now, and Winona, sullen, releases Doug from her grip.

"So . . ." I press forth, even though it's risky. "I guess I'm just wondering if we need to reshoot this scene?"

"For the eighth time," mutters Doug, nursing his forearm.

Winona's studying the grass, and I hold my breath, waiting for a response I'm not sure I'm ready to hear.

At last, she climbs the flat stone steps leading up to her front door. "Why don't you see for yourself."

Upstairs, I settle in front of Winona's computer to view the current cut of the film. It starts with an unassuming Winona as the older sister of Doug's character, walking past the two boys playing their hand-slap game. Then the story shifts to just Doug and Sai, who are shown running down the Palermo sidewalk, full of spirit and laughter. They burst into the 7-Eleven and make a mess of the candy section before my voice interrupts them, accusing Doug of shoplifting. Watching the boys' faces fill the camera, I can see how effectively Winona has captured a sense of unease and claustrophobia.

"This is excellent," I say, turning to Winona. But she only frowns, jotting something down in her notebook.

Now Doug and Sai are talking as they loiter along Palermo Avenue. Doug is upset by the accusation, but Sai doesn't understand. The gulf between them widens, and they quarrel. Then Doug pushes Sai, Sai pushes back, and Doug gets knocked to the grass.

But then Doug springs up again and hoofs it down the street. Sai scrambles after him, feet pounding on the sidewalk until he stumbles and falls. Doug, still running, turns his head just in time to see the tumble, and he gradually slows down. There's a moment of silence as he considers what to do. Then a car approaches—we hear its roar before we see its dazzling chrome—and it's Winona behind the wheel of her dad's vintage convertible, rocking a pair of shades. She rolls down her window and surveys the situation. *Get in,* she seems to suggest to Doug, and he obeys. Then she cruises over to Sai and offers him a ride, too. After he climbs into the back seat, Winona drives them all off into the sunset.

After it's over, I'm grinning ear to ear. I've seen a lot of Winona Wilson films, and this is the best one yet. "That was a masterpiece," I rave, swiveling around to face Winona. "Like, I really—" But I pause when I notice she isn't listening. "What are you doing?"

Winona is still scribbling notes, so wildly I can't even read them. "I think that Palermo Avenue scene needs something more," she says, more to the page than me. "Or maybe less?"

I wrestle the notebook away from her so that she'll stop writing. "Hey, what's up with you?"

"Nothing," she retorts, lunging to retrieve her notes. "I just need this to be really great. A few more changes and—"

"But you could keep making changes forever," I point out. "You'll never be done at this rate. How are you going to submit it?"

"Well, maybe I won't!"

The catch in her voice makes me sit back and release her notebook, which she snatches to her chest.

"You can't *not* submit it," I say. "You won't even have a shot if you don't enter."

"Yeah, but then I can't be rejected, either." Winona's so quiet when she says this, I almost don't even hear her. But understanding dawns on me, and I finally put all the pieces together. *This* is why she rewrote so obsessively. *This* is why she pushed to reshoot so many times. Because if something isn't finished, it can never really be judged. You'll never have to reckon with the fact that maybe it—and you—didn't live up to your expectations.

And boy, do I know what it's like to not live up to your own expectations.

"This is the real deal, Eliza," Winona says. "And I guess . . . especially because I've now literally put myself into the film, I don't want to know that it's not good enough. I don't want to know that *I'm* not good enough."

Smokey, perhaps sensing an opportunity in the way that only dogs can, trots into the room and rests her head on my lap, wispy brows twitching as she regards Winona, then me. "Maybe the thing about the real deal is that it doesn't work that way," I venture, petting Smokey's head. "Maybe it's not that you're either good enough or you're not. Maybe it's just about the process."

Winona reaches over and scratches Smokey's back, which precipitates some serious tail wagging. "Maybe."

"Anyway," I remind her, "you've said yourself that the festival panelists might be a biased authority. If they don't get your work, maybe it's on them."

"Yeah," Winona replies glumly, "but at the end of the day, they're still the authority." Her notebook slips from her lap, but she doesn't pick it up. "Like, it still means something to win an Oscar or make it into the Criterion Collection. I still want the recognition. And I feel like if my work isn't absolutely perfect, what chance do I even have?"

"Winona," I cut in. "Does that not sound like something your dad would say? It's not your job to be perfect!"

"I know," Winona groans. "I know."

"And yes, you might get rejected, maybe for unjust reasons, but the best thing you can do right this moment is shoot your shot. So shoot it, because your film is really good. Definitely good enough to submit." Winona starts to brush this off, but I don't let her. "I'm serious. I'm sorry I've been useless lately, but I swear I'd tell you if there was anything I thought you actually needed to change. You know I would."

Winona stretches out on the floor. "That's true," she says slowly. "But let's be real, your judgment has been a little questionable these days."

The observation, though not inaccurate, still makes my insides fold into a heap.

"I'm sorry about the Len situation, too," I say, rueful. "Really."

Winona has stopped petting Smokey, so now they're both looking at me with the same *What gives?* expression. "What did you think was going to happen when word got out?"

"To be honest, there wasn't very much thinking involved."

A snort escapes through her nose, and that's when I finally lay out the whole story for her. The kiss. The hookup. The way Serena found out. The revelation about the manifesto. "And, well," I say. "You know the rest."

"That's some shitshow, Eliza."

"I know. I should've just told you everything earlier."

"Why didn't you?" Winona's forehead wrinkles, but her question seems more hurt than angry.

The answer rises up from deep inside my chest, and as much as I want to ignore it, I can't. "I was afraid," I admit. The words come out feeling cramped and inadequate, but they're the truth. All my bravado about not fearing anything was, in the end, unjustified. "I was worried that you, more than anyone else, would think I'd become a disappointment, that I'd lost sight of what was really important. And that you'd be right."

Winona strokes the top of Smokey's snout. "I probably *would* have been hard on you," she agrees. "Like I was hard on Serena." Sighing, she ponders the carpet for a long time. "Like I am on myself."

"Well, unlike you or Serena, I did kind of ruin the whole feminism thing."

"No, you didn't." Winona leans back onto her elbows, eyeing me. "But you also didn't exactly make it easy for anyone to stick up for you."

A fresh wave of exhaustion hits me then, and I feel ready to buckle underneath it all—the backlash of the past few days, the bad decisions I made, and everything that came before. "Yeah," I say wearily. "Sometimes I think I shouldn't have bothered with any of it."

"You don't really believe that," Winona says. "And neither do I." Her gaze becomes stern, and I shut my eyes, preparing for more censure. "However, the next time you decide to make the patriarchy into your boy toy, I would appreciate being informed before Serena Hwangbo. I don't think that's too much to ask of your best friend."

I laugh, almost wilting with relief. "Noted."

"Especially if said boy is gonna come around asking me where you are."

"What?" My cheeks redden.

"Don't worry, I wasn't that nice to him."

"But what did he even want?"

At this, Smokey drops her head dismissively to the floor, and Winona's eyebrow flies up. "What do you think?"

Later that night, while I'm sprawled across my bed, trying to memorize some Spanish vocabulary words, Winona texts me to say that *Driveways* has officially been submitted for consideration for this year's National Young Filmmakers Festival. I respond right away with **!!!!!!!**, and for the next few minutes, we exchange basically nothing but a series of celebratory emojis.

Then my phone buzzes with another type of notification. Someone, it seems, has just commented on Natalie's original Insta post, which still happens occasionally. I swipe through the screenshots like a masochist, filling with fresh anger and humiliation as I reread my own words.

But then I get to the last part, the two paragraphs that I didn't actually write.

> *I thought my esteemed colleagues at the* Bugle *were better than this. They are not. They never have been. In the three decades that this paper has been in existence, only seven of the editors in chief have been female. That's 19 percent. That's lower than the percentage of women currently in Congress. We're talking about Congress, people.*

Today, the Bugle *could have done a small part to bend the arc of the moral universe. Instead, it has elected yet another male to do a job that, on just about every criterion, should have gone to a far more deserving female. I'm disappointed, I'm indignant, and I'm insulted—but maybe I'm not surprised.*

That's when I realize something. If Len was the one who posted the manifesto, then . . . he must have written that ending.

What could it mean? Was he just full of shit? Like, was it supposed to be a parody of something that I would have written?

Or did he really mean it?

I imagine him standing there in the newsroom, counting the portraits of female editors in chief on the wall, or sitting in his stupid Princeton chair in his room, googling the number of female members of Congress.

Hanging my head over the edge of my bed, I check to see if *Life: A User's Manual* is still where I discarded it. But of course it's there, splayed open so that the first fifty pages or so are bent out of shape. Instinctively, I reach down to rescue it, smoothing the creases before I remember, mid-swipe, that I'm not supposed to give a rat's ass about whether I've ruined Len's book.

I flip to the end of the offending tome, which concludes with chapter 99. If Perec had properly followed his own knight's-tour-through-the-apartment-building conceit, there should have been one hundred chapters—one for each room. But he didn't. He purposely omitted a chapter, just to break the system. This, I've since learned from researching the guy, was Perec's thing: he believed that structural constraints could be the raison d'être of a work, but true creativity and meaning came from embracing a *clinamen*, or an intentional deviation from those constraints.

So Len was right when he told me Perec was all about rules. And though I refused to listen, he also hinted about how that meant breaking them, too. People think this makes Perec's work more humanistic, or at least, more philosophical. Because I guess nothing in life is as orderly as you expect it to be.

I pick up my phone again and reload the last messages I got from Len:

I fucked up, Eliza.

I'm sorry.

Can we please talk?

I think about responding, but instead I hit the lock button and turn out the light. In the dark, I curl up on my side and bunch the edge of my comforter close to my chest.

Goddamn Len. Every time I think I've got him figured out.

39

IN THE MORNING, I'M IN FIRST PERIOD CHEM, trying to get ahead on my US history reading, when the morning announcements kick off with the sound of Otis Redding.

I look up, and it's Winona's *Pretty in Pink* prom promo video. She got this senior, Jada Williams, captain of the Willoughby dance team, to dress up as Duckie and lip-sync to "Try a Little Tenderness"—just like in the movie. Jada, wearing a tan blazer, dances energetically through the quad and enjoys every second of it. As the final shot fades out, the words *Pretty in Pink* appear in neon magenta, and below that, *Willoughby High School Prom* and *Tickets on sale in the quad*. Everyone claps when it's over, including me.

I'm about to turn back to reading about the Cold War détente when I hear an unexpected voice coming from the TV.

"Hello, Sentinels. This is Len DiMartile."

"And this is Serena Hwangbo."

"Please stand for the Pledge of Allegiance."

I remain stuck in my seat for a full five seconds after everyone else has gotten up, and as I scramble to my feet, I can't stop staring at Len. Today he's wearing a pastel flannel, the plaid made up of faded pinks and yellows. He stands next to Serena, who is at least a foot shorter, and they both turn slightly, their hands placed over their hearts.

On the other side of their chests, though, they're both wearing *I AM A FEMINIST* buttons. Len's is particularly notable for the piece of masking tape covering the word *FEMINIST*. In its place, written in Sharpie, is the word *SLUT*.

I glance over at James, who, suspiciously, doesn't show any surprise.

"Hey," I whisper. "What's going on?"

"Just wait and see," he answers cryptically.

So, for maybe the third time this year, I pay attention to the morning announcements. Of course, I don't actually retain a single fact that's uttered by either Len or Serena. The whole time, I'm feeling antsy, wondering what's going to happen.

"Okay, Len," says Serena, finally. "I heard you have a special announcement?"

"Yeah," he replies, nodding. He's not as cute on TV as he is in real life, but the likeness is enough that my heart speeds up anyway. "Well, as I'm sure everyone knows, the *Bugle* staff recently elected me to be the editor in chief next year."

People around me are peeping in my direction now. I pretend not to notice.

"And there's been a lot of opposition expressed against this, much of it reasonable." Len clears his throat, and he sounds unusually nervous. There go his fingers into his hair. Now my curiosity is *really* piqued.

"I agree that we haven't had enough female students in leadership positions at Willoughby, especially in the roles of school president and *Bugle* editor in chief. The numbers are a travesty, and I regret that I had nothing to do with improving them. Because feminism, contrary to popular belief, isn't about hating on guys like me. It's about all of us working toward equality, together." He looks into the camera now, a level, unflinching gaze. "But that's not the only reason why I'm stepping down."

The class breaks into a murmur, and even Mr. Pham stops grading quizzes to listen.

"I'm stepping down because I'm the one who posted Eliza Quan's manifesto on the *Bugle* home page. That was conduct unbecoming of a *Bugle* editor in chief, and a violation of basic journalistic integrity. Not to mention messed up." He stuffs his hands in his pockets. "So, I'm sorry. For everything. But I can't accept the position, because it's not the right thing to do."

He faces the camera one more time, and it feels as though his eyes are locked on mine.

"Thanks, Len," says Serena, like she's merely engaging in a run-of-the-mill announcement handoff. "It takes courage to admit when you're wrong, and I think you've done it beautifully." She gives the camera a little knowing look, which also, strangely, feels meant for me. "But I want to ask you about one more thing."

I'm still transfixed, and so is everyone else.

"Tell us about that button you're wearing." Serena points at his shirt.

"Oh yeah," says Len. "As I'm sure you also know, there have been some pretty ugly rumors going around about Eliza and me. So I just wanted to set the record straight. Whatever Eliza gets called, I should be, too. It's not fair that only she has to deal with that crap."

"That's very noble of you, Len," says Serena. "But I'd take it one step further." She reaches over and peels the tape off Len's button, so that once again it reads *I AM A FEMINIST*. Then she crosses her arms and speaks into the camera. "I think we should all stop calling each other names. I've been guilty of it, too. But I believe we should work to build each other up, not tear each other down. And to me, that's important enough to run a campaign on."

Behind her, a banner unfurls, showing Serena dressed as Rosie the Riveter, brandishing a bicep in the classic manner, with a headline that says *Hwangbo for President!* as a replacement for *We can do it!*

"That's right, I'm officially announcing my campaign to run for school president!"

You have to hand it to her. The girl knows how to send a message.

In the background, there are sounds of whoops and cheers, and someone throws a shower of red, white, and blue confetti into the frame.

"And that's all we've got," Serena cheers. "Good morning, and good luck!"

Right before the video clicks off, Len pops into the frame with a V *for Victory* sign. "Vote for Serena," he says, and then it cuts to black.

As Mr. Pham turns off the TV, James raises his eyebrows at me.

"How does it feel to be the new *Bugle* editor in chief?" he asks.

My jaw is still hanging open, but no words come to mind other than the ones I finally decide to text Len:

Okay, let's talk.

40

AT THE END OF THE DAY, I WAIT FOR LEN BEHIND the art studio, leaning against the wall of the portable building. The street that borders this edge of campus is pretty quiet, and though you can hear the distant din of sports teams practicing, the only real sound here is the wind occasionally rustling the yellow grass.

I slide down to the ground and pick at the little white clovers, the kind that Kim liked to make into necklaces when we were in elementary school. She always had a knack for doing it properly: piercing one stem with her fingernail and stringing the next blossom through the slit, the bud securing itself. I, on the other hand, when I bothered with such things, could only accomplish the task by clumsily tying each stem to the next. But that was the price you paid for brute force and impatience.

I'm trying out Kim's method now, bungling together a string of clovers almost two feet long before I realize that Len still hasn't shown up.

When I check my phone, there's no message other than his last one, agreeing to meet me here. I text him again, but in response, there's only a painful, drawn-out silence.

Where could he be? Part of me wonders if he's not coming after all. Did he go through all that trouble with the morning announcements just to stand me up? My chest constricts in protest. *That doesn't really seem like him,* it insists.

Embarrassment rushes to my cheeks, and I start to tear apart my clover chain, one blossom at a time. What do I really know about what Len is like? I can't believe that after all this, I'm still giving him the benefit of the doubt. I, Eliza Quan, *don't* give people the benefit of the doubt.

Halfway through my clover destruction, however, I pause. I could keep sitting here, ripping apart stem after stem, my resolve hardening into something familiar and fitting, yet also deeply unsatisfying. Or, I could admit that maybe I don't want that anymore.

I tie the remaining length of the flower chain into a bracelet, and then I hop to my feet. I don't have to give Len the benefit of the doubt. But I *can* give him another chance.

Back in the quad, the after-school crowd has mostly thinned. It occurs to me, however, that I have no idea where to begin looking for Len. I reach for my phone again, trying to think of someone I could text. Serena, maybe?

Then, a few feet away, I hear a tap on the window of a nearby classroom. And, after a few seconds, another. I move closer to investigate, and that's when I see him. On the other side of the glass, he's crouched over a desk, catapulting a paper clip that lands with another soft clink against the windowpane. When he catches my eye, he pantomimes texting and waves his hands in a desperate gesture. *No phone*, he mouths.

So that's what happened: Len has landed himself in detention, and he got stuck with a teacher who's actually strict about collecting everyone's phones. I would be lying if I said I wasn't just a *little* bit gratified that something, at last, has caught up to Len. But I do need to talk to him, I realize. The urge increases its grip on my nerves with every passing minute, and if I wait until after detention has ended, there won't be very much time before Mom gets here to pick me up.

I have no plan whatsoever, but that doesn't stop me from dashing over and finding myself fully, brazenly inside the classroom before I realize the faculty member in charge of detention today is—

"Dr. Guinn!"

He looks up from an issue of *The Atlantic*, peering at me over his glasses. "Hello, Eliza," he says. "Just visiting today?"

"Actually . . . ," I say, and then I stop, because I don't know how to end the sentence. Inappropriately, or maybe appropriately, I find myself wondering what Len would do. Then an idea flashes in my mind. "I have a question."

Dr. Guinn folds up his magazine and sets it on the desk. Everyone else, confused and excited by this interruption to detention, waits for his response. It arrives after a long pause:

"May I presume that this involves our friend in the back row?"

All eyes turn toward Len, who stops mid-slouch in his seat, both legs stretched into the aisle.

"That's the thing, though," I say. "He isn't exactly my friend." Out of the corner of my eye, I notice Len releasing the slightest of winces.

"I would think, then," says Dr. Guinn, massaging his brow, "that you would feel a certain justice in the consequences that have unfolded?"

I decide not to answer that. "Dr. Guinn," I say instead, vaulting my voice over the space where his question hangs in the air. "Wasn't it you who once talked about the importance of connection?"

Dr. Guinn's eyebrows, almost invisible in their sparseness, rise in mild surprise. He isn't expecting this, which is exactly what I'm counting on.

"You said we should try to connect to those who disagree with us," I continue. "To those we feel have done us wrong."

"I believe we had this discussion, yes."

"But bridging that kind of divide requires both sides to extend, as you put it, a hand over the trenches." I gesture now at Len, who is still wearing his *I AM A FEMINIST* button. "Sometimes we don't do it very well, and sometimes it's not really enough." He sinks a little lower in his seat. "But I think it's worth acknowledging each other when we try."

Dr. Guinn's arms are in their usual crossed position, his

mouth pressed into a thoughtful line that's halfway to either a smile or a frown. "What are you proposing, Eliza?"

Okay, here it goes. "I think Len tried today," I say, pointing at him. "It kills me to admit it, but I will, because I'm trying, too." I take a step forward, and though Len remains quiet and unsmiling, his eyes brighten. "I don't think he should be punished for finally doing the right thing. For once."

Dr. Guinn reclines in his chair. "You're asking for Len to be released from detention."

I nod, glancing at the clock directly above Dr. Guinn's shiny head. "There's only about forty minutes left at this point," I say. "I think he's earned at least that much of a reprieve."

A silence ensues as Dr. Guinn checks his watch and, finding it apparently in need of a wind-up, twists the metal knob on the side until it clicks to a stop. Again, the entire room is mesmerized. At long last, a reply is issued. "Very well," Dr. Guinn says. "Reprieve granted."

The atmosphere crackles into a celebration, which is kind of odd when you think about it, because I've only gotten Len out of detention and no one else. But Len, being Len, has jumped up from his seat and is already being offered high fives by the kids around him. Shouts of "All right, DiMartile!" and "You the man!" pile on him, and as I watch him get congratulated for doing precisely nothing, I conclude that some things, it seems, never change.

Or maybe they can. Len, giving a slight shake of his head, flourishes a hand toward me, like an actor gesturing to the orchestra during a curtain call, and someone else adds, "Yeah, give credit where it's due!"

On our way out, Dr. Guinn regards both of us. To me, he says, "We may never entirely see eye to eye, Eliza, but your tenacity is, and always has been, a force." I am still figuring out whether he means this as a compliment when he hands Len his phone. "And you, sir, I will see back here tomorrow."

"Tomorrow?" I ask Len, when we're outside.

He grins at me, wide and warm and familiar. "If you don't mind, I'll need to be liberated from detention about four more times."

"I don't know if you're worth the trouble!" But I laugh, and it feels nicer than I expected.

Len's happiness is obvious, though keyed up with a furtive, skittish energy. His fingers fly through his hair before he pulls his baseball cap down over his eyes. I have never seen him like this, and also, at the same time, I know exactly how he's feeling.

"Can I buy you a drink?" he says, voice breaking a bit over the words.

At the Boba Bros counter, Len orders what's on the weekly special board for himself, and then, before I can say anything, adds, "And a lavender tea with almond jelly, please. With soy milk and half the sweetener." He steps back, making space for me. "Right?"

It is exactly my usual order, and when my face involuntarily lights up, I can feel his tension dissolving into a kind of satisfied knowing. It's almost smug, his relief. That's why, when he brings the drinks out to where I'm waiting on the strip-mall lawn, I point at the other one. "I'd like that today, if you don't mind."

This throws him off, like I knew it would. But he hands the cup over without any questions. "It's *hojicha*," he says, lowering himself to the ground beside me. "A Japanese green tea."

I take a sip and am struck by how different it is—rich and full like cinnamon, or burnt sugar, but without the harsh aftertaste. It's not bad, actually. New, but somehow still comforting.

In the quiet between us, Len chews on his straw more than he drinks, and we spend a few minutes just watching the cars go by. Finally, I say, "That was some announcement you pulled this morning," just as he says, "Listen, I'm really sorry, Eliza."

After a tentative pause, Len fumbles forward. "I'm sorry for posting the manifesto, and for not telling you about it. Without a doubt, it was incredibly stupid. But your description of me was so ruthless that . . . well, honestly, I did kind of want to see how funny it would be to provoke you." Guilty patches of pink spread across his cheeks.

I jab my straw inside my cup. "Yeah, I know, that's how you pretend things don't hurt you. By being a jerk."

Len's face knots up in remorse. "I swear, it was mostly meant to be a dumb, self-deprecating joke. I didn't even think anyone but you would see it before we took it down. I tried to get James and Powell to, remember? But then it just became this whole thing I didn't know how to stop."

He touches my wrist, fingertips light against my skin, and lingers over the clover bracelet, gently, before dropping his hand back into the grass.

"I obviously didn't think things through. And then I was just afraid to tell you the truth." He's taking large gulps of his tea now, draining the cup at an ill-advised rate. "I'm sorry for being a coward, I'm sorry for breaking your trust, and I'm sorry for everything that happened because of me. And for all the shitty things I said."

"You *were* shitty."

Len tries to hide his reaction in his cup, but all that's left are almond jelly cubes and ice. "Yeah," he says, sounding forlorn.

"But you weren't always wrong." Now I sigh into my tea. "I also said some really shitty things. And I'm sorry." I straighten my legs out in front of me, and he does the same. The sides of our jeans touch. "I've been afraid, too. And also wrong in a lot of ways. I thought I knew everything about everyone, but I guess sometimes I didn't even really know myself." Facing him, abruptly overcome by an urgency to make sure he hears what I'm about to say, I reach for his hand. "I don't think you're a coward."

"Anymore?" he quips. But he closes his fingers around mine.

"We could all be cowards." I lean my forehead into his shoulder. "Or we could all not."

He rests his chin on my head, and it feels natural to fit together, finally, in this easy way. "Wise words from the new *Bugle* editor in chief," he agrees.

"Wait." I sit back with a jolt, seized by a realization. "Does stepping down mean you have to quit the *Bugle*?"

"No, I'll stick around as a staff writer. Unless, of course, you're kicking me off?"

A smile stretches across my face, big enough to rival his. "Your ethics record *is* a little spotty."

"Well, I'm turning over a new leaf." He adjusts the brim of his cap forward so that its angle is impeccable. "And, to start, as a disclaimer, I can't cover any more baseball games. Conflict of interest and all."

I ambush him with a hug, and my question comes out like a squeal. "You're going back?" I think my enthusiasm astonishes both of us.

"That's the goal," says Len, laughing.

"Wow, good for you! Maybe I'll even show up to a game sometime."

"*Maybe* you'll even develop an abiding love for the Willoughby team."

I grab his hat and place it snugly on my head. "You never know with these things," I say, smirking, and lie back in the grass, hands behind my head.

Len stretches out, too, so that the two of us are side by side under the springtime sky, and all at once, the afternoon feels infinite, like the entire universe exists in the specific golden warmth of what's here before me, right within my grasp. And even though there's so much I don't know—so much that I can't know—I've also never felt more sure of myself.

One Month Later

"A LITTLE HIGHER, MAYBE. MORE—WAIT, NO, now that's too much."

Len throws me a look over his shoulder, his outstretched arms holding a framed portrait up against the wall. "You know you can reach this, right?" he says. "I don't think you really needed 'an extremely tall person' for this."

"You got me." My face breaks into a fiendish grin. "The truth is, I just needed *you*." After all, the symbolism of the gesture—my portrait being hung in its rightful place by the boy who nearly deposed me—was simply too great to pass up.

Even though said boy is very cute, especially when allegedly grumpy about being bossed around.

I breeze over and lean up to kiss him on the cheek, but then I stop, squinting at where he's positioned the frame. "Maybe a little to the left?"

It's lunchtime, only a few days before the year is over for good, and my editor's portrait has just arrived in the mail from Eton Kuo '88, the illustrious artist himself. James, who handed me the package this morning, was maudlin about the whole thing. "Man," he said, watching me tear open the envelope. "It feels like only yesterday I was getting mine." When I slid the drawing out, he declared it a masterpiece, and then, his voice growing shaky, added, "I'm proud of you, Quan. I really am."

The portrait, if I may say so myself, is a pretty good likeness. Sure, my forehead's a little wide, and I'm not sure I scrunch my face up *that* much ("You do," said James), but I hear that one shouldn't have such stringent expectations in life.

"This is good, Eliza," Len insists, marking the wall with a pencil before grabbing a hammer from the counter.

I'm about to protest when Natalie, flushed and out of breath, pops her head into the newsroom. "Hey," she says, "they just finished counting the votes for the student-council election. Serena won! She's the new school president."

"That's amazing!" Clapping my hands together, I can barely keep my feet on the ground. Between this and Winona learning that she made it into the National Young Filmmakers Festival, this has been a bombshell of a week!

"I'm gonna run out to the quad," says Natalie, grabbing the camera from the cabinet. "Serena just posted that she's doing a surprise livestream in five. See you out there?"

"Yeah," I call after her, waving as she gallops out the door. Then I remember that Len and I are in the middle of my portrait installation. "Do you mind if we finish this later—"

But Len just stands there, flipping the hammer in his hand

before setting it back on the counter, and that's when I notice that he's already done hanging up my portrait.

And what do you know? He was right. The frame is aligned just fine.

"It's perfect." I beam at him, and then reach for my latest sweater alternative, one that I've been wearing a lot since I decided it's perfectly reasonable—dare I say even fun—to switch up my wardrobe occasionally.

"Nice jacket," observes Len, as I thread my arms through the leather sleeves. I laugh when he pulls me in close, pretending to inspect the embroidered name on my chest. "Who's DiMartile?" he murmurs into my hair. "You like him or something?" I almost let him move down to my lips, but then I lean back playfully.

"Well," I say, "*he* certainly likes me."

Len's smirk takes its time spreading across his face. "Oh yeah?" he says. "I thought you didn't care about being liked."

I stand up on my toes, slipping my arms around his neck. "*I* can care about whatever I like."

Then I draw him into a knockout of a kiss—a real one this time, long and full of all kinds of potential—before leading him out to the quad, his hand in mine, to discover what the future is like when girls, finally, take charge.

Acknowledgments

This book would not exist without the many individuals who, thankfully, liked Eliza enough to give her (and me) a shot:

First, a big thank-you to my agent Jenny Bent, whose reactions to things are almost always the same as mine, only wiser and more hilarious—and whose unshakable belief in this story has made all my dreams come true. Thanks also to Gemma Cooper, whose fabulous taste and sound judgment have been an invaluable part of Eliza's journey across the pond. And to the rest of the Bent Agency team, especially Claire Draper, Amelia Hodgson, and Victoria Cappello.

Equally huge thanks go to my editors: the fierce and savvy Mabel Hsu, as well as the eloquent and always gracious Stephanie King. I am indebted to both for their keen guidance and tireless support. And because they laugh at my jokes in the comments.

Much gratitude to the team at Harper: Karen Sherman, Lindsay M. Wagner, and Gweneth Morton for their impeccable attention to detail; Molly Fehr, Amy Ryan, and Fevik for a gorgeous cover; and Allison C. Brown, Aubrey Churchward, Jacquelynn Burke, Tanu Srivastava, and Katherine Tegen for all their enthusiasm and support. Same to Rebecca Hill, Sarah Cronin, Katharine Millichope, Kevin Wada, Stevie Hopwood, and Katarina Jovanovic from the Usborne team—thank you for creating a beautiful UK edition and making me feel like part of the family even from this many time zones away.

Many thanks to the friends who always acted like writing a book was a perfectly reasonable way to spend my time, especially those who helped me finish this one: Trish Smyth, who inspired me to start writing again; Lei'La' Bryant and Lucy Claire Curran, who have long been my biggest champions; Ayushee Aithal, who listens to all my rants and provides excellent gut checks; and Alice Lee, whose critical judgment I have found indispensable since we were twelve.

Thank you also to everyone who took the time to read full or partial drafts, including Avi Francisco, Christina Liu, Krystal Gregory, and Riya Kuo.

Much love and appreciation to my parents, who supported my writing from the beginning. Also to C., who inspired an important character.

And finally, to J. I couldn't have done it without you.